THE
WIFE
NEXT DOOR

BOOKS BY RONA HALSALL

Keep You Safe

Love You Gone

The Honeymoon

Her Mother's Lies

One Mistake

The Ex-Boyfriend

The Liar's Daughter

The Guest Room

THE
WIFE
NEXT DOOR

RONA HALSALL

bookouture

Published by Bookouture in 2022

An imprint of Storyfire Ltd.
Carmelite House
50 Victoria Embankment
London EC4Y 0DZ

www.bookouture.com

ISBN: 978-1-80314-160-2
eBook ISBN: 978-1-80314-159-6

For my early readers, who make my books so much better
Mark, Kerry-Ann, Gill, Sandra, Dee, Wendy and Chloe –
thank you!

PROLOGUE

She looked up at the patch of blue sky, visible through the tops of the pine trees, ragged round the edges like a torn piece of cloth. Was this the last piece of sky she would ever see? She shivered in the cool of the shadows, terrified by the thought. *My son. He needs me.*

Her body lay on the chilly ground, her head resting on a damp patch of moss, the prickle of heather against her face. She was in a dip, something digging into her back. A broken branch, she supposed. She'd tried to move before now – it could have been minutes ago, or hours – but that had brought a pain so fierce she'd blacked out for a while. Now, even breathing brought a stab of pain to her stomach, making her resort to the shallow breaths she'd once been taught for childbirth. It helped a little, but not enough. Tears ran down her cheeks, the taste of salt in her mouth. How long could she hold out? How much longer would her body keep going before it started to shut down, drained of its lifeblood?

She'd thought she was at the beginning of a new phase in her life, her heart full of hope that the past was behind her and she could begin again with a new love, a new partnership to nurture and cherish her child. They'd been so excited about the house, but she knew now it had all been a fantasy. Nothing had been real. Could she have known? Should she have worked it out sooner?

That was all academic now. The most important thing was hanging on to the thread of life, grasping it with all her might, the thought of her son keeping her strong.

She moved her hands, sticky with congealed blood, tried to press harder on the wound to stem the bleeding. Pain seared through her, making her gasp, then whimper. She was starting to fade, she could feel it. Slow breaths, she counselled herself. Slow breaths. Focus. Just take it one at a time.

Please find me, she whispered in her head. Someone please come and find me.

CHAPTER ONE

Jess stared at the shiny bunch of keys in her hand, new and unfamiliar, her heart fluttering with excitement. A gust of wind whipped at her hair, flicking it in her eyes. She tucked it behind her ears, twisting it into a dark knot at the back of her head as she studied the houses in front of her. A pair of attractively designed three-bedroom semi-detached properties, each with a patch of lawn at the front, a weeping cherry tree planted in the middle, and ornamental grasses in a patch by the door. Block-paved drives provided parking for two vehicles, and a garage nestled at the side of each house. The front doors gleamed in the sunshine, a mere three feet between the two of them. Like a pair of Siamese twins, she thought, her eyes sliding from one house to the other, inseparable but with their own personalities.

The houses were on a new estate in Peel, a small fishing town on the west coast of the Isle of Man. An island in the middle of the Irish Sea measuring all of ten miles wide and thirty-three miles long, it was part of Great Britain but had its own government, which had been established over a thousand years before, when the Vikings came. It was a small island with a big personality and a determination to be the master of its own destiny.

Identical pairs of properties stretched up the road behind her and into the estate. It was a development designed for families, located on the edge of town. A few minutes' walk down the road there was a big playground for the kids and a swimming pool, and next door to that was her son Toby's primary school. The secondary school he would be going to in a couple of years was accessible through the estate – no busy roads to walk along, no need for buses, and he'd have schoolmates on his doorstep. Absolutely perfect. Really, she couldn't have hoped for a better solution to a problem that had gnawed at her for the last few months. How to separate from her husband, Rob, while making the change as easy as possible for their son.

She smiled to herself. This was the ideal solution.

A shout made her turn. Rob and his new partner, Carol, were walking up the road towards her. He was tall and lanky, his blonde hair slicked back; she was small and equally blonde, her hair in a trademark messy bun. They went well together, Jess thought as she watched them approach, glad that he'd found someone who was more his type: corporate and ambitious and just a little too intense at times. Her mind added 'boring', but she swept that thought away as uncharitable. Carol could be fun when she'd had a couple of drinks to loosen her up. Sober she could be a bit reserved, with a tendency to disappear into herself, like she had a million things going on in her head. That didn't detract from her thoughtfulness, though, and she was a lovely mum, very sweet to Toby and her own son, Mo, always keen to take them on outings together and play games with them.

Rob had messaged earlier to say they were having lunch at the pub on the edge of the estate while they waited for the removal van to arrive. Jess had left them to finish off at the house she'd shared with Rob for almost ten years while she dropped Toby at her mum's, on a neighbouring estate. It had been a mad few days trying to get the packing finished, sorting their possessions into boxes marked *His* and *Hers*. Unpicking a union that had been tightly sewn together until just a year ago hadn't been easy, but when was packing up a house ever easy, never mind separating?

This wasn't like your normal break-up, thought Jess, proud of the way she and Rob had been able to manage the process. There was none of the high emotion her friends had been through, none of the bickering and sniping, and they'd negotiated their way to what she considered a fair division of everything they owned. She would admit, though, to twinges of sadness that it hadn't worked out, as much for her son's sake as her own.

Rob and Carol stopped in front of their own front door, holding hands. Jess's smile widened. This was going to work, she could feel it in her bones, her body almost fizzing now. *I've done it.* She'd made it to the starting line of a brand-new phase in her life. Her friends couldn't believe it. She couldn't quite believe it herself.

She gave them a thumbs up, and Carol smiled, gave her a wave. Jess turned to admire the house again while she waited for her new partner, Ben, to join her. This was what they'd decided: they'd all go into their new homes at the same time, a symbolic gesture. It was about equality, the fact they were in this together; a demonstration of their commitment to make it work.

It almost hadn't happened. Theirs had been the last properties available on the development, and she knew they'd been lucky to secure them. She'd rung the developer as a last resort, not really expecting them to have anything available. After all, the estate had been completed weeks ago, and most of the houses had been bought off plan before a single brick was laid.

'You're in luck,' the sales executive had said.

Jess was hunched over her desk in the library and sat up a little straighter. She'd spent many a lunch hour ringing estate agents, and had expected to draw a blank again.

'An investor has pulled out at the last minute. We have a pair of three-bedroom semis available. Can I send you the details?' The sales executive laughed. 'It's funny, I just got off the phone to the investor, so you couldn't have timed it better.'

Jess's mind whirred into action as she opened the email that arrived a minute later. She chewed her lip as she scanned the details. The price might be achievable at a push. There was no time to dally. She had to secure this deal now, or the chance would be gone. Her heart gave a little skip. Houses next door to each other – how perfect was that? She could already see it working in her mind, the kids coming and going as they pleased, ready-made childcare on the doorstep. A companion for Toby in Mo, too. Her mouth curved into a satisfied grin and she rang the sales executive back.

'Can I put down a deposit?'

Really, she should have consulted with the others first, but they'd had so many discussions about this issue, she knew they'd approve. Hadn't Rob joked the other night that they needed either one great big house or two next to each other? Both had seemed unachievable given the state of the housing market and the lack of suitable properties in their price range, but this was doable. Identical homes. What could be fairer than that?

It had been a bit of a struggle sorting out the finances in the middle of divorce proceedings, though. And Ben was stuck until his house was sold, which was proving tricky because there was modernisation work to be done, something that had put off a couple of prospective buyers. In the end, Rob had bought both the houses; it had stretched his finances to the max, but it was the only way to make it work. 'We can sort it out once the divorce is settled,' he'd said in his usual laid-back way. Unflappable. That was Rob. It helped that he worked for a finance company, of course. Favourable rates for employees.

Was it fate? She liked to think so, liked to see it as the universe approving of their plans. Unlike her mother, whose comment on the subject had been, 'You've had some daft ideas in your time, my girl, but this... well, it's just bonkers, if you ask me.' Of course, Jess hadn't asked her, but when did that ever stop her mum from offering an opinion?

Unfortunately, Jess's parents had never been able to speak to each other again after they'd separated, an ocean of bitterness and resentment keeping them well and truly apart, with neither of them having a good word to say about the other. That experience was the basis of her mum's comments, but Rob was the opposite of her dad, being a well-balanced, reasonable human being, liberal in his views and always on the side of reason. And that was why Jess was confident this was the best possible answer for all of them.

Admittedly, it wasn't an arrangement that would suit most divorcing couples, but her relationship with Rob was as strong as ever, despite their decision to start new lives with different people. *My decision*, she reminded herself. *I was the one who started all this.* For months, that thought would have sparked a sense of guilt about uprooting her son from his life, but this arrangement had changed everything. What she felt now was an overwhelming sense of peace, a sense that her troubles were behind her.

CHAPTER TWO

Arms circled her from behind, scooping her up, making her scream. Ben held her tight against his body, a waft of his citrus aftershave filling her nostrils.

'Gotcha! We're going to do this properly,' he said, starting to carry her up the driveway towards the front door. 'Not that I'm superstitious or anything, but... now we're engaged, I think we need a practice run for when we get married.'

She tipped her head back so she could see his face.

A lovable rogue. That was probably the best way to describe Ben. Dark curly hair and big brown eyes that you could lose yourself in. Strong arms from years working as a carpenter and joiner. He was a bit of a free spirit, a player, you might say, who'd travelled widely in the past, working his way round the world until his grandma became ill. He came home to look after her, because his sister had three young kids so couldn't cope with caring for their gran as well. It was an experience that had made him grow up fast, he'd told Jess. And after his gran had died, he'd stayed on in her little terraced cottage in the centre of Peel.

He'd been brought up by his grandparents after his mum

died in a riding accident, and they doted on him and his sister. The identity of his father had always been a mystery, but the man clearly hadn't been interested in bringing up his son, so Ben had given up worrying about that side of his parentage. 'My grandparents probably didn't take enough notice of what I was getting up to as a teenager,' he'd said when he first introduced Jess to his fourteen-year-old daughter, Ruby, the product of a casual relationship when he'd been a teenager. Ruby's mother, Darcey, had not been the one for him, and they'd soon parted ways, but he'd done everything he could to support his child, determined not to follow in his own father's footsteps. For the past couple of years, Ruby had lived with him during the week while her mum worked night shifts as a nurse.

Jess let her head rest on his chest, a surge of love for this man and his spontaneity rushing through her. Rob would never dream of doing something like carrying her over the threshold, not being a romantic in any shape or form. Her former husband was like a well-loved dressing gown, something you put on when you needed a bit of comfort in front of the fire on a cold winter night. Ben, on the other hand, was like a bright summer dress, with the promise of sunshine and adventure.

He spoke to a part of her that had been in hiding for most of her adult life, and in his company she could allow herself to be the person she wanted to be. A little bit daft, enjoying early-morning swims in the sea, kayaking trips, dancing the night away, singing along to the radio at the top of her voice. It felt like she'd been reborn now she'd found someone who enjoyed everything she did. As though she'd shed a skin and was glowing in fresh vibrant colours.

Even some of the regulars at the library had noticed a difference in her demeanour, commenting on how well she looked. As much as anything, that had given her the confidence to move her relationship with Ben to the next level. He was good for her, there was no denying it. And a happy mum was much better for a child than a miserable, distracted one with no energy. Even her own mother, who was her ex-husband's number one fan, couldn't argue with that.

She passed Ben the keys and he opened the door, carrying her through into the open-plan living space, then turning in a circle, the biggest smile on his face. 'This is it, love. This is where you and me start our life together.'

He bent his head, and as his lips met hers, it felt like her world was still spinning. She never ceased to be amazed at the effect this man had on her. They'd been seeing each other for almost a year now, and still she was besotted. She'd never felt like this with Rob, even at the start of their relationship.

'Oh for God's sake. Put her down, Dad. You don't know where she's been.' Ruby had flounced into the room with a cardboard box, which she dumped on the windowsill as she glared at them over the top of her pink designer glasses.

Jess reminded herself that the girl wasn't always like that. At times she could be sweet as apple pie, but she was anxious about the move, and rudeness seemed to be her default setting when she was below par in any way. Of course, Ben didn't pull her up for it, his parenting style being to treat her more as an equal than a child. There didn't seem to be any boundaries, with bad behaviour put down to teenage hormones. Now that he and Jess were moving in together, however, things would have to change. Still, there was plenty of time for that. Today, nothing was going to spoil Jess's good mood.

'You can take your stuff straight up to your room,' Ben said, picking up the box and handing it to his daughter. 'Come on, let's go and have a look, see where you're going to put everything.'

As they disappeared upstairs, Jess studied the boxes and bin bags stacked against the wall. Ben had brought some of her stuff over the night before in his work van. Apart from a few more boxes, a suitcase of clothes and some carrier bags of bits and bobs, this was the sum total of her possessions. Not much to show for a nine-year marriage. But then the house she and Rob had been living in hadn't been theirs. It belonged to Rob's parents, who had moved to Tenerife when his dad's arthritis had deteriorated. He was so much better in the warm climate that they'd stayed, pleased to have Rob to look after the house back on the Isle of Man.

In all their time together, she and Rob had never bought any furniture. She supposed it was good, in a way, that they hadn't had to negotiate who would have what, and she loved the fact that she and Ben would be starting afresh, nothing tainted with memories of her previous relationship. Ben was only bringing a few sentimental items that had belonged to his grandparents, most of the furniture in his own house being well and truly worn out.

She walked through into the kitchen area. Her hand stroked the granite worktop, her eyes lighting up at the brand-new appliances. It was going to be wonderful after her old kitchen with its wonky cupboards and leaky tap, the chipped tiles on the floor that were impossible to clean. This place was sparkling.

She did a happy little dance, laughter bubbling up inside, excited to start unpacking and making the house their own.

CHAPTER THREE

Jess drove to her mum's bungalow with a grin still stuck on her face. They could easily walk here from the new house, but her arms ached from carrying boxes and her legs were tired with running up and down the stairs. She felt sweaty and grubby, but her new home was really taking shape. In fact, it was looking fantastic. She'd spent so much of her life living in other people's houses, it was a novelty to have a blank canvas and organise everything how she wanted it. Ben had let her get on with it, saying interior design wasn't really his thing, and she loved that he trusted her to create their new home.

The new furniture had arrived as planned, which was a relief because you never knew if delivery promises would actually be kept. They'd put loads of stuff away already. Ben had been busy constructing the bunk beds for Toby's room and putting up shelves. Even Ruby had shown willing, and Jess had left her making the beds, on the understanding that she'd get a takeaway on the way home from picking up Toby.

After her earlier rudeness, Ruby had actually been laughing and smiling, and had become quite agreeable once her room had started to take shape. She'd been allowed to choose her own bedroom furniture, and Jess had treated her to some new bedding and matching cushions as a surprise. Thank God she liked them. It had been a risk, but it was worth it to see the delight on her face, and Jess allowed herself to hope that the two of them could become closer in time.

Ben's old house, stuffed full of his gran's knick-knacks and photos, was very much Ben and Ruby's domain, with Jess as a weekend visitor. The new house would change that dynamic completely, and she wanted to believe there were already signs of that happening.

Although organising the move had been stressful, she felt a sense of euphoria now it was done. She parked the car and practically skipped up her mum's driveway.

'Ah, there you are,' her mum said as she poked her head out of the lounge. 'We're just finishing off a game of chess.'

Jess grimaced, aware that these games could take hours. She looked at her watch. 'Oh dear. I said I'd get a takeaway for everyone. We haven't eaten yet, so I was hoping to get off pretty soon.'

Her mum took the hint, flapping the problem away with her hand. 'It's okay, we can put it on hold and finish next time he's here.' She beamed at Jess. 'I'm hoping I'll see a lot more of him now you're close enough for him to walk here. You were miles away before.'

Jess had to smile at that. Their old house was only a couple of miles outside Peel. Not exactly far, but it did mean a car or bus journey to visit.

'It's going to be great.' She pulled her mum into a hug, a cloying floral scent filling her nostrils. She coughed as it caught the back of her throat. 'New perfume, Mum?'

Her mum released her and smiled. 'I thought I'd treat myself. They had a sale on. You like it?'

Jess averted her eyes. 'Lovely.' Perfume was her mum's

latest passion, but she was far too liberal with it. 'It'll be fantastic for Toby to be able to come up here more often.'

Her mum's face became more serious, and she pulled the lounge door closed so Toby couldn't hear what she was about to say. 'Look, I know it's your life and it's for you to decide how to live it, but are you really sure this is the right thing to do? I mean... moving next door to Rob, it's a bit... idealistic, I suppose is what I'm trying to say. There's bound to be problems. I don't know a single relationship that's broken up without some sort of bad feeling.'

Jess leant against the wall, wondering if she had the energy for this now. How many times was she going to have to explain herself? One more time, it seemed.

'Look, Mum. I know you and Dad had a bad break-up.' Her mum huffed at the understatement. 'But we're in a different situation. When I spoke to Rob about things, it turned out he'd been feeling the exact same way about our marriage. We were friends who became lovers, who ended up married because I fell pregnant with Toby. If our contraception hadn't failed...' she shrugged, 'maybe we would have parted company sooner.'

Her mum sighed, exasperated. 'But you still love each other, that's what I don't understand.'

Jess put out a hand and patted her mum's shoulder, knowing she was having more problems adjusting to the break-up than any of them. 'I love him as a friend, and that's not going to change. Honestly, this isn't something we've undertaken lightly, you know that. We talked for months about it before we decided to separate. But once we'd both had a chance to think about a different life for ourselves, we couldn't unthink it.'

She sighed, a ripple of sadness washing over her. But endings *were* sad, that was the nature of them. Even if you had a new life to look forward to.

'We both knew we weren't living the lives we wanted, but we didn't feel we could change things because of Toby. Now he'll be able to see both of us whenever he wants. And we'll be happier and better parents because of it. Plus he'll have a big sister in Ruby, and he got the little brother he always wanted in Mo.' She gave her mum a reassuring smile. 'Honestly, this is win-win for all of us. You included, because you've inherited a couple more grandchildren.'

She thought she'd hit the jackpot with that last comment, because she'd had years of questions about when there might be a brother or sister for Toby. But her mum still looked worried.

'I do hope Rob will continue coming round. You know he's like a son to me.' She gave a sniff, blinked a few times.

Jess gave her another hug. 'Don't you worry about that. You know he adores you.' Oh dear, she really hadn't considered what effect the break-up of her marriage would have on her mum. She'd always doted on Rob, and they had a very easy relationship, which Jess had been grateful for. It wasn't like that for everyone, and her friends were always telling her how lucky she was. Still, this was her life, not her mum's, and anyway, things probably wouldn't be that different. 'He'll still be part of the family, Mum. He's Toby's dad, after all, and we'll be sharing parenting. We're just... blending.'

Her mum pulled away, shaking her head. 'Blending!' She gave a little snort. 'I just don't see how it's going to work. There'll always be friction. What does Ben think about it?'

Jess laughed. 'Oh, he was on board straight away. You know what it's like with him and Rob. They're inseparable these days.' She laughed. 'Always off cycling together. In fact, I think Rob sees more of Ben than I do.' This was the truth, and if anything was a source of friction in their relationship, this was it.

Her mum fiddled with the buttons on her cardigan. 'It's just weird, if you ask me.' She held up a hand to stop Jess responding. 'I know, love, I know. My experience isn't your experience. And if it's going to work for the kids, then that's great. Better than all the aggro you had to put up with when you were growing up, that's for sure.' Sadness turned down the corners of her mouth. 'I wish it could have been a bit more amicable with your dad, but some people... well, they're just not that easy to deal with, are they?'

'Oh, Mum, it's not your fault he ran off with that woman. I don't blame you at all for things being difficult. I'm sure I'd feel differently if Rob had had an affair, and he'd probably feel the same towards me, but that's not what happened.'

Her mind took her back to the day it all began, the crumbling of her marriage.

CHAPTER FOUR

THEN

They were at a school reunion. Jess hadn't really wanted to go, but her mum had encouraged her because she'd been a bit down for the best part of a year, with no idea why she was feeling so low. Life had lost its sparkle, and every day it felt like she was going through the motions, following the same old routines, seeing the same people. Even her job at the library no longer filled her with enthusiasm. In fact, nothing did. She went to bed every night feeling relieved that the day was over and anxious that she'd have to do it all again in the morning.

Rob thought she was depressed and kept urging her to see the doctor. Jess had no intention of taking medication so didn't see the point in seeing anyone, but she was struggling to work out what was wrong with her. She had an amazing husband, so thoughtful all her friends were jealous. A lovely son. They had no mortgage, because they were living in Rob's parents' house. They had holidays, savings in the bank. Life was good, wasn't it?

She kept trying to shake herself out of it, but nothing made any difference. Reluctantly she agreed to go to the reunion, putting on the new dress Rob had persuaded her to buy. He had such good taste when it came to clothes, so much better than her. She got out the curling tongs and tried to make her shoulder-length hair more glamorous, but when she looked in the mirror, she just saw the same worn-out version of herself. This was not who she wanted to be. Methodically she applied makeup, hiding the dark rings under her eyes, the sprinkling of spots that covered her chin. Then she pinned on a smile. The camouflage was complete. She could do this for a night, couldn't she? Do it for Rob?

Her husband was a man who needed to feel that his life was a success. He'd been head boy at school. The popular one with good looks and an athletic physique. Way out of her league, she'd always thought. It turned out that the real Rob was quite different to the persona he projected, but he didn't want his old school friends to know that. This reunion was him living up to expectations, something that was still important to him all these years after they'd left school behind. Especially since many of his old crowd were coming over from London, where they now lived, a few of them working in the City and making significant money. Though Rob had stayed on the island, preferring to swim in a smaller pond when it came to work, he was undoubtedly successful too, a senior manager in a finance company.

She touched up her lipstick, then stood and smoothed her red satin dress. It felt so lovely and cool against her skin, shimmering in the light, showing off the auburn tints in her dark hair. The final touch was a pearl choker that had belonged to Rob's grandmother, and now she looked like someone who'd stepped out of a 1950s movie. She slipped her feet into matching red satin shoes, then, with a sigh, pulled her shoulders back and went downstairs. It's just one night, she reminded herself. Just one night.

Rob was waiting for her in the lounge, chatting to her mum, who was babysitting Toby for the night. They both looked up when she entered, their hushed conversation halted mid-sentence. An awkward silence hung in the air. *They've been talking about me.* She knew they had. It happened a lot at the moment. Her lips twitched in annoyance. *Cool it. Don't say anything.* It really wasn't worth it. They were worried about her, that was all.

'Sweetheart, you look fabulous,' Rob said, his eyes lighting up with relief. She wondered if he'd thought she wouldn't wear the dress. Whether she'd spurn it for something more modest.

'You're so glamorous,' her mum said. 'I wish I could wear red, but it makes me look haggard.' She pulled a face, and Rob laughed.

'You couldn't look haggard if you tried, Helen.'

Her mum's eyes travelled down Jess's body and back up again. 'You've got such fabulous legs, you should be proud to show them off.'

Rob came over to Jess and took her hands, giving them a squeeze, his voice excited. 'I knew that dress would look good on you the minute I saw it. Honestly, love, you could be a model. Everyone will be so impressed.'

Jess smiled, trying to hide her irritation. 'I'm glad you both approve. I was wondering what I'd wear now I've lost weight, so I'm glad you persuaded me to buy it.' She'd had a look through her wardrobe a week ago and had realised she had absolutely nothing suitable. A passing comment to Rob, and the next day he'd shown her the dress online.

She looked at him now in his black suit and white shirt. A red silk handkerchief in his top pocket, the same colour as her dress. Meticulous. Perfect. Reliable. And completely predictable. Surely she should feel a rush of pride that this man was her husband. That he took such good care of her. But maybe that was the problem. Maybe she didn't want to be a songbird in a gilded cage.

The reunion was well attended, and she felt like she had on her wedding day, all the smiling making her cheeks ache as she talked to people she no longer knew and others she couldn't even remember. When things started getting rowdy, she had to fight the urge to call a cab and go home. But Rob was in his element, holding court just like he used to when he was at school, surrounded by a circle of friends.

She was too exhausted to make small talk, so she went to the bar to get something to drink and wait it out. Ben was the barman for the night, earning some extra money helping a friend who ran the catering company. Their eyes met and something happened to her that had never happened before. She felt like she'd been jump-started. They stared at each other for a moment before his face creased into a grin.

'What can I get you?'

'Just... um... just a glass of water, please.'

His eyes didn't move from hers. Her mouth was dry, her body flushed with a sudden heat. She perched on a stool, heart thundering in her chest, not quite sure what was happening.

'You don't want anything with that water?' He raised an eyebrow, a crooked smile on his lips.

'No thanks. I'm not really a drinker. Ever since I had my son...' She shrugged. 'I don't know. Pregnancy did something to me and I just don't fancy alcohol any more.' She pulled a face. 'How boring is that?'

He laughed. 'Not boring at all. Got to listen to your body.' He leant towards her, spoke in a conspiratorial whisper. 'I don't drink much either. But don't tell anyone. It's not a good look for a barman.' There was a mischievous twinkle in his eyes, and she felt drawn to him like she'd never been drawn to anyone in her life before. 'Push the boat out and have a slice of lemon. Or even lime.'

She laughed. 'Go on then, I'll have one of each. And some ice.'

'Steady on,' he said. 'We don't want you mixing your drinks.'

They fell into an easy conversation, starting with school and working their way from there. They'd both been born and brought up on the island, so there was always going to be common ground: people they knew, things they'd done, places they'd been. She'd known his gran, it turned out, a keen reader who came along to the book club she ran at the library.

She found out that Ben was the same age as her and had a teenage daughter. He was happy to talk kids, and they shared anecdotes in an exchange that flowed so naturally and absorbed her so completely, she was shocked when Rob put an arm round her shoulders and she realised almost everyone had gone home.

After that night, she felt different in a way she was reluctant to admit to herself, let alone anyone else. She kept running over the conversation with Ben in her mind, catching herself laughing at things he'd said. An inner glow had been ignited, and she enjoyed the replays with a sense of guilt, but also delight that she had this thing that was just hers to enjoy.

The following week, Ben walked into the café where she was having lunch and came to join her. Then he was in the library, in the supermarket, the fish and chip shop. In fact he seemed to pop up everywhere, and every time they met, they would fall into a conversation that she didn't want to end. The draw to him grew stronger, until it reached the point where she could no longer deny that she was developing a crush on him.

She was appalled, torn in two by her wayward thoughts. In the end, she confided in her workmate, Pam, who was a bit of a mother figure to her. They were sorting out books to go back on the shelves.

'Look, love, for what it's worth, you've been more like yourself these past few weeks. I was wondering what had changed.' Pam shrugged. 'You can't help who you fall in love with, that's a fact, however hard you try. Another fact is that living a lie will destroy your health. So even though it's hard, I think you need to be honest with yourself. And with Rob, for that matter.'

Jess was horrified. She had no intention of acting on her

emotions, however strong they might be. 'I can't break up my marriage on the basis of a crush, can I?'

'That's not what I'm saying. But there's clearly something that's not working for you with Rob.' Pam turned away, carried on sorting the books. 'Talk to him.'

Jess pondered on that for another week, until she finally plucked up courage to have a difficult conversation with her husband. She had a speech all worked out, and she was waiting for the right moment, but then his pernickety behaviour, his insistence on watching his preference on TV sparked a row, and she blurted it out.

'I can't live like this any more,' she snapped, springing to her feet.

He switched off the TV, turned to face her, bewilderment in his eyes. 'What do you mean?'

'You and me being married... It's just... not working.' She gasped, biting her lip, alarmed that she'd finally voiced her thoughts. 'That's what's been making me ill.'

He blinked. A nervous smile wavered on his lips. 'Of course it's working. You're just going through a bit of a rough patch. You've been so much better since the school reunion. Maybe you need to take some time out? Have a career change or retrain or something?'

His hand reached for hers and she snatched it away, clasped it to her chest, where she could feel the pounding of her heart. *Am I really going to do this?* She took a deep breath. It wasn't too late to stop, but she'd taken that first step and she knew she had to be brave and have the conversation.

'Look, Rob.' She swallowed, sweat coating her palms. Her voice faltered as she wondered where to start. 'You are the best friend I will ever have and... Well, at the beginning, we sort of fell into this relationship, didn't we? We somehow evolved from friends who dated other people to friends who got horrendously drunk and ended up sleeping with each other.' She risked a glance at him then, noticed his expression was one of concentration, not anger. He was listening, not reacting. She carried on, 'When our contraception went wrong and I fell pregnant with Toby, you know I wasn't sure about marriage. I mean... we talked about it, didn't we?' He gave the smallest of nods, acknowledging that he remembered. 'But then I thought about my parents' relationship, which had started with a big romantic falling-in-love, and I saw how that ended and I thought loving you as a friend would be enough. That we'd never fall out – and we don't, but...'

She sighed. It wasn't that Rob had done anything wrong. In fact, he did everything right. But she didn't connect with him at a fundamental level like she did with Ben. And now she'd found that connection, it had become an umbilical cord, a source of energy and sustenance that she hadn't known existed.

'There's a missing element,' she went on. 'And I only just realised that's why I've been having a bad time recently. Friendship isn't enough. I... well, I need to be in love.' She took a deep breath and looked him in the eye, steadying herself for the hardest thing she'd ever had to say. 'And I'm sorry, Rob, but I'm not in love with you.'

There, she'd done it. Her gaze fell to the floor as her heart flipped, her hands clasped tightly together. After a moment's silence, she glanced at him again, dreading his reaction.

'I think we need a drink,' he said, getting up and heading off into the kitchen.

She let out the breath she'd been holding. It was better than she could have hoped for. At least he didn't seem angry with her. Instead, he was buying a bit of time by going off to get a bottle of wine. He usually did that when he had a thorny problem to sort out – took himself off for a quiet moment before he reacted. She'd always liked that about him, his measured responses. No panicking.

She waited, perched on the edge of the sofa, too anxious to

relax. Had she done the right thing? Then she thought about the excitement that ignited her inside whenever she saw Ben. That feeling of being properly alive. It wasn't that she was planning on starting a relationship with him; it was just that he'd shown her what might be possible. What she was missing.

Rob came back a few minutes later with a bottle of Rioja, two glasses, and a smile on his face. Now that wasn't what she'd been expecting.

He pulled a cushion onto the floor and flopped down on the other side of the coffee table, opening the bottle and pouring two glasses. He pushed one across to her, then folded his legs into his familiar cross-legged position. He'd meditated all his life, his father being a yoga teacher, and had kept up a daily habit. She'd always thought it was why he was so calm, but try as she might, she couldn't replicate his practice, her mind too busy to allow her to settle. She took a sip of her drink, then another, while she waited for him to say something.

'You and me... we are absolutely on the same page,' he said eventually.

Her eyebrows shot up her forehead. She hadn't been expecting that either. She'd been anticipating a rigorous defence of their marriage, him trying to convince her of how strong it was. She took another sip, thrown by his comment. 'We are?'

He nodded. 'Absolutely. You see... I've been thinking the exact same thing. On the one hand, I've wanted us to stay together for Toby, but on the other, I have found myself... developing feelings for a work colleague.'

Her mouth dropped open, her body sagging back into the sofa as relief took all the strength from her muscles. 'You have?'

He looked up from under his lashes. Sheepish. 'I'll admit, the attraction has been getting stronger. And just like you, I was beginning to think there was something missing from my life.

Something I would never get to experience if we stayed together.'

She could hardly believe what she was hearing.

'Oh thank God it's not just me,' she said, knocking back the rest of her drink.

'I didn't know how to tell you.' She gave a strangled laugh and he filled up her glass, smiled at her. 'But you did the hard work for me.'

He caught her eye then, and she gazed at him, the closeness between them undeniable, not sure what she was feeling about anything any more.

'Tell me about the woman you met at work,' she said, remembering how they used to discuss their dates all those years ago when they'd been at uni. It felt familiar and comfortable and surreal at the same time.

He drained his glass, then refilled it and settled himself on his cushion. 'She's called Carol.' He gave a sigh, a dreamy expression in his eyes. 'Smaller than you, but long legs, wavy blonde hair. Absolutely stunning. Ambitious. Smart. Really kind-hearted as well. She's got a son called Mo, who's a few years younger than Toby.'

'Reverting to type, then.' Jess laughed. 'You always went for the blondes at uni, I remember that.'

'What about you?' he said, taking a sip of his wine, his eyes meeting hers over the rim of the glass. 'Have you met someone?'

She hesitated, then nodded and looked down at her hands, not sure if she was relieved or uncomfortable about all this. 'He's called Ben. He was behind the bar at the school reunion. I keep bumping into him in town.' She caught his eye again, and he held her gaze. 'It's not that I'm arranging to see him or anything; we just seem to go to the same places. He's got a child too, a daughter he dotes on.'

They chatted about their respective crushes, how they felt, what was important to them, and agreed that whatever happened, they didn't want to traumatise their son or make him decide who he wanted to live with.

'Let's not rush into anything,' Rob said. 'Let's just give each other permission to date and see how it pans out. Maybe we'll get it out of our systems and decide that what we have is best for us after all. Or maybe we'll fall in love with other people. But let's keep it fluid.'

She smiled at him, loving him more in that moment than she had for years. 'Fluid. I like that.'

CHAPTER FIVE

'Earth to Jessica, are you receiving me?' Her mum reached out and grasped her hand, giving it a tug to get her attention. 'You were miles away.'

'Oh, I was just thinking about Rob and Ben and Carol and...' Jess gave a quick smile. 'I know it sounds strange, but we're all sure it's worth giving it a go.'

'Well, love, I don't mean to go on. I know people have different ideas now to when I got married. But if anything happens and you need a place to stay for a while, you're always welcome here.'

'I know, Mum.' Jess was thinking that running home to her mum and her I-told-you-so's was probably the last things she'd be doing. Anyway, it wouldn't go wrong. They were committed to the cause. All of them.

Helen gave a satisfied nod, clearly feeling better now she'd said her piece. Jess hoped that would be the last of it. Nothing was going to take the shine off her day. Nothing.

Her mum bustled into the lounge and Jess followed. Toby looked up from the coffee table, where he was studying the chessboard, fingers hovering over a bishop, ready to make his move. His face fell when he saw her. 'I can't go yet. We haven't finished.'

Helen put a hand on his shoulder. 'I'll leave it set up, then we can finish off next time.'

He smiled then, his mouth full of teeth that seemed too large for his face. Big blue eyes, floppy blonde hair, just like Rob. The only things he seemed to have inherited from Jess's side of the family were his lopsided ears and her mum's square chin. When she really stopped to think about it, Jess was always amazed that she'd managed to make this quirky child, this living, breathing person.

Unfortunately, after a long and traumatic labour, she'd lost pints of blood and been told it would be dangerous to her health to go through another pregnancy. Toby was the only child she'd ever have, which had been a big disappointment to him, as he longed for a sibling to play with. Now, though, he would have two, and she felt that out of the three families, he was the one who was most looking forward to the new living arrangements.

He loved having a younger stepbrother who looked up to him, and it seemed to have been a real boost to his confidence. The mean kids at school, who teased him about his ears and his geekiness, didn't bother him quite so much any more.

She ruffled his hair. 'Tomorrow we'll walk over here from the house so you know the way, then you can come any time you like.'

His face broke into a delighted grin. 'For real?'

'Absolutely. It's not as far as you'd think.'

Helen was practically rubbing her hands together. 'We can do some baking if you like. It's going to be great.'

Toby jumped up and gave his gran a hug, then he got out his phone and took a picture of the chessboard, grinning as he slipped it back in his pocket. He wagged a finger at her. 'That's so you don't cheat.'

Helen gasped in mock horror. 'As if I'd do a thing like that.'

'She does, Mum.' Toby came and slipped an arm round Jess's waist, and she reached down to give him a kiss. 'I have to keep an eye on her.'

Jess laughed, because she'd had the same problem playing games with her mum when she'd been a child as well. Helen hated to lose, that was the trouble. Way too competitive, not to mention always being right. But she was a fabulous gran to Toby, and Jess could see she'd have to be careful or she'd end up monopolising him.

They said their goodbyes and headed off towards the Chinese takeaway down on the harbour, Ben's favourite.

When Jess got home, all the lights were on in the house, and she could hear laughter through the open window. Her ex-husband's laughter.

'I've got to tell Dad about what happened this afternoon,' Toby said, leaping out of the car the moment they stopped.

Jess watched him go. She hadn't a clue what he might be talking about. But then he was the sort of child who compart-mentalised his life. He talked to her about school and the books he was reading, and he talked to Rob about astronomy and maths, his two main interests. How they'd produced a mathe-matical whiz she'd no idea, as she herself was pretty clueless. Rob was not far ahead, but he had the ability to wing it. What did happen this afternoon? she wondered. No doubt she'd find out soon enough.

She picked up the takeaway, slung Toby's bag over her shoulder and headed into the house. She'd thought they were going to have an evening to themselves tonight, but it looked like there was going to be a family gathering. The sound of Carol's laughter, loud and unrestrained, made her wince. Had they been drinking? Then Rob's booming guffaw burst through the kitchen doorway, and she knew for certain that they had.

She stopped for a moment, leant against the wall. A headache throbbed at her temples, the euphoria having worn off. She was weary after the move and the stress of organising everything, bone tired with all the physical lifting and carrying. She couldn't face a boozy night, wanting nothing more than to eat, then have a nice hot bath and go to bed.

They'll understand, she told herself, loitering for another moment in the lounge. She noticed that Ben had put their moving-in cards up on the mantelpiece, and she went to look, picking up each one to see who it was from. So much goodwill, from friends and old neighbours and work colleagues, it filled her with a warm glow.

She picked up the last card, a cartoon picture of a house on the front. *Congratulations on your new home*, it said inside. And underneath, in big, bold handwriting were the words: *Welcome to your nightmare, bitch.*

CHAPTER SIX

She gasped, the card dropping from her hands. Who would send such a horrible message? And what was Ben doing putting it on the mantelpiece alongside all the others?

Before she could pick it up, Ben came into the room.

'There you are.' He took the takeaway bag off her, led her into the kitchen, and before she could say anything about the card, she was thrust into the centre of an impromptu house-warming party.

Everyone was there, the whole blended family, and she was thrown for a minute, the vitriolic message of the card at odds with the noisy, cheerful gathering. She gave herself a quick talking-to, making herself push the shock of it to the back of her mind. Sour grapes, that was all. Somebody who was jealous that they had navigated an amicable separation. But still the question lingered – who would bother to do that? It felt malicious, menacing. It's just a card, she told herself, plastering a smile on her face.

Mo and Toby were shuffling through packs of Pokémon cards, heads together, oblivious to everything going on around them. Ruby was getting plates out of the cupboard, Rob and

Carol were laughing about something. It was relaxed, jovial, like their usual Friday gatherings, a tradition they'd started months ago to prepare the kids for the move. Except this was different. This was in her new home. And someone hated her for it. The very thought made her shiver.

She looked round the table, flustered. 'I don't think I've got enough food for everyone.' Ben put the bag on the table and started unloading the containers. She caught Rob's eye. 'I thought you guys would be sorting out your house. I wasn't expecting—'

Rob held up a hand, stopping her. 'It's okay, we've eaten, don't worry about us. We just brought some bubbly round as a housewarming gift.' He held up a huge bottle of champagne, half empty now.

Carol giggled. 'I'm sorry, but we started without you.'

She didn't look sorry. She looked sozzled. Rob was flushed, and Ben gave a little shrug, like it wasn't his idea but there was nothing he could do. 'There's a glass here for you, love.' He pushed an empty champagne flute towards Rob. 'Fill her up.'

The sight of Toby and Mo dashing out of the room distracted her. The thump of their feet running up the stairs told her they were going to check out Toby's room. She smiled then, all thoughts of the malicious card swept from her mind as she wondered what her son would make of the decor. She hoped he'd like the map of the night sky they'd put next to his bed, the constellation duvet cover and his very own desk. He would sleep in the top bunk, and there was a sofa underneath that could turn into a bed when Mo or one of Toby's friends stayed over.

'I'll just nip up and make sure everything's okay.' She glanced at Ben. 'Can you sort out the food? I'll be back in a minute.'

Toby was sitting on his bunk, tracing the constellations on his poster with his finger, muttering their names under his breath. Mo was asleep on the sofa, curled up like a cat, his black hair flopping over his eyes, his thumb in his mouth. Her heart melted. He was such a gentle child, a bit nervy at times, but he looked up to Toby like he was some sort of superhero. It always surprised her how children that age could fall asleep in an instant, but it had been an exciting day for him and the poor boy was obviously worn out.

Toby put a finger to his lips, then pointed at Mo. She nodded, whispering, 'I know, it's okay, I won't wake him.'

She beamed at her son, eyes stinging. *This is what it's all about. These little guys.* She checked herself. And Ruby. She mustn't forget Ruby, making sure she put as much effort into her relationship with her soon-to-be stepdaughter as she did with the boys.

'This is so cool, Mum. I love it. I really, really love it.' Toby leant down and flung his arms round her neck, giving her a sloppy kiss on the cheek. 'And I really, really love you.' He kissed her again. 'I'm so glad we're all going to be next door and everything. And I can see Dad and Mo and Carol whenever I want.' He pulled away and frowned. 'That's how it's going to work, isn't it? Or will there be rules about when I can see Dad, like Patrick in my class? He can only see his dad at weekends, and he says...' his voice faltered, 'a week is a long time without your dad.'

She stroked his hair, waiting for the lump in her throat to melt away, hating that her innocent child had a mind full of worries. 'You can see your dad whenever you want, and Mo can come here whenever he wants. We're going to be one family, living in two houses.'

He buried his face in her neck and she thought she felt the dampness of tears against her skin.

'Come downstairs and have something to eat,' she said, clinging to the practical so her emotions wouldn't get the better of her.

'I don't want to eat with the grown-ups, it's too loud.' He was very sensitive to noise, and even up here she could hear the guffaws of laughter.

'Okay, well you can have your food in your room, but just this once. We're not going to make a habit of it.' She was loath to spoil his excitement about the new house and she knew he'd be careful, as he hated mess. 'You can try out your desk while you're eating.'

Thankfully they'd had laminate flooring put in all the rooms, as Mo was asthmatic, but it was practical for the inevitable spills as well. Young boys and new carpets were not a good mix. There was a rag rug by the bed to add a bit of comfort, but she knew Toby would like the simplicity.

When she re-entered the kitchen, a sudden burst of laughter jarred through her. Toby was right, it *was* loud. She watched him wince as he grabbed his plate of chicken fried rice, then scurried back up the stairs. Ruby had disappeared as well, probably ensconced in her room with her headphones on as usual. Self-contained, Ben called her, seemingly unworried by her detachment from the rest of the family.

Jess flopped into a seat, grabbed her glass of champagne and took a few gulps before picking up her fork and starting on her plate of king prawn curry and egg fried rice.

Ben was telling one of his shaggy dog stories, which she was pretty sure held only a fleeting resemblance to the truth, but he did like to get people laughing and he had a quirky sense of humour that never failed. She ate steadily while the others talked, the volume getting louder, their laughter more raucous. Her headache was stronger now, throbbing at her temples, the words on the card floating in and out of her mind, refusing to go away.

'Cheer up, love, it might never happen.' Carol was looking at her, a big smile on her face, eyes shining. She was having a good time and Jess was happy to see it. She knew there was sadness in Carol's past, but she didn't know all the details and hadn't liked to ask. She supposed she would find out in time. Over recent months, although there had been little chance for them to sit down together and have a good old heart to heart, she had seen Carol become more relaxed and start to open up a bit.

She swallowed her mouthful of food. 'Sorry, I was zoned out there.' She forced a smile, not wanting to break the celebratory mood. 'It's been a full-on day, hasn't it?'

Ben waved the champagne bottle at her. 'You're way behind. Come on, darling. We're celebrating the first chapter in our new lives.'

She emptied her glass, feeling the bubbles fizzing in her mouth, a burst of warmth spreading through her. Ben filled it up. 'Let's toast to that then.' Her eyes travelled round the table. 'To our new lives.'

I just need a couple of drinks, then I'll forget about that card.

But she couldn't forget about it. She was itching to go and have another look, see if she'd made a mistake, misread it maybe, and it was just a joke.

Later, when their neighbours had gone home and she was alone with Ben, she returned to the lounge to retrieve the card and show it to him.

But it was gone. She searched the floor, thinking it might have slithered under the sofa or the armchair, but there was no sign of it.

'I thought you'd like me to put them up,' Ben said when he came into the room and found her reading each one in turn, sure that someone must have seen the card on the floor and put it back on the mantelpiece. She couldn't quite remember what the picture on the front looked like – there were a lot of similar designs.

She glanced up at him, carried on with her search. 'I do, that was really thoughtful of you, but there was one in particular that I wanted to show you.' She put the last card down, frowned. 'It's not here, though.' She scanned the room, hoping she might have overlooked it, her hands gravitating to her hips.

'Who was it from?'

'That's the thing. It wasn't signed. But it had this horrible message in it. I wanted to show you to see what your take on it was. Whether it might be a joke.'

He came over to her and wrapped her in a hug, sensing she needed comfort. 'What did it say?'

'It said "Welcome to your nightmare, bitch".' She felt him tense. Her voice cracked. 'Big scrawled writing, like the person had been really angry when they wrote it and had been pressing so hard the pen nib nearly went through the card.'

Ben stroked her hair, held her tighter. 'Wow, that's horrible, no wonder you're feeling a bit jittery. I didn't see anything like that when I put them up. Ruby helped me. We opened all the envelopes together and read the messages. She was really chuffed that so many people were wishing us well. I think it made her feel better about the whole moving-in-together thing.'

'You read all of them?' She pushed back, studied his face. 'Are you sure? I thought maybe you'd put it up there not real-ising what was written inside.'

'I'm positive. They were all lovely.' He pulled her closer, kissed the top of her head. 'Maybe you didn't read it right.'

She felt unsure now, but she could still picture it in her mind. 'It was there. Honestly it was.'

'There's always someone wanting to rain on happy people's parades,' Ben said. 'I'd forget about it if I were you.'

'You're missing the point, though.' She pulled away from him again, caught his eye. 'Someone must have come in here and put that card on the mantelpiece and then taken it away again. And the only people who could have done that are part of this family.'

He laughed. 'Well that can't be right, can it? We're like the bloody Four Musketeers aren't we, in this new venture of ours. You, me, Carol and Rob. All for one and one for all. No, love, there must be another explanation.' He thought for a moment. 'I mean, there's been all sorts of people in and out of here today. And if it was on the floor, maybe one of the others thought it was rubbish and just threw it away.'

It was clear to Jess that he didn't quite believe her, and without the evidence there was no way to convince him she wasn't imagining things.

She took his point, though, that lots of people had been in and out of the house. Ben's ex, Darcey, had called in to drop off some things for Ruby. Rob had been over the previous day to go round with the property developer, making sure everything was in order before they moved in. Pam from work had brought a cake. A couple of their new neighbours had popped in to introduce themselves. In reality, it had been pretty hectic.

'You're tired, love. We all are. It's been a hell of a thing getting the move done, and I'm so proud of you, the way you got stuck in and made it happen. The kids' bedrooms look fantastic, and I love the colours you picked for our room and downstairs.' He sighed a happy sigh, and she could see the love in his eyes. 'You're a miracle-worker, that's what you are.'

This is what I should be thinking about, not some stupid card.

The tension seeped from her shoulders, and she caught his hand, entwining her fingers with his, enjoying the roughness of his skin against the softness of hers.

'We did it,' he murmured, his eyes fixed on hers. 'You and me. The dream team.' She leant against him, sinking into the comfort of his embrace. 'Forget about the party-poopers. I've waited so long for someone like you to come into my life, and I'm not going to let anyone mess this up for us. Okay? I'll always keep you safe. Always.'

Music was playing softly through the speakers. He'd set it all up earlier, with Alexa in charge of the playlist. These were end-of-the-night songs, the smoochy numbers she remembered from school discos. She wrapped her arms around his neck, closed her eyes and followed his lead as he led her round the room in a slow dance.

He meant every word he'd just said. He *would* always be there to look after her, whoever might want to make her feel ill at ease. She smiled to herself, deciding that she needed to learn to trust a little more and control a little less. There was nothing to worry about. Nothing at all.

CHAPTER SEVEN

After a restless night, the next day was glorious. Ben was snoring gently, and she knew it would be a while before he was ready to get up. It was still early, just past seven, but she was a morning person by nature and enjoyed a bit of quiet before her family rose.

Feeling thankful that she hadn't drunk enough to suffer a hangover, she hopped out of bed and crept down the hallway, peeping into Toby's room. Mo had stayed the night, because Carol was feeling a bit worse for wear when Rob had finally decided it was time to go back to their own house. Instead of being in the sofa bed, though, he'd climbed up into Toby's bunk and they were curled up together, their faces so peaceful it brought a surge of emotion that filled her chest. Mo was a lovely addition to their family, quite chatty once he relaxed and a perfect companion for Toby.

This was exactly why they'd bought houses next door to each other, she thought as she crept out of the room, poking her head round Ruby's door. She looked peaceful too. It seemed everyone had slept well in the new house except her, the horrible card still niggling at her.

She made herself a coffee in the new machine and hugged the mug to her chest, trying to accentuate the positive and push the negative out of her head. A new life with Ben and their wedding to look forward to. She'd hardly dared hope it would happen after her dithering. She'd never been good with change. Maybe that was why she'd stuck with Rob – better the devil you know. But now she'd taken the plunge, she was looking forward to a different future. Okay, so last night's gathering hadn't been what she'd wanted, and the card had shaken her up, but it had been a busy and stressful day. Maybe she'd imagined it after all.

She'd enjoyed herself once she'd had some food and a couple of drinks. Ben with his stories, Carol with her pithy quips and Jess and Rob as the audience. That was how the dynamic seemed to work. Ben and Carol had an easy friendship, but then they knew each other from many years ago, when they'd gone out together for a while.

It was a small world on the island, the community intertwined with family connections past and present as well as old school friends who popped up in each other's lives. You couldn't fall out with people when you lived in a place like that, and you never passed someone you knew without stopping for a chat. It could feel very inclusive and supportive that way. At other times, it could feel claustrophobic. It just depended on where you were at with your life. Inevitably there was gossip, and Jess knew that her new living arrangement had sparked a lot of interest and conflicting opinions.

She didn't care what anyone else thought, though, confident that she and Rob were doing what was best for their family, and if she was pressed about how things would work, she had ready answers.

Her coffee smelt delicious, and she took a sip, savouring that first taste. But there was something niggling at her, and she let her mind travel back to their gathering the previous evening to see if she could work out what it was.

She'd always enjoyed their get-togethers. In the past, the situation had been different because she'd only really seen Ben at the weekends so they didn't disrupt the kids' school routines. Their Friday evenings were the start of their time together, so it was always something to look forward to. And it was planned, so she was ready for it. She wasn't sure how she felt about impromptu gatherings like last night, though.

What will it be like if Rob and Carol treat our house like a second home?

That was her niggle. She hadn't thought about it before now, really, the focus being on the kids being able to drift between houses as the urge took them. They hadn't talked about the adults and what the boundaries were going to be.

It was a special night, she reminded herself, taking another sip of her coffee. We'd just moved in. Things will settle down.

Remembering the card, she put her mug down while she had another search round in the lounge, but it was nowhere to be seen and she was happy to believe that she might have imagined it. Stress and tiredness could do funny things to the mind, and she closed the door on that particular worry.

The sun was streaming through the windows and she decided it would be lovely to have her morning coffee in the garden, start making plans about what they might do with the space. At the moment, it was just laid to lawn and frankly a bit boring. She wanted flower beds and a vegetable patch.

She opened the patio doors and stepped outside. That's when she noticed the fence between the two houses had been taken down.

When the heck did that happen? She could have sworn it was there yesterday when they were moving in. Certain of it, when she thought back, because they'd sat in the garden to have a cup of tea and a breather in the afternoon. Had she looked after that? She'd heard Rob and Ben out there a bit later, but she'd been busy sorting out the bedrooms, and hadn't taken much notice.

Her heart sank. It wasn't what they'd agreed. They'd asked for a gate to be put in so Toby could go round to his dad's whenever he wanted and Mo could come round to play. She hadn't agreed to the fence being removed completely. Now they had no privacy at all. With the best will in the world, this was a step too far in terms of blending.

She went back inside, her benevolent mood gone.

There was a lot they hadn't discussed, she realised, finding a box of cereal in the cupboard and pouring herself a bowl. She functioned better when she'd had food, knew she was prone to being a bit negative when her blood sugar was low. As she munched her way through the granola, a knock on the window startled her, and Rob walked in without waiting to be asked.

'I thought you'd be up.' He grinned. 'Looks like we're the only early birds today. I got bored waiting for Carol to wake up.' He laughed. 'I'm not sure she'll be up to much today, not after last night.'

Jess thought it was best not to comment. After all, it was none of her business any more. She didn't want to sound bitchy, but she was surprised at how much Carol had been drinking. It seemed a bit out of character really, but she supposed she was entitled to kick back once in a while.

'Is everything okay?' she asked before she could stop herself. She could tell Rob wanted to talk. 'Sit down. Let me get you a coffee from our fancy new machine.'

He sank into a seat, ran a hand through his hair. 'Thank you. It's probably nothing.'

'What's nothing?' Ben appeared, his comment finished with a yawn. He was still in his pyjamas, looking all ruffled.

'Coffee?' Jess asked, grabbing another pod for the machine and passing Rob his mug. 'So... what's the problem?'

Rob spooned sugar into his drink, staring at it as he stirred.

'That's the thing, I don't know the precise details. I just over-heard a weird conversation the other day. Carol was practically hissing at whoever was on the phone. You know, like really angry, telling them to never call her again.'

Jess looked up. 'That doesn't sound like nothing,' she said, passing Ben his coffee. 'Have you spoken to her about it?'

Rob shook his head. 'I tried, but she refused to say anything much. Just said it was a work issue and it had been sorted. Then she went off on one about me eavesdropping on her private conversations.' He caught her eye. 'I had to back off. Mo was there, and you know how upset he gets about raised voices.'

Jess nodded, wondering if it was an odd coincidence that she and Carol were both feeling threatened... or was she making two and two equal five?

'Maybe you just have to believe her when she says it's sort-ed?' Ben said, stirring sugar into his drink.

Rob didn't look convinced. 'If we were still working at the same place, it wouldn't be a problem. You know, I could look out for her. But now she's moved to a new company... well, I haven't a clue what's going on.'

'She was pretty relaxed last night,' Ben said, brow furrowed. 'I mean, she was on great form. Honestly, mate, I'd take her word for it. Maybe she'll tell you what it's about if you don't press too hard. You know, give her a bit of space.'

Rob nodded. 'Yeah, you're probably right. It's just... I thought she seemed, well, scared. And if anything happened to her... Christ, it doesn't bear thinking about.'

Ben nodded. 'I know. Just keep an eye out for her, that's all you can do.'

The room fell silent, each of them lost in their own thoughts, Jess trying to figure out if there might be a connection or if she was being paranoid.

'Anyway,' she said eventually, deciding it was time to change the subject, 'what happened to the fence?'

The men looked at each other.

'I meant to talk to you about that,' Ben said, pulling a face. Rob gave him an encouraging nod. 'Thing is, we all decided it's a better space for the kids to play in without the fence. You know, easier than opening and shutting the gate all the time. We're going to put a barbie pit in and a pizza oven. And a bit of decking with a canopy where we can all sit when the weather's nice. Footie nets for the boys and...' he glanced at Rob, who gave him a thumbs up, 'we've got a shed lined up for the bikes. We did agree on that, didn't we?'

Jess held up a hand, heart sinking. 'Wait... just wait a minute. *We* didn't decide anything. Or is it you two making all the decisions now?' Heat rushed to her cheeks, and her eyes flicked between the two men; neither was apparently willing to answer the question.

'Well... it was actually Carol who suggested the fence should go,' Ben said eventually. 'She said it was ugly and the garden would look better and be more useful without it. Then I put it to Rob and he could see the logic, so we got on with it.'

She glared at him.

He held up his hands. 'We didn't think you'd mind.'

Anger seemed to have paralysed her vocal cords.

'I'll admit the shed was my idea,' he continued. 'But we do need somewhere to put all the bike stuff and to work on them.'

'There are two perfectly good garages,' she pointed out. 'Couldn't you use one of those?' She caught the glance Ben sent to Rob, and her irritation spiked. Was she going to be included in any of their schemes? It didn't look like it. 'Oh, you've got other plans for the garages, have you?'

Rob looked uncomfortable. 'We thought we could turn one into a den for the kids. You know, we've got the table football and the ping-pong. That could go in there.'

Jess could feel her frustration about to burst out and took a calming breath before she spoke. 'Can't the other one be for the bikes?'

Rob shrugged. 'If that's what you want. Okay, well I've already got the play stuff from Mum and Dad's stashed in our garage, so we'll set it up there.' He winked at Ben. 'Looks like your house is Bike Central.'

The men high-fived and Rob left before Jess could return to the subject of the fence, feeling that somehow she'd been outmanoeuvred. But that wasn't her priority now.

'Has Carol said anything to you about being in trouble at work? Or somebody bothering her?'

Ben took a long sip of his coffee before answering. 'Nope.'

'I'm just wondering if it might be connected to that horrible card. You know, somebody who doesn't approve of our new living arrangements.'

'Nah, love. I think you're barking up the wrong tree.' He reached across the table and took her hand. 'Carol's problems are nothing to do with us. Don't start thinking you need to get involved. She's perfectly capable of sorting out her own life without you and Rob butting in.'

Jess wasn't convinced, but if Carol had told him something in confidence, she didn't expect him to divulge it. She'd just have to find out for herself.

CHAPTER EIGHT

It was a strange sort of a day after that. Ben and Rob disappeared into Rob's garage for long periods of time on the pretext of creating the children's playroom. Jess suspected they were setting up the Xbox and 'testing' it. Carol was nowhere to be seen, so Jess was supervising all the kids. Not that she really minded. Ruby was happy to spend time alone, setting up shots of her room for her Instagram account. The boys were up and down the stairs, in and out of the houses, exploring possibilities for new games, like a couple of excited puppies.

The sun was shining, the day was warm, and she gave herself a talking-to. She had to stop this paranoia and enjoy their new home. This was what they'd hoped for, wasn't it? Truth be told, it was as relaxing a time as she could remember with the kids. She grabbed her book, picked up a blanket and settled on the lawn for a bit of uninterrupted reading.

Ten minutes later, Toby came running to find her, worry etched across his face.

'Mo wants his mummy, but we don't know where she is,' he panted, sliding to the ground beside her.

Jess put her book down, puzzled. 'She's not at home?' She'd assumed Carol was sleeping off a hangover.

He shook his head, his big blue eyes brimming with tears. 'We've looked all over for her.'

She put an arm round him and pulled him close, gave him a kiss, wondering what had got Mo so upset. The boys had been having a lovely time only minutes before. 'Doesn't Daddy know where she is?'

'He says we can't go in the garage and if we have a problem we have to come and find you.'

Jess got to her feet, Toby grabbing her hand and pulling her towards the house next door. 'He's in his bedroom, Mum, he's crying and it's my fault.' His bottom lip was quivering. 'I think... I did something to upset him.'

'Hey, it's okay,' she said, bending to give him another hug. She couldn't bear to see him upset like this. He was the centre of her world, and her happiness revolved around his. If he was sad or upset, then so was she. 'What do you think you did?'

He gave a dramatic sigh. 'We found a dead mouse by the back door. And we started talking about things dying, and I said "like your daddy", and then he burst into tears and got really angry and said his daddy was only dead in England but he was alive in Turkey. And I said you can't be dead in one place and alive in another, but he wouldn't believe me, and then he started hitting me and said he hated me and he wanted his mummy. But we couldn't find her.'

Jess's heart sank. Death was such a hard concept for children. The finality of it. Poor Mo. She could remember one of her first conversations with Carol. The boys were playing with Ben and Rob while the women cleared up after the meal.

'It's so lovely seeing Mo smiling and laughing,' Carol said as she cleared the table while Jess stacked the dishwasher. 'It's been so tough for him without his dad.'

'Are you divorced?' Jess asked, glad of the opportunity to find out a bit more about Rob's new partner.

There was a loaded silence, and she wondered if she'd overstepped the mark.

'He's no longer with us,' Carol murmured, her face hidden by a curtain of hair as she bent over the table. 'He... he died in a fishing accident.'

'He died?' Rob hadn't mentioned a word about this, and Jess felt wrong-footed, horrified that she might have caused upset.

'Hmm-hmm.' Carol nodded, clearly finding it hard to talk.

'I'm so sorry.' Jess straightened up, not sure whether to go and give Carol a hug, deciding in the end that it probably wasn't what she wanted. After all, they hardly knew each other. 'I didn't mean to pry.'

'No, it's okay.' Carol looked up, gave an over-bright smile. 'It's been hard for Mo to adjust to our new situation. And me, to be honest, as a single parent. Turkey is so different to anywhere else we've lived.' She passed Jess a stack of plates. 'I think he misses his grandad, too. They were very close.' She gave a big sigh. 'But he blamed me for everything, so I felt I couldn't stay.'

'Oh, that's tough. On you and Mo.' Jess put a hand on her shoulder, gave it a sympathetic rub, thinking she'd never seen Carol looking vulnerable like this. 'I'm sorry you've had such a hard time.'

Carol went back to the table and started collecting the empty glasses. 'Thank you. But I think we've turned a corner now. Mo loves Rob, he really does. And Toby is such a great friend for him.'

Jess smiled. 'I feel the same about Mo.' She laughed. 'And you, for that matter. I'm glad Rob's found someone who can relate to him better than I ever did. You two were made for each other.'

It felt strange saying it, but she really meant it. Carol appeared to be intensely ambitious. Just like Rob. She lived and breathed her work. Just like Rob. And they seemed to have the same quirky sense of humour, constantly sharing secret jokes and quoting from favourite films that Jess hadn't even known he liked.

Their relationship had shown her a whole new side to her husband and given her the confidence to move on with her own plans, knowing that he'd be much happier with Carol than he'd ever been with her. Of course she still cared about him, but she was delighted that he seemed to have found his soulmate, just as she'd found hers.

Rob kept telling her how intelligent Carol was, how she was destined for big things. It was obvious that he was incredibly proud of her. Jess felt the only thing she'd ever done to make him proud was to bear him a son.

Personally she thought ambition was overrated. Surely the most important thing in life was being happy in your own skin? Money was important, of course it was, but only to the point where you had enough. After that, she wasn't really interested, had no desire to be wealthy. Having family time was worth more to her. That was where she and Rob differed. He yearned for wealth, to be seen as a success.

He'd spent much of the time they'd been together chasing his dreams. First he wanted to be top of the sales team in terms of income. Once he'd achieved that, he wanted to be team leader, and after that, branch manager. Now he'd reached that goal, he was looking to head up the European division. And all the time his son was growing up and he wasn't there to experience those little milestones that Jess treasured. He was a great dad, but he just wasn't there enough, and Toby felt it.

Thank goodness Ben was different. He wouldn't be too busy for sports day or parents' evening or the school play. He wouldn't put work before family. Maybe that was part of the attraction for her. Some part of her maternal instinct kicking in, subliminally making her seek a better mate to nurture her young.

The fact that Rob and Ben were opposites was perhaps why they got on so well. Ben was happy to let Rob plan their cycle rides, their fitness regimes, their excursions away. But he was also able to say no, which Rob respected.

She halted her thoughts and concentrated on her son, who was pulling her across the garden and towards the open patio doors of her husband's house. *Am I supposed to ask before coming in here?* They hadn't really talked about it, how it would work on a day-to-day basis. That was the whole point, though, she reminded herself. Then corrected her assertion. *Not for the adults.* They couldn't just wander into each other's houses at will. That would be awkward in the extreme.

She glanced around, hoping Carol would appear and she could hand back the problem of her upset son. 'Carol?' she called, stopping just outside the patio doors, not wanting to go any further.

She waited. No reply. Cleared her throat, resisting Toby's attempts to drag her into the house. 'Carol, are you there?'

Silence.

'Come on, Mum.' Toby tugged impatiently at her arm. 'I told you she's not here.'

Still, the idea that she was intruding in a space that wasn't hers wouldn't leave her. It didn't help that she recognised some of the furniture as things she'd shared with Rob for all those years. His parents had suggested that he take what he wanted as they were going to put their place on the market now it was no longer needed. She swallowed, uncomfortable, as she crept upstairs, feeling like a burglar, senses on high alert in case Carol came home and found her there. She'd most likely popped out for some shopping, and the supermarket was only a short walk away, five minutes tops. Surely she'd be back soon.

Mo was face down on his bed, sobbing so hard his whole body was shaking.

Her heart went out to him. 'Hey, sweetheart.' She sat next to him, put a comforting hand on his back. 'It's okay, Toby didn't mean to upset you. Really he didn't.'

'He shouldn't say my daddy's dead.' Mo turned his head to the side to look at her, eyes burning with a fire she'd never seen before, his face blotchy and red. 'That's a horrible thing to say. He's not like that mouse. He's not.' His little fist thumped the mattress.

Toby sat down beside her, silent tears rolling down his cheeks. 'I'm sorry, Mo. I'm really sorry.' He reached for the younger boy, then pulled back. 'Please don't be mad at me.'

Mo made no response, but after a few minutes, his tears started to subside and he pulled himself up and curled himself against Jess's body, his arms snaking round her waist. She held both boys to her, wondering how on earth she could make this better without being misleading. Dead was dead, but how you explained it to a five-year-old who thought otherwise, she wasn't sure.

It's not your job, she told herself. You don't know the facts. Carol needs to do this. She took a couple of deep breaths. All she had to do was smooth over the upset. No explanations needed. In fact, distraction was probably the order of the day.

'I don't suppose either of you would like some ice cream?' she whispered. 'I think it's what we need to make us all feel better.'

'I don't want to talk about dead things,' Mo insisted.

'No, we won't, will we, Toby?' She hugged both boys a little tighter.

'Nope.' Toby shook his head, face solemn. 'No dead stuff. Promise.'

'Pinky promise?' Mo asked, crooking his little finger.

'Pinky promise,' Toby said, catching Mo's finger with his own and shaking.

Then Mo was sliding off the bed and Toby was hugging him and telling him he was sorry again.

Jess followed them downstairs, out into the garden and back into her own house, so distracted by her thoughts of ice cream that she didn't notice what was on her kitchen floor until she felt the crunch under her feet. She looked down, her hands flying to her mouth. The new set of mugs that she'd taken out of the dishwasher and left on the side, ready to put away, were smashed on the tiles. All of them.

They'd been a housewarming present from her mum. Bone china, with an intricate floral pattern. A sob caught in her throat, and she sank into a chair. How could this have happened? It wasn't as though they could have been blown off the worktop, even though she'd left the patio doors open when she'd gone next door with Toby. Had somebody been in here and done this? She really couldn't think of another explanation. Unless Ruby... No, she wouldn't. Would she?

The shock seemed to paralyse her. It was like she herself had been violated, rather than her crockery.

'What's the matter?' Toby asked, before his eyes settled on the scattering of broken china. 'Oh dear.' His eyes met hers. 'How did that happen?'

She swallowed, tried to gather herself, not wanting the boys to see how upset she was. 'There's been a bit of an accident,' she said, her voice over-bright. 'Let me clear this up, then I'll bring your ice cream outside. Okay?'

Toby and Mo nodded and went to sit on the lawn, while she scanned the mess, the weight of what had happened, the maliciousness of the damage, pressing on her chest until she could hardly breathe.

CHAPTER NINE

She took pictures to show Ben, then cleared up the mess and dished out the ice cream. Once the boys were settled with theirs, she took a bowl upstairs. Ruby looked up as she walked into her room, a scowl painted across her face.

'What about knocking before you come in?' she snapped, tucking her phone behind her as though hiding evidence.

Jess held up the bowl, stretched her mouth into a smile. 'I brought ice cream.' Did the girl look guilty? She thought she did.

Ruby's scowl lifted for a nanosecond before settling back in place. 'You still need to knock.' She held out a hand for the bowl, a look of petulant frustration on her face. Such a pretty face when she smiled, Jess thought, hoping that this animosity might fade sooner rather than later, now they were all going to be living together.

'Of course,' she said with a forced grin, deciding that now was not the time to try and discuss manners. 'I'll try and remember.' Her hand tightened round the bowl and she had to fight the temptation to turn around and leave the room. *Does this child even deserve ice cream?* If she'd spoken like that to her own parents, there would have been consequences, but Ruby's parenting to date didn't seem to include any such thing. 'We'll have to sit down soon with your dad and work out the house rules, won't we?'

Their eyes locked, and they stared at each other for what felt like minutes but was probably only seconds. Eventually Jess gave in and handed over the bowl, a curt nod being Ruby's only acknowledgement of the favour.

Teenage girls. Was there anything in life that was trickier to deal with? Maybe teenage boys, but she would have to wait a few years to see how that worked out.

She tried to make her voice nonchalant. 'I don't suppose you've been down to the kitchen in the last half-hour, have you?'

Ruby narrowed her eyes. 'Why?'

'I'd put a new set of mugs on the side, and when I came back inside, they were smashed all over the floor.' Her eyes didn't move from Ruby's face, checking for a reaction.

'Those ones from your mum?' Ruby looked genuinely shocked. 'But they were lovely. I was going to claim one for myself. You know, so I could have a nice mug just for me up here.' Her expression was one of genuine disappointment, and Jess felt that she was telling the truth.

She plodded back downstairs, picked up her own bowl of melting ice cream and spooned it into her mouth. When was Ben going to come back? He'd been messing about in that garage all morning. She picked up her phone and messaged him. Since they'd moved in, she'd hardly seen him, and now she really needed to talk to him about the broken mugs and the fact that she suspected someone had been in their house.

The boys had finished their ice cream and were now playing with the Swingball she'd set up in the garden earlier. She checked her phone. No reply from Ben. Maybe he'd been distracted, hadn't heard the ping of her message. He was only in the garage next door, but now she was worried about an intruder, she didn't want to leave the house, or the boys, unattended. She chewed on a nail, watching the boys play outside, not sure what to do. Unease pulled at the back of her neck, bunching the muscles, making them ache, while her mind searched for an innocent explanation for the broken mugs.

She picked up her phone again, scanned through the pictures, unable to get away from the impression that it was a deliberate act of sabotage. Somebody messing with her mind, trying to make her frightened, and on top of the horrible card, she couldn't deny they were succeeding.

She hurried to the front door, thinking she could shout Ben from there and he'd hear her. That was when she noticed the cars were gone from next door's drive. He might still be in the garage, though. She called his name, waited for an answer, but there was nothing. She messaged him again, slipped back inside to check the boys were okay.

It was clear the other adults had all gone out and left her home alone looking after three children, worried about an intruder while they did goodness knows what. There was only one other person she could turn to: her mum.

'Hello, love.' Helen answered on the second ring. 'I was just thinking about you, wondering how you're settling in. I forgot to say I'm at work today. Julie asked if I could cover for Frankie. So I've only got a minute.'

Helen was a hairdresser, but she normally had Saturdays off so she could spend more time with Toby and Jess.

'Okay, I'll be quick,' Jess said, the words tumbling out of her mouth. 'Something weird has happened and the others have disappeared and I'm here with the kids and I'm not sure what to do.'

'Steady on. Why don't you calm down and take a deep breath. It's not like you to sound so flustered.'

Jess did as she was told for once, sinking into a kitchen chair as she took a moment to gather her thoughts before telling her mum about the card and the broken mugs.

'Well, I have to admit that does sound a bit odd. But you know, there's always people who are jealous, so I wouldn't worry about the card.'

Jess sighed, realising that nobody could understand how menacing it had felt unless they could see it for themselves. The anger in the way it had been written had been as disturbing as the message itself.

'And the broken mugs...' her mum continued. 'Do you remember a couple of years ago, when things started getting broken in the house and I got myself all worked up about having a poltergeist or something?' She laughed. 'Turned out it was the neighbour's cat, didn't it?'

Jess closed her eyes, relief flooding through her. That was it. A cat. The patio doors had been open, and it would be typical of a neighbouring feline to come and have a nosy. 'Oh, Mum, I do remember that, and you're right. It could have been a cat.' She could visualise it now, sitting on the worktop, paw swiping at the mugs one by one. Just the sort of thing a cat might do.

'Look, love, I've got to go. I've got a client waiting for her colour to be rinsed off. I'll see you later, shall I?'

They said their goodbyes and Jess disconnected, happy that the mystery of the broken mugs had been solved and deciding that she would just have to forget about the card. As her mum had said, put it down to petty jealousy and leave it at that.

She messaged Ben again, annoyed now that he hadn't responded. What if it had been a real emergency and she'd needed help? Despite her mum putting her mind at rest, her body still felt like it was on high alert, and she was unsettled and twitchy. Her stomach grumbled and she checked the time, surprised to see it was almost one o'clock. She knew there was little food in the house and had been planning on going shopping once Ben had finished messing about in the garage. Now she decided the easiest thing would be to take the kids out for lunch. Make an adventure of it. If the others could go out, then she could too.

Ben had fixed a little rack on the kitchen wall for all their keys, and she'd put her car keys on the first hook on the left. But now they weren't there. She stared at the empty hook, trying to remember when she'd last had them. It would have been the previous night, when she'd brought Toby home from her mum's. Maybe she'd forgotten to hang them up after the shock of the card. But even if she'd left them on the worktop, Ben would have hung them up; he was a stickler for putting things away. He said it came with being a tradesman, because if you didn't look after your tools, you couldn't do the job. A place for every-thing and everything in its place. She liked that about him, the way he looked after his things.

Had she left them in her jacket pocket? That was a possibil-ity, and she went to look, but apart from a packet of tissues, her pockets were empty. She proceeded to turn the house upside down, but there was no sign of her keys anywhere. She'd driven home, so obviously the keys had come into the house with her. So where were they now?

Another mystery. That was three now. It couldn't just be coincidence, could it?

Don't be so paranoid, she told herself. They'll turn up. I probably can't see for looking. Or perhaps Ben picked them up for some reason?

She tried to think whether there was anything in her car that he might need, but drew a blank. All his tools were kept in his work van. Her car was merely a way for her and Toby to get from A to B, and she kept very little in there apart from a bag of beach stuff in the boot.

Her stomach grumbled again, but she was stuck at home until the others turned up, so any thoughts of eating out had disappeared. A quick inventory of the kitchen cupboards told her it was going to be pasta and pesto for lunch. Not very exciting, and she knew it wasn't Ruby's favourite, but if that was all she had, there could be no arguing.

She checked her phone again. Still no message from Ben.

Where on earth was he?

Her mind went into overdrive, the strange events of the morning niggling at her.

What if somebody took the keys?

What if it wasn't a cat that broke the mugs?

What if the person who wrote the card has been in my house?

CHAPTER TEN

The sound of a car pulling into next door's drive shook her out of her panic and she ran to the window. Ben got out of the driver's seat of Rob's car, then Carol got out of the passenger side. Jess watched as Ben leant against the bonnet while they talked, then gasped when Carol threw her arms round his neck and gave him a kiss. Not on the cheek, but full on the lips. Ben's hands were perilously close to Carol's buttocks, she noticed, hackles rising.

Carol moved away from him, Ben laughed at something she said, then smacked her on the bum as he sauntered across to their own front door. She could actually hear him whistling, like he hadn't a care in the world.

Heat rose through her body, hands tightening by her sides as the front door opened and in he walked.

'Hey, love. What's for lunch? I could eat a scabby donkey, I'm that hungry.'

It was a moment before she could trust herself to speak.

'We haven't got anything in.' The chill in her voice like a blast of Arctic air. 'Unless you want pasta and pesto again.'

The expression on his face told her he was unimpressed.

'I'll nip to the shop for something, shall I? It's great having the supermarket on the doorstep.' His eyes lit up. 'I know, shall I get a Subway? Toby loves that, doesn't he? And Ruby.'

Jess folded her arms across her chest. 'Where have you been?'

The smile fell from his face. 'What do you mean?'

'I've been messaging and you didn't answer.'

Was he blushing? She was sure he was. He gave a quick laugh, his eyes not meeting hers. 'Oh, I left my phone in Rob's garage, idiot that I am.' He looked worried then. 'Why, has something happened? Are the kids all right?'

Her jaw tightened as she wondered whether to tell him about the mugs and the lost car keys. But those weren't the main things bothering her. 'I didn't know where you were. Where any of you were.' Her voice had a flinty sharpness to it that refused to be softened. Not after what she'd just seen. 'And how come you and Carol are so friendly all of a sudden?'

'Hey, what's got into you? Me and Carol have always been friendly.' He stuffed his hands in his pockets, a frown creasing his brow. 'What's this about?'

She sighed, hating the way she sounded. It was true that Ben and Carol had always got on well, but...

'I just saw you kiss her.'

He laughed and walked towards her, gathering her to him in a way that usually made her feel loved. Today, though, it didn't feel like that. Today it felt like he was hiding something. She pulled away and he looked puzzled. Hurt even.

'Look, there's friendly and then there's stepping over the line.' She pointed out of the window in the direction of the driveway. 'That kiss was more than friendly.'

'That was Carol, not me. Honestly...' he held his hands up in surrender, 'wasn't me that started it.'

'But your hands,' she hissed, 'which you have full control over, were on her bum.'

He rolled his eyes. 'So shoot me now. It didn't mean anything. I didn't even realise that's what happened, but if it's what you saw, then I'm sorry.' His voice had grown hard. 'I'll make sure it doesn't happen again.'

He glared at her. She glared back, feeling petty now, then dropped her gaze, tears stinging her eyes. This was not what she wanted their life together to be like, and she wasn't normally prone to jealousy. She trusted Ben, didn't she?

She sighed, not sure how to make this right now.

'Carol had a bit of an accident,' Ben said. 'She went out for a drive, found herself on the hills behind Ballaugh – you know, the road up to the mountain? Anyway, she swerved to miss a pheasant and ended up in a ditch. We had to go on a rescue mission and Rob stayed with her car, waiting for the tow truck, while I brought Carol back.' He looked a bit sheepish now. 'She was just saying thank you, but I can see what it might have looked like.'

Jess swallowed. Was that the truth?

'Ballaugh? What was she doing up there?' The moors at the back of the village stretched up over the hills, the roads rough after years of neglect and a pounding from the weather. Carol was not really an outdoor person and it seemed out of character for her to head up there on her own. Spectacular views, though, out over the sea towards Scotland and Ireland, so maybe that had been the attraction.

Ben shrugged. 'Honestly, I have no idea. She said she just wanted a bit of space. Mo was okay with us all at home, so it was a chance to get out on her own. Be a bit impulsive. That's not something a single mum can do too often.' He shrugged again, his gaze meeting hers. 'You can't blame her for wanting a bit of time to herself, can you?'

She went to him then, wrapped her arms round his waist, rested her head against his chest. He held her to him. 'I'm sorry,' she murmured. 'I didn't mean to start a fight.'

He stroked her hair. 'It's okay. I can see it might look a bit... well, off, if you didn't know the context.'

'I suppose it's going to take a bit of getting used to. This new living arrangement.'

He bent and kissed her. 'We'll settle in, love. Don't worry, it'll be fine. At least we're all friends, and as long as we talk through any problems, we'll find ways to make it work.'

'It felt weird, me being here on my own and you three disappearing like that.' She held him tighter, comforted by the steady thump of his heart. 'It's been a bit of a strange morning, to be honest.'

He gave her a squeeze. 'Why don't we see if there's anything I can rustle up for lunch while you tell me all about it?' He clearly understood that she didn't want him disappearing again, even if it was just to get some food. He was good like that, picking up on the unsaid, whereas Rob had been oblivious.

She nodded, letting her arms drop before following him into the kitchen, watching while he scoured the cupboards for ingredients.

'Pasta and pesto it is then,' he said eventually, glancing over his shoulder at her. 'How many am I cooking for?'

'Better make it five, I think. The boys have been glued together all morning, apart from a bit of a falling-out. But they seem to be fine now.'

She could see them out of the window playing some kind of chase, Toby pretending to be a monster out to devour Mo. She smiled, happy to see them having fun.

'A couple of odd things happened,' she said, telling Ben about the mugs smashed on the kitchen floor. She showed him the pictures on her phone, then had another look herself. 'Is it just me, or does it look like they've been dropped in a sort of pattern? You know, a pair there, another pair there and the final pair here.' She pointed at the screen as he looked over her shoulder. 'Mum thinks it was a cat.'

He laughed. 'I think your mum has hit the nail on the head. A hundred per cent cat-like behaviour. I'm not seeing a pattern, just broken mugs. Anyway, why would someone bother to do that?'

'To scare me? Same as the card.'

'You mean the card that's disappeared?' He tipped pasta into the pan. She bristled, but bit back her response, not willing to reignite their argument. He glanced at her and must have registered the expression on her face. 'Sorry, love. I don't mean to be dismissive, but you've got to ask yourself why anyone would bother. I mean, it's not normal behaviour, is it?'

'No, it's not. And that's why I'm scared.' Just saying it made her fear more real. 'The worst thing, though, is my keys have gone missing.'

He frowned. 'Your house keys?'

'And car keys. I put them on the same ring last night, and I swear I hung them on the rack, but they're not there now. I was going to take the kids out. That's when I noticed they'd gone.'

'You sure they're not just in a pocket somewhere? Or a drawer or a box or something?' He glanced around the kitchen as though he might magically spot them. 'It was pretty mad here yesterday, wasn't it?'

'I've looked everywhere.' Her eyes met his and she voiced her real concern. 'What if someone's taken them?'

'Oh come on. Enough of this paranoia.' He leant against the worktop, a hand raking through his hair. 'You have to stop looking at everything as though it's suspicious. Nobody is out to get you. You're just seeing things that aren't there.'

She ran her tongue round dry lips. Was he right?

CHAPTER ELEVEN

A little while later, Ben was dishing out pasta into five bowls when Carol appeared at the patio doors. She walked into the kitchen, smiled at him before swinging her gaze around the room.

'I was looking for Mo.' She appeared distracted, a bit flustered. 'I'm sorry, I lost track of time and realised he hasn't had anything for lunch.'

'They're upstairs,' Jess said, setting the cutlery on the table, irked that Carol had just come in without being invited. She held her tongue, thinking she needed to talk things through with Ben and decide what they wanted the protocols to be before she raised the subject. A bit of privacy would be nice, though.

'I've made him lunch,' Ben said, bringing the dishes over to the table. 'He might as well stay for a bit if you fancy more time to yourself.'

'Rob's still waiting for the tow truck.' Carol gave an exasperated sigh. 'I'd booked lunch for us all at the Hawthorne, but it's not going to happen now.'

Ben reached into the cupboard, pulled out another bowl. 'There's plenty if you want to stay. Nothing fancy, but...' He scraped the remains out of the pan. 'I always do way too much pasta.'

Carol seemed undecided for a moment, then she gave him a full-wattage smile. 'You're such a bloody treasure,' she said, sitting at the table, her eyes flicking to Jess for a millisecond before fixing back on Ben. 'You've got a keeper here, Jess. I wish Rob knew how to cook. Honestly, he's hopeless. Can't even microwave things.'

Jess frowned. 'He's not that bad. He used to do the cooking a couple of nights a week and we survived quite well.'

'Beans on toast, was it?' Carol laughed.

Jess opened her mouth to defend her ex-husband, but closed it again when Ben flashed her a warning glance. No need to pick a fight. Whatever gripe Carol had with Rob, it was their business and not hers.

She picked up another set of cutlery, placed it on the table. 'Maybe you can change your reservation to this evening instead?'

Carol was staring out of the window, lost in thought, and seemed not to hear her.

Jess decided to ignore what she felt was a snub and went to round up the children, who thundered down the stairs and into the kitchen in a babble of chatter. Ruby sat next to her father and started an intense conversation about her Instagram account and the fact that she'd had some bitchy comments on her latest post. 'I need to change that duvet cover,' she said. 'It's not right for my image. I need something more edgy. I saw this cool one online.' She thrust her phone in front of her father, a picture of the cover she wanted on the screen. 'Can I order it? It's only thirty pounds.'

'Sure you can,' Ben said, not really looking.

Jess felt a twitch of annoyance tug at her mouth. Ruby had been delighted with the bedding when they'd put it on. Now it wasn't good enough. She was worried that social media was turning her into someone she wasn't, with her constant striving to maximise her likes. It was a game with no winners, she thought. Especially when it came to their budget.

Once again, she bit her tongue. She'd wait until she and Ben were alone. Then she could get everything out in the open about Ruby and her behaviour and the need for ground rules so they could be consistent with their parenting.

Carol's phone pinged with a message. Her eyebrows shot up her forehead and she tapped in a quick reply. A couple of seconds later, another message pinged. The colour drained from her face, and she stood, her cutlery clattering to the floor.

'Everything okay?' Jess asked, startled by the sudden change in demeanour.

Carol's phone started ringing then, and she darted for the door. 'Got to take this,' she said, leaving the rest of them looking at each other, their eating halted mid-chew.

Jess stood. 'I'll... um, go and make sure she's all right. It's probably just Rob ringing about the car.'

'Yeah, you're probably right,' Ben said. 'She seems a bit jumpy, doesn't she? You don't think it's to do with the conversation we had with Rob earlier, do you?' He was choosing his words carefully so the children couldn't get involved, and Jess nodded, thinking he was probably right.

She hurried through the garden and halted by the neighbouring back door. Carol was nowhere in sight. She couldn't just walk into their house the way Carol had walked into hers; it didn't feel right. Better to set a precedent and go to the front door, she decided.

She was walking round the side of the house when she heard Carol's voice floating through the open kitchen window.

'I told you before, never ring me again.'

Jess stopped, pressing herself against the wall.

Carol was speaking again. 'No, no, that's never going to

happen.' Silence for a moment, then, 'Please, don't. I beg you. Please.' She sounded panicky, distressed.

Jess crept round to the front door. What on earth was going on?

She rang the doorbell, waited. Rang the bell again, but Carol didn't answer.

CHAPTER TWELVE

Jess went back to her own house to find Ben stacking the dishwasher.

'I thought the boys could chill out for an hour or so,' he said, nodding towards the lounge, where Toby was flicking through the film choices on the Disney Channel. 'Mo was almost falling asleep in his lunch, and from what they've told me, they've had a busy morning.'

'Good idea.' Her eyes met his. 'We need to talk.'

He raised an eyebrow, finished putting the cutlery in the tray, then slammed the door shut and switched the machine on.

Jess closed the double doors that separated the dining area from the lounge and filled the kettle, leaning back against the worktop next to him while it boiled.

'I heard Carol on the phone to someone. She sounded really scared.'

Ben frowned. 'Rob seemed concerned about someone from work, didn't he? I suppose we'd better tell him when he gets back. What do you think?'

She was about to reply when the patio doors opened and

Carol walked in, her face red and blotchy, like she'd been crying.

'Where's Mo?' She sounded frantic, her eyes raking round the room.

'He's watching a film with Toby.' Jess pointed to the lounge. 'He was—'

Carol ignored her and wrenched the doors open, picked her son up from the sofa and marched out the way she'd come.

'Carol...?' Jess followed her, watching as she hurried back to her own house. 'Is everything okay? Carol...' The only answer was the door banging shut behind her.

Ben appeared at the patio doors. 'Well that was weird. What's going on?'

Jess pulled him outside, not wanting Toby to overhear. 'I don't know, but I have a feeling... Whoever was on the phone was threatening her. She was pleading with them not to do something.'

Ben gave a low whistle, looking thoughtful for a moment. 'Tell you what, shall I try and talk to her? See if I can find out what's going on?'

Jess pictured Carol's arms around Ben's neck a little while earlier. The kiss. The last thing she wanted was him going round to see her, but she didn't want to appear jealous, deciding on nonchalance instead. She shrugged. 'You know her better than me.'

'She was sort of... anxious when I brought her home earlier. Pretending she was okay, you know, but I could see something was bothering her. I thought it was just the shock of running the car off the road.' His eyes studied the back of the neighbouring house. 'Maybe it wasn't.'

Jess pulled her phone out of her pocket. 'I'll give Rob a ring, make sure it's not just the two of them having a spat.' She reran the overheard conversation in her head, paused. 'I honestly don't think she was talking to him, though. She told whoever she was speaking to not to ring her again. No, it was definitely someone else. But perhaps Rob knows who it is.'

Ben ran a hand through his hair. 'Christ, this is awkward, isn't it? Maybe we shouldn't interfere.'

'There's no harm in going and checking she's okay.' Jess gave him a shove towards the neighbouring house. 'Do your charm offensive.'

Ben gave her a quizzical look. 'What? After you told me off for that kiss before?'

She sighed, frustrated. 'Well you don't need to bloody kiss her. Just make sure she's okay. I mean, you'll be lucky if she even answers.'

Ben strode across the lawn, Jess watching as he knocked on the patio doors, peered through the window, then walked round the side of the house. She rang Rob, but it went straight to voice-mail. She left a message urging him to call back.

A few minutes later, Ben returned. 'You were right, she's not answering.' He shrugged. 'We tried. I'll have a word with Rob later, if you like.'

Jess nodded, uneasy. 'I don't suppose there's anything more we can do. He's not answering his phone.'

Ben put his arms round her, pulled her into a hug. 'I'm sure it's nothing to worry about.' He kissed the top of her head. 'Let's stop worrying about the neighbours and spend a bit of time thinking about us, shall we?'

They spent the rest of the afternoon unpacking the last boxes and finding homes for things. Toby enjoyed helping, and Ben even managed to prise Ruby out of her room for a little while.

The events of earlier in the day had been pushed to the back of Jess's mind, so she was surprised when the doorbell rang and she found Rob standing there.

She smiled. 'Did you get the car sorted out?'

He looked uncomfortable, restless, his hands stuffed in the pockets of his jeans. 'Yeah, yeah, took all afternoon, but these things always take longer than you expect, don't they?'

'Are you coming in?' She stood to one side to allow him through.

He shook his head. 'Not now. Carol doesn't know I'm here, but I just wanted a quick word.'

He beckoned for her to come outside, clearly not wanting anyone else to hear. She folded her arms across her chest. 'What is it?'

'Carol's in a bit of a funk.'

Jess nodded. 'I know, she had this phone call earlier and—'

'I just wanted to ask you not to talk about her late husband with Mo. Apparently he's got himself confused and worked up about things and... well, it's just better if the subject doesn't come up.'

'It wasn't me who brought it up,' she snapped, not willing to just stand there and take a telling-off.

He sighed, rocked back on his heels. 'It's better if you let Carol deal with it her way, okay?'

'I was just trying to help.' There was a defensive note in her voice, her arms tightening across her chest.

He glared at her. 'It didn't help.' His tone was unexpectedly harsh. 'It's just created a load of aggravation, so, you know, just butt out is all I'm saying.'

With that, he turned and left. She watched him stalk through his own front door, slamming it behind him.

Wow, he's had a bad day, she thought, not used to seeing him so annoyed. She wondered what Carol had said, whether she'd told him about the threatening phone call. She thought not. Thought all this fuss about Mo was a displacement activity to mask the real reason she was upset. The child had been fine all afternoon, everything forgotten. The only reason he might be tearful now was the indignity and unfairness of being dragged away from the film he'd been enjoying with Toby.

Why doesn't she want Rob to know? She shook her head and went back inside, reminding herself it wasn't her problem.

In the kitchen, Ben walked in from the garden, a big grin on his face. 'Look what I found on the lawn,' he said, holding up her bunch of keys. 'The boys must have been playing with them.'

CHAPTER THIRTEEN

'What? You're kidding me.' She couldn't believe what she was seeing.

He held out the keys and she took them off him, studying them like she'd never seen them before. Checking they were really hers. 'But... I looked outside. And they definitely weren't there.'

She sank into a chair, suddenly exhausted. The day had thrown so much at her, she wasn't sure she could cope with anything else, and she had the distinct feeling that somebody was messing with her. Playing tricks. She had scoured the garden, along with every inch of the house.

Ben passed her a mug. 'I made us coffee.' He studied her face, his eyes clouded with concern. 'Are you okay? You're looking a bit... stressed.' He nodded towards the keys still clutched in her hand. 'I thought you'd be pleased to have them back.'

'Oh, I am.' She reached over and grabbed her handbag from the back of the chair, stuffing her keys inside where she knew they'd be safe, not daring to look at him in case she burst into tears. 'It's been a peculiar sort of a day. So many ups and downs, people getting upset with me.' She swallowed, struggling to keep her emotions in check. 'I've just had a right telling-off from Rob, and now these keys mysteriously reappearing...'

Ben gave her a sympathetic smile. 'I think everyone is a bit stressed, what with the move and the new living arrangements.' He stirred sugar into his drink, looking thoughtful. 'Poor Rob's had all the faff of dealing with Carol's car. You know he hasn't got the patience for that stuff. Hates it when things go wrong and he has to wait for people to turn up.' He walked over to where she was sitting, gave her shoulder a gentle rub. 'Best to leave them to sort themselves out.' He bent to give her a kiss. 'And like I said, the boys were probably playing with the keys, nothing mysterious. I mean it's easy to get paranoid about stuff that's perfectly innocent, isn't it?'

She leant into him, took a deep breath, noticing how fast her heart was beating. He was probably right. *I'm getting worked up about nothing.*

'I think we need to relax now, get everything back in perspective.' He took her hand, glancing towards the lounge. 'Come on, let's watch the rest of this movie with Toby. Have a family snuggle on our wonderful new sofa.'

She let him pull her from her seat. Watching an animated film with her partner and son was exactly what she should be doing.

Toby's face lit up when they settled next to him, and a little while later, Ruby appeared and joined them too. She cuddled up to her dad and soon she was as wrapped up in the movie as Toby was.

This is what it's all about, Jess thought as she finally allowed herself to relax. Her family enjoying a bit of downtime together. Rob had never been interested in kids' movies. His brain was too busy. He'd rather be researching something on the internet, listening to a podcast or watching a self-development tutorial. He was constantly trying to improve, learn more, get better at whatever skill he'd decided to master. There was no time in his world for mindless relaxation. Ben, however, had mastered the art. Another thing she found attractive about him

Perfect, she thought, as she enjoyed the warmth of her son tucked next to her and Rob's arm round her shoulders. The stress of moving, the uncertainty as to whether they were doing the right thing, wondering what was best for Toby. It was all worth it if this was the end result.

She must have drifted off to sleep, because she woke to find herself alone on the sofa, the house quiet, a fleece blanket tucked round her legs. Bleary-eyed, she yawned and stretched, still groggy with sleep. She checked her phone. Almost 7 p.m. She'd been out for a couple of hours. But sleep had evaded her for the last few weeks, so it was no wonder she'd succumbed.

'Ben?' she called. No reply. She walked through to the kitchen, looked out into the garden. Rob and Carol had set up their barbecue in the far corner and were organising chairs round a table. She watched them for a moment, then turned away, still sure that taking the fence down had been a really bad idea. She didn't want to be watching her neighbours all the time, whether it was accidental or not. Especially as they both seemed to be cross with her. It felt awkward, like she was spying on them.

Her eyes settled on the note on the worktop, scrawled in Ben's spidery writing.

Hey gorgeous,

Toby has gone to see Rob and play with Mo. I've taken Ruby over to Darcey's. They're off to Liverpool on a mother–daughter shopping trip tomorrow for a couple of days.
    I'll pick up something for tea on my way home.

Love Ben XOXO

She looked out of the window again, saw Toby carefully carrying a plate loaded with what looked like burgers. He must have been in the kitchen when she'd looked out before. Rob ruffled his hair, took the plate off him and put it next to the grill. Toby skipped back towards the kitchen, to get something else for their meal, no doubt. Carol was right behind him, saying something that made him laugh.

Jess turned away, shaken by what she was feeling. Jealousy? Regret? It was hard to say, but watching her son with his other family was making her feel distinctly uncomfortable.

Oh God, this is going to take some getting used to.

Now she was suddenly alone in their new house, and it felt strange. Too new and unfamiliar to feel like home yet. She drifted from room to room, assessing what still needed to be done, working out what extra bits of furniture and storage they might need to keep the place looking tidy. But even as she told herself not to, she couldn't help glancing out of the window to see what was happening next door.

She watched Carol crouching down, hugging Toby. Her son was laughing. Carol was tickling him. He was clearly having a lovely time. *Without me.* Her heart lurched and she turned away. It was what she'd wanted, she reminded herself. A fully blended family. But she hadn't expected to feel left out. Surplus to requirements.

She was putting clothes away in her wardrobe, as a means of distraction, when the doorbell rang. Glancing out of the window, she saw the top of a grey head that could only belong to her mother. She dashed downstairs.

'Mum,' she said, beaming as she threw the door open. 'What a lovely surprise.'

Helen held up a plate of cupcakes, chocolate and vanilla judging by the colour. They looked delicious.

'I've been experimenting,' she said as Jess ushered her inside. 'A new cookbook.' She laughed. 'You know I can't resist all those lovely pictures. Anyway, I thought it was something me and Toby could do together.' Jess took the plate, her mouth watering. 'Not bad for my first effort, don't you think?'

'They look fantastic. Fancy trying one with a cuppa?'

'Great idea.' Helen glanced around. 'Well, isn't this looking nice?'

'I'll give you a guided tour if you like.'

'Of course I'd like.' She gave Jess a nudge. 'Come on, put those cakes down and let me have a nosy.'

Jess laughed and led her through to the kitchen diner. 'Isn't this great? Look how clean it all is. None of those wonky cupboards and worn-out worktops I put up with for years in Rob's parents' house.'

Helen nodded. 'Very posh.' She went to look out of the patio doors. 'Oh.' She turned, looking surprised. 'A shared garden? That's not very private, is it?' She pulled a face. 'I'm not sure I'd like that. Still, I'd better go and say hello to Rob and Toby. I think they saw me, and it would look rude if I just ignored them.' She darted back into the lounge and picked up the plate of cakes. 'Back in a tick.'

Jess watched as her mum strode across the lawn. Toby rushed towards her, Mo not far behind, and she bent down, listening to them both, showing them the cakes. Rob came over to greet her, gave her a kiss on the cheek and a hug. Then Carol walked out of the kitchen and her mum's face changed, an expression of shocked surprise written all over it. She was laughing, as was Carol, and they fell into animated conversation, like two people who knew each other. Which was weird, because her mum had never met Carol.

When her mum was free at weekends, it was Jess who made arrangements to see her with Toby and Ben, while Rob and Carol had time together with Mo. She really hadn't prioritised formal introductions between her mum and Carol, leaving that up to Rob. It was his relationship at the end of the day, and she hadn't wanted to interfere. But Helen's expression and the way the two of them were talking now suggested that they knew each other quite well. The little touches on the arm, the eye contact. It all suggested familiarity.

Rob said something and pressed a drink into Helen's hand. She laughed and took a sip, and Jess knew she'd be there for a while now. Enjoying herself while Jess was on the outside looking in, a spectator watching her son interacting with his family. A family that didn't include her.

Her hand clutched at her chest, as though she could rub away the pain in her heart. This wasn't how it was supposed to be. The walls seemed to close in on her, pressing the air out of her lungs. She had to get away from this feeling of rejection. Quickly she scribbled a note, then grabbed her handbag and pulled out her keys, deciding she'd drive over to Glen Helen and have a walk up the river. Just for a little while, to get everything sorted out in her head. It was a wooded valley full of magnificent beech trees with a waterfall at the end. A wonderfully peaceful place, which was exactly what she needed to calm herself down. It was only a ten-minute drive, so she'd be back when Ben returned.

The front door slammed behind her and she jumped into her car, reversing out of the drive and down to the junction with the main road. Within seconds, she realised something wasn't right. The car was pulling to the left and there was a peculiar slapping noise. She stopped by the side of the road and got out to look.

The back tyre on the passenger side was completely flat. She stared at it, knowing there hadn't been a problem yesterday when she'd brought Toby home. Yet another inconvenience. Was it a coincidence, or one more trick someone had played on her?

CHAPTER FOURTEEN

It took Jess half an hour to change the tyre, the bolts being stiff, and by the time she was finished, she was feeling hot and flustered and angry. Once she'd removed the flat tyre, she could see there was a clean slice through it, like someone had stabbed it with a knife. It wasn't the sort of puncture you'd get just by running over something in the road. This was deliberate.

It was one more thing to add to the list of mysterious incidents.

As Ben had said, there could be innocent explanations for the mugs and the keys, but she was certain this was malicious damage and proof that someone had a vendetta against her.

She thought about the message in the card. *Welcome to your nightmare, bitch.* Was this the start? Was there more to come? Her heart was racing, adrenaline pumping round her body as she tried to think who would do this to her.

As far as she knew, she had no enemies. She was generally a happy-go-lucky sort of person, and she'd always led her life trying to treat others as she wanted to be treated herself. You had to be like that when you lived in a small rural area, and it was what she loved about life on the island. That sense of community, the kindness of strangers. But somebody must hate her, and she wondered what she'd done, unknowingly, to cause all this trouble. If she could work it out, she'd go and apologise, see if she could make amends, because she really wanted it to stop.

Was this about Ben? she wondered, aware that he'd broken a few hearts over the years. Could it be an ex-lover who was jealous of their relationship? Someone who was trying to frighten her off? It was the only possibility she could think of, because it had all started when they'd moved into the house, and she was the sole target. Nobody was making trouble for Ben. Or Rob. But... Carol was having problems, wasn't she? Could it be the same person, trying to disrupt their blended family? Someone with moral objections? After all, their plan had raised a few eyebrows, so she couldn't discount it.

With her mind full of possibilities and no firm conclusions, she loaded the tyre into the boot and slammed it shut, desperate to speak to Ben. He'd messaged her to say he wouldn't be long.

She was getting plates and cutlery ready for their meal when her mum stumbled into the kitchen, steadying herself against the back of a chair. 'Rob said to tell you that Toby's staying over at theirs tonight,' she slurred. Her eyes were sparkling, face flushed. She giggled. 'I shouldn't have had that second glass of Prosecco on an empty stomach. It's made me go all squiffy.'

Despite feeling a little annoyed that her mum had come to see her but ended up next door, Jess was genuinely pleased to see her looking so happy.

'I'll get you a coffee, shall I?' She flicked the kettle on. 'Can't have you drunk and disorderly. You might never find your way home.'

Helen wagged a finger at her. 'No, no, no. No need for that.

Rob said he'd give me a lift.' She beamed. 'Such a thoughtful man.' Jess couldn't argue with that, and she knew he doted on her mum as much as she doted on him. Helen glanced around. 'Talking of which, where's that fella of yours?'

'Oh, he took Ruby to her mum's. He's on his way back now. Shouldn't be long if you want to wait a minute and say hello.'

Helen shook her head, let go of the chair. 'Another time. My lift will be waiting. Just wanted to say goodbye.' She steadied herself and headed for the front door, using the walls and furniture to keep herself upright. How many glasses had she had? Jess wondered, deciding it must be way more than two. Her mum was clearly drunk.

'Looked like you were having a nice time out there,' she called after her, wincing inside as she said it. She couldn't help herself and there was a trace of something in her voice that she didn't like. Did that sound bitter? Jealous? She thought it might.

Her mum turned, her hand grasping the handle of the lounge door as she swayed. 'Oh, it's a lovely set-up they've got, and Carol was telling me about their plans for a garden office so she and Rob can work from home.'

'Right.' Jess tried to hide the surprise in her voice. Nothing had been said to her about a garden office. But then it was their garden so she supposed they could do what they wanted with it. She switched to the thing that was really puzzling her. 'Do you and Carol know each other?'

Helen laughed. 'We do! I hadn't put two and two together, to be honest. But I do her hair. Have done for quite a few months now. The salon is near her office and she popped in on the off chance one day, and here we are – now she's with Rob, she's practically my daughter, right?' She gave another giggle, a sound Jess hadn't heard from her mum in years. 'It's a small world on the island, isn't it?'

The honk of a car horn made Jess jump.

Helen let go of the handle and staggered towards the front door, Jess following, worried that she might fall over. 'See you soon, love. We'll have to do the guided tour another day, won't we?' She gave a little wave as she headed down the drive.

Jess stood watching as Rob opened the passenger door for her mum and got her settled in the car. He spotted her and gave her a grin and a thumbs up before getting in the driver's seat and reversing out of the drive.

What an unsettling day it had been, she thought as she gazed after them. Quite apart from the acts of mischief against her, there was an issue with boundaries, both emotional and physical. Mentally she felt as though she'd had a day out on a rough sea and had landed back on shore feeling thoroughly shaken up, her legs unsure whether they could trust solid ground.

Her eyes clouded as she stared into the distance, only shaken from her thoughts when Ben arrived home a few minutes later. He parked his van behind her car and started up the drive, then stopped and peered into the border where the ornamental grasses had been planted. Bending, he picked something up, turning it in his hand. The light of the dying sun glinted off it, and as he came closer, Jess could see exactly what it was. A knife.

'How the heck did this get in the garden?' he asked, holding it up for her to see.

Her hand went to her mouth. It was identical to the boning knife from the new set she'd just bought.

'Oh my God. That's just creepy,' she gasped, feeling the blood drain from her face. She held on to the door as her world seemed to shift. It didn't seem like mischief any more. It felt like something far more sinister.

'It is ours, isn't it?' Ben asked, looking puzzled. As well he might. There was no reasonable explanation for one of their new knives being planted up to the hilt in the front border.

'I... I don't know,' she stammered. 'I'd have to check.' With her heart thundering in her chest, she turned and hurried to the kitchen, checking the knife block on the counter. And there it was – the empty space where the boning knife should have been.

CHAPTER FIFTEEN

Jess covered her face with her hands. Someone had been in her house, taken the knife and used it to slash her tyre. That same someone must also have taken her keys and broken the mugs. Did that make sense, or was she jumping to conclusions? She burst into tears, sobs heaving through her body as her hopes for their wonderful new life crumbled to dust.

'Hey, what's going on?' Ben said, laying the knife on the worktop, along with the pizza boxes, so he could gather her in his arms. 'Come on, love. Speak to me.'

But she couldn't, and she had to wait until her sobs had subsided and she could catch her breath, while he stroked her hair and told her it would be okay.

'It isn't okay,' she said eventually. 'It really isn't. I've had a horrible day, all these weird things happening and people being funny with me and my mum dumping me to go and get sloshed next door, and then I was going to go for a drive out to Glen Helen to clear my head and I had a flat tyre. And do you know what? Someone had stabbed it with a knife. And then you find the very knife in our flower bed.' The words came out in one big long breath, but saying them made her feel worse. Even more scared than she'd been before.

Ben led her to the table and sat her down before sinking into the chair next to her, his arm round her shoulder. 'Why didn't you tell me about the tyre? I would have come and sorted that out for you.'

'I don't need you to sort things out for me. I'm perfectly capable of doing that myself,' she snapped, her voice sounding halfway to hysterical. 'What I do need is for you to listen to what I'm telling you. Someone is out to get me.'

He rubbed her shoulder. 'Steady on. Let's not jump to conclusions.'

'It's not coincidences. It's not.' She grasped his hand, pulled it from her shoulder, frustrated that he didn't seem to be acknowledging her fears. 'Somebody wants to scare me, and I don't know if this is about the house, or about you and me. Or even about us all living next door to each other. I just can't work it out.'

He gave a big sigh and sat back, his hand rasping over his stubble. 'Bloody hell, love. Don't go all dramatic on me. I thought you were the sensible one.'

'I am the sensible one. That's why I'm worried. I mean, when you get a card saying "Welcome to your nightmare, bitch" and then horrible things start happening, you've got to think it's all connected, don't you?'

'I don't know, love. I mean, it seems pretty harmless stuff, doesn't it? Broken mugs, missing keys and a flat tyre? All of that could have been the boys.'

'You're not thinking straight,' she insisted, her teeth clenched. 'It could *not* have been the boys because I was with them when the mugs were broken.'

'You're connecting things that might not be connected. That's what I'm struggling with.' His eyes met hers. 'The boys could have been playing with the keys. That's possible, isn't it?'

She thought for a moment, then nodded. Because he did have a point. 'They wouldn't have taken the knife, though. Toby knows not to go near knives.'

Ben looked thoughtful, his hand scratching at his chin again. He was worried. She could see he was. He cleared his throat. 'Where was Ruby when all this was going on?'

'In her room. She was doing pictures for her Insta, but I'll admit I wasn't taking too much notice, not with the upset with the boys and everything else that was happening.' She looked at her hands, her fingers tugging at a hangnail. It wasn't good enough, she realised. Her job was to keep an eye on all the kids, not just the boys. 'I'm sorry,' she mumbled. 'Did she say something?'

She glanced up then, caught the steely expression on his face, and her heart sank. Yet another thing that hadn't gone right today.

'Yeah, she did say something.' He sighed. 'She said lots of things... silly things. You know... She's a bit idealistic. Young for her age emotionally. I suppose you could call it naïve.'

Jess stared at him, wondering if he was going to tell her what had been said, but the silence told her that wasn't going to happen.

'Well go on then. You can't just throw a comment like that out there and not elaborate. What did she say?'

She saw him thinking, no doubt editing the words in his mind to make them more palatable. 'I can't really remember her exact—'

'Oh no you don't.' She tapped a finger on the table. 'That's a cop-out if ever I heard one. Just tell me.'

He grimaced. 'She wants me and Darcey to get back together. Says she doesn't want a stepmother. She has a mother and doesn't need another one. Especially... a bossy one.'

Jess reeled back in her chair like he'd just slapped her across the face.

He held up a hand, quickly backtracking, a note of panic in his voice. 'I was quoting Ruby there. It's not that *I* think you're bossy. And it's not going to happen. I don't want you worrying about that. It's never been on the cards. Honestly, me and Darcey, we're just mates. Maybe not even that.' He shrugged. 'I really don't know how you'd describe our relationship.' He looked away. 'It's just something Ruby has got in her head.'

'I'm not sure what you're saying here... You think Ruby might be the one doing all these things?'

He pulled a face. 'It sort of figures, doesn't it? Causing trouble to create a rift between us?'

Jess thought about it for a moment, wondering if it was possible. Her heart ached with the knowledge that Ben might be right. Ruby had been in the house all the time. She'd had the opportunity.

Although she was saddened by the idea that her future stepdaughter might want to split her and Ben up, in a way it was a relief. She took a deep breath. This was solvable. Ben could make it all stop. In fact, they could do it together.

'We need to sit down with her and talk about this,' she said. She knew she'd get nowhere on her own, given Ruby's antagonism towards her. Bossy? Of course she'd see her as bossy, given that Jess was the only adult in the girl's life who actually tried to set boundaries. She couldn't trust Ben to have this conversation on his own, because Ruby got away with murder on his watch. All she had to do was turn on the tears and his resolve would melt to mush.

He reached for her hand, and this time she didn't resist, but let him entwine his fingers with hers. 'I promise. When she gets back from Liverpool, we'll definitely do it.'

There wasn't much more she could say. She had his promise, and Ruby was away, so there was nothing to be done for the time being. But the not knowing left her feeling agitated, on

edge. What if Ruby denied it, but still carried on causing trouble? She frowned and glanced up to see him watching her.

'Don't look so worried,' he said, the backs of his fingers
brushing her cheek. 'I'm determined this is going to work for us.
Whatever Ruby thinks, she can't stop us from being together.'
He leant over and kissed her on the lips, a kiss so tender she had
to believe him. 'I love you with all my heart and I can't tell you
how much I want us to be married.'

'Even if it'll cause trouble with your daughter?' She'd never
considered before that this might be a deal-breaker, but what if
it was? Her breath caught in her throat, the idea of their relationship being dictated by Ruby too horrifying to consider.

'Please don't worry about it. She's not going to stop me
making you my wife.' He smiled at her. 'Now we've got the
move out of the way, it's time to start thinking about the
wedding, isn't it?'

She looked away, her heart skipping a beat. There was
information she hadn't shared with him yet, and she knew he
wasn't going to like it.

CHAPTER SIXTEEN

Before Jess could speak, Ben stood up.

'I'm starving. Come on, let's eat, then we can start to think about wedding plans now we've got an evening to ourselves. Maybe sort out a date and a venue.' She could sense his excitement in the way he practically bounced over to the worktop to grab the pizza boxes, then went to the fridge, pulling out a bottle of Prosecco. He held it up. 'We can pretend it's champagne, can't we? I think we should celebrate the positives instead of letting ourselves get dragged down by the negatives. I'm sure everything will settle down with the kids.'

That was typical of Ben; he was a glass-half-full type of guy. But she was still worried about Ruby and her mischief, and now she had to explain about the wedding as well.

He put everything on the table, opened the bottle and poured them each a glass.

'To us,' he said.

She clinked her glass against his, gave a tentative smile. 'New beginnings.'

'Yes, that's a good one.' His smile broadened. 'New beginnings.' They both took a sip of the sparkling wine, then helped themselves to slices of pizza.

'It's funny,' he said, 'but I honestly thought I'd never get married. Just didn't imagine I'd find someone I'd want to spend the rest of my life with.' He laughed. 'Then you came along, and I knew straight away you were special.'

She looked down at her food, her stomach churning with nerves. It was lovely to hear him say that, but it was making things harder.

Just tell him, before this gets any worse.

She took a gulp of her Prosecco. 'Ah, about the wedding... I know you don't want anything fancy and we can get it organised pretty quickly, but... I think Toby might need a bit more time to get used to the new living arrangements.'

The smile dropped from his face. 'What? But you promised. Once we'd moved...'

'I know. I know what I said.' She studied her food, unable to meet his eye, the heat rising to her cheeks. 'I just think... Now we're officially living together, there's no rush, is there?'

He stared at her for a moment, mouth hanging open, clearly shocked. 'Why are you stalling on this?' His voice had a hard edge to it, a note of hurt, and she realised her excuse wasn't working. Anyway, it wasn't fair to blame Toby for a delay that had nothing to do with him.

'Well, um... there's still a few things to sort out before we can finalise the divorce.'

He put his slice of pizza down, his attention focused on their conversation. 'But you signed the papers ages ago. I was under the impression you were nearly there. Free and single and available to marry me.'

She closed her eyes for a moment, took a deep breath. 'There was a bit of a mix-up with some of the paperwork. I could have sworn I'd sent it back. In fact, I can remember giving it to Mum to stick in the postbox on her way past. But it seems the solicitor never got it, and it was weeks before I found out.'

His expression said he didn't believe her. 'How on earth does that happen? What, everything you signed just went missing?'

She nodded. 'Yep, that's about it. I've been on to the post office, but they can't find it anywhere.' She sighed. 'I've just got to do that bit all over again, and it took me ages because it had an inventory of everything and how it's being split.'

His face was starting to redden, and she could hear the frustration in his voice. 'But everything's been physically split now anyway. Why does it matter?'

'It has to be in writing, apparently. And it's all the money stuff as well.' She flapped a hand, trying to make light of it. 'So tedious. But I'll get round to it now that we're here and I don't have to think about organising the move any more.'

'You don't seem to be in much of a hurry. Just agree to everything and let Rob's solicitor get on with it.'

She sighed, looking at her congealing food. 'It's not that simple. And like I said, Toby could do with a bit of time to acclimatise to things and—'

Ben's hand slammed onto the table, stopping her in her tracks. 'Look, we've bent over backwards to make life easy for Toby, but when are you going to think about me?' There was a stony glint in his eye, and she was too shocked to respond. She'd never seen him like this before. 'Darcey was right,' he snarled. 'Our relationship is all about what *you* want, isn't it?'

With that, he got up and walked out of the room, stomping up the stairs.

Tears stung her eyes. Should she go after him, tell him how hurt she felt? It wasn't her fault the divorce papers had got lost, was it? *But I should have told him when it happened, rather than keeping it a secret.*

Her napkin was scrunched in her hand and she swiped at

her eyes, annoyed with herself for creating this problem in the first place. Crying would do no good. She stood and climbed the stairs, an apology ready on her tongue.

Ben was sitting on the bed, his head in his hands.

'I'm sorry, love,' she murmured. 'I should have told you about the delay. But I promise I'll get everything back to the solicitor as soon as possible.' She sat next to him, put an arm round his shoulders. 'It doesn't need to stop us making wedding plans.'

He looked thoroughly dejected, his shoulders slumped. 'I'm not going to push you if you're not ready. You need to want this as much as I do or it's not going to work.' His eyes met hers and she could see the sheen of tears. 'I just don't think you do.'

Her heart lurched. 'I do. Really I do.' She grasped his hand. 'I love you so much. It's just that divorcing someone is a really long and tiresome process, and I want to get it right. All the details matter, especially with a child involved. And they all take time to think about.'

He brought her hand to his lips, kissed her knuckles, and she knew she was forgiven.

'Carol and Rob have already planned their wedding,' he said, 'so there's no reason for any delays. He's keen as mustard, and I think they're hoping for a baby.'

Jess swallowed, feeling a weight land on her chest, squashing all the breath from her lungs. It all felt very sudden. 'Who told you that?'

'Carol did. She's already booked the chapel.'

'Wow.' It was all she could think of to say. 'I'd better get on with that paperwork then.' The thought of it made her limbs feel like leaden weights, pinning her to the edge of the bed. She turned to Ben. 'I don't suppose you fancy going through it with me, do you?'

He grinned at her, obviously delighted to have been asked. 'Of course. We'll have it done in no time.'

She found the box with all her personal admin and put it on the coffee table, while Ben brought the rest of the Prosecco. The thick manila envelope was on the top of the pile, and she pulled out the contents.

Her hand flew to her mouth, appalled at what she was seeing. Someone had used bright red lipstick to scrawl *WHORE* over every page in great big letters.

She looked at Ben, who was clearly as shocked as she was, the silence between them as thick as sea mist.

'Christ,' he said eventually, 'I'm going to have to have that conversation with Ruby, aren't I?'

Jess was appalled that the girl had been so angry she would have thought to do such a thing. She felt attacked, violated, and she hurried upstairs, locking herself in the bathroom to give herself time to think. Any relationship with Ben included a relationship with Ruby. That was how it went with second marriages. But could she really face these ongoing attacks? However much she might love Ben, could she live with the malignant threat that Ruby appeared to represent?

Her mind took her back to the start of things, when the idea that they should live as a blended family had first come about.

They were just dishing up the evening meal when a piercing scream had filled the air. The adults all looked at each other. 'Ruby?' Carol said, frowning. Then they heard more screams, like little warriors on the warpath, and Rob and Ben dashed up the stairs, leaving Jess and Carol in the kitchen.

Jess listened, appalled. 'God, that sounds worse than usual.' She put the serving spoon down, wiping her hands on a tea towel, ready to go and find out what was happening, worried for her son, who really was no good in a fight.

Carol put a hand on her shoulder, holding her back. 'Let the men sort it out. Honestly, it's better.'

Jess sighed. She had a fierce maternal instinct, which always concluded that her son couldn't be in the wrong, and Carol was much the same. Then the blame game started, and it never ended well. They'd learnt that from experience. So now the men were the designated troubleshooters.

'I don't know why they have to fight,' Carol complained. 'I mean, they have all the gadgets they could want here, but somehow one of them is always using what another one wants.'

'Yes, but there's not a lot of room up there for the three of them, and I know Ruby's at an age where she likes her own space.'

'Do you think that's it? Are the boys winding her up again?'

'It was her screaming, wasn't it?'

They stopped and listened. The screams had come to a sudden halt, replaced by the rumble of male voices. Negotiations or arbitration or warnings of consequences. It could be any one of those things.

Then there was the thump of feet down the stairs, and Ruby, her face red and tear-stained, flew past them and out of the back door. Ben jogged after her, rolling his eyes at Jess as he went past. A few minutes later, the boys came down, looking sheepish, Rob following behind.

'Okay, lads,' he said, 'wash your hands and sit at the table, please. Food's ready.'

Carol frowned. 'Is that blood on Mo's face?'

Jess gasped when she saw the long scratch right down his cheek. Then she noticed Toby was clutching his ear and he'd obviously been crying.

She caught Rob's eye. 'What the heck happened up there?'

He sighed. 'The boys crept up on Ruby when she was doing her homework and put a spider on her neck. She went ballistic. Had Mo pinned to the floor when we got up there. And she'd given Toby a belt round the ear.'

Jess leant against the worktop and gave a sigh that seemed to travel all the way up from her feet. How much more of this fighting could she take?

'Let's talk about it later,' she heard Carol say. 'When Ben gets back and the kids are watching a movie.'

That was when it started, the plan to buy houses close to each other where the children could all have their own space and not be on top of each other.

'Think about it,' Ben said later that night, when she'd gone home with him and Ruby. 'There'd be ready-made childcare on the doorstep. Imagine how much freedom that would give us all.'

He had a point, she supposed, but she wasn't a hundred per cent convinced. She liked the status quo, to be honest. Her still living in the same house as Rob, both being parents to their son. Toby didn't experience anything different except his parents sleeping in separate rooms. It was a big step moving in with Ben. Was she ready?

But the following Friday, there was another fight between the kids, and that made up her mind. They needed space, and she had to put their needs over her own reservations.

'Look,' she said to the rest of the adults, 'I'm in. Let's do it.'

Now she huffed to herself as she sat on the edge of the bath. Look what a stupid idea that had turned out to be. She'd ended up living with a little monster.

All she could do was hope that Ben was true to his word and would be able to talk Ruby round.

CHAPTER SEVENTEEN

Jess woke late after a rare lie-in, stretching as she blinked in the morning sun. Now that she knew it was Ruby behind all the trouble, she felt a lot better. It was the not knowing that had made things scary.

'Morning, sleepyhead,' Ben said, placing a tray on the bed, the smell of coffee and hot buttered toast filling the air. 'A treat for my lady.'

She grinned and sat up, plumping her pillows before reaching for a slice of toast.

Ben hopped into bed and took a slice for himself. 'Isn't this the life? A chance to be alone for once.'

Jess sighed. It felt like she was on holiday with the freedom to properly relax. Life could be a lot worse, she told herself as she sipped her coffee, letting all the concerns of the previous day melt away.

It was after midday by the time they finally got up and dressed. She was glowing, feeling so alive she thought she might burst. Things had turned a corner, she was sure of it, and Ben had promised again to speak to Ruby as soon as she got back from her shopping trip with her mum.

'I'll go and get some groceries, shall I?' he said, peering into the empty fridge.

'Brilliant. I'm going to nip next door and see what Toby's up to. I thought I might take the boys out this afternoon, go up to the ropes course at South Barrule. It's a nice day, should be fun.'

'Good idea. Me and Rob are out on the bikes, remember. We're off up to Ramsey today.'

'No worries.' She headed for the front door, a spring in her step. 'I won't be long.'

Next door, she rang the bell. Carol answered, giving her a fleeting smile as she stepped back to let her in. Jess felt that same unease as she walked through a house furnished with belongings that used to be in her own home.

'I thought I could take the boys out this afternoon,' she said before they entered the kitchen, not wanting to announce it in front of the boys just in case Carol had other plans for her and Mo.

Carol seemed flustered, her fingers playing with a strand of hair. 'Oh... I don't think...' She glanced down at the floor. 'I'm sorry, but I've already arranged to take them swimming.'

'But it's a lovely day. I thought they'd enjoy being outside.'

She chewed at her lip. 'Look, Jess. Nothing personal, but I really don't want you taking Mo anywhere for the time being. Not if you're going to fill his head with rubbish about his father.' There was a spark of annoyance in her eyes that Jess had never seen before. 'Something you know nothing about at all.'

The words stung as hard as a slap, making Jess take a step back.

'What? Look, I didn't even mention his father to him.' She sighed, not wanting to fall out with her neighbour. 'It was Toby who upset Mo. I just tried to comfort him.'

'Well you've made a hard situation even harder.' Carol's chin quivered. 'It's best if you don't refer to his father at all, okay? I'd rather he forgot about him.'

Jess's eyes widened. Carol wasn't listening and her stand-point seemed harsh. Surely as he got older Mo would want to know more about his heritage rather than pretend he'd never even had a father. Then she remembered the phone conversation, and her mind made a leap.

She dropped her voice, worried that the boys might overhear. 'His father *is* dead, isn't he? Or is that just something you want Mo to believe?'

A look of horror flashed in Carol's eyes, and Jess knew then she was onto something.

'Are you calling me a liar?' Carol's voice rose, a flush colouring her cheeks.

'No, that's not what I meant. It's just... if we're going to be co-parenting our children, I need to be clear about Mo's past, so I can answer his questions and concerns as and when they come up.'

'You're not co-parenting my child,' Carol hissed. 'Whatever gave you that idea?'

'But that's what this is all about, isn't it? Moving in next door to each other so we're one family.'

Carol huffed. 'Mo is my son and I'll parent him in the way I see fit. I don't need you interfering and confusing him.'

Jess folded her arms across her chest, not sure how to respond.

'What's going on?' Rob popped his head round the door.

She turned to him, relieved. 'A bit of a misunderstanding, that's all.' She could almost see the animosity radiating from Carol, could feel imaginary daggers digging between her shoulder blades.

He came into the room, already dressed in his Lycra cycling gear. It was a hobby he'd only recently rediscovered, although he'd been a keen cyclist when he was younger. A bad fall had put him off for a while, but now he was a real enthusiast, taking the opportunity to get out on his bike with Ben whenever they could organise it. He said it helped take his mind off work, and he was certainly looking better for it, his athletic physique back to how he'd been as a young man.

He went to Carol and put his hands on her shoulders, looking into her eyes. An intimate gesture that made Jess feel out of place.

'You okay, love?'

Carol clung to him, her head turned away from Jess. It looked like she was shaking. Was she crying?

Jess felt a flutter of panic in her chest and decided to cut her losses. 'Look, I'm sorry if I've said something out of turn. You get on with your day and I'll see Toby later, okay?'

Rob looked at her over the top of Carol's head, his face set in a neutral expression that meant he was really pissed off. 'Yep. Sounds like the best idea.'

Jess closed the front door behind her, aware that she was trembling.

Well that was awkward, she thought. And how come it was okay for Carol to parent Jess's child, but not the other way round? In fact, hadn't Carol made arrangements without even asking her? Shutting her out, almost. At least Jess had the manners to come and discuss her plans first, not just assume it was okay.

She felt thoroughly discombobulated, like her feathers had been ruffled and she couldn't get them back into place. Nothing was as it should be, and she was left with a lingering feeling that there was something strange going on with Carol. Something her neighbour didn't want anyone else to know about.

CHAPTER EIGHTEEN

Two days later, Jess still didn't have her son home. She'd hardly seen him apart from fleeting glimpses when he'd dashed in to gather his swimming stuff and then to find his binoculars.

Rob was working, but Carol had time off over the summer holidays and had planned a full agenda of activities. She'd taken the boys to the wildlife park, then today they'd gone up to Ramsey to play bowls and have a picnic on the beach. Not that Jess had spoken to her after their previous conversation – the way Carol had suddenly turned on her made her reluctant to go round. It had seemed completely out of character. Up to now, Carol had always been so friendly towards her, a little nervous at first, but once she'd got to know her better, she'd opened up about her past and the hardship she'd faced when she'd first moved back to the island.

Jess remembered their first proper heart-to-heart. They'd been making a salad for tea, Carol chopping peppers, carrots and cucumber for the boys to dip in hummus.

'My family didn't want to know me when I told them I was staying in Bodrum and marrying a Turkish fisherman,' she'd sighed, sadness pulling at her mouth. 'It was a magical time in my life. You know, I was at that age when anything seems possible, no fear of the future. But my mum thought I was throwing away my degree and my career and dad was furious at me for upsetting Mum.' She carried on chopping. 'I thought it might be different when I came home. But they still wouldn't speak to me.'

'Families can be so difficult,' Jess said, thinking about her own torrid upbringing and the constant aggravation between her parents. 'But at least you have Rob now. And me and Ben.'

Carol smiled then. 'You're right. I'll have a new family. Ben was telling me that only the other day when we had lunch.'

Jess tried to hide her surprise that Ben and Carol had met up. It was the first she'd heard of it, but she wasn't his keeper, and he was a sociable guy. 'It's funny you and Ben knowing each other, isn't it?' She cringed, aware that she was fishing for information on their shared history, hoping it wasn't too obvious.

Carol laughed. 'It's such a small world on the island. I sort of love it, because you never know who'll end up sitting next to you in a restaurant or café. Or standing next to you at the bar. Or being your new boss. Best to be friendly with everyone, I've found.'

Jess thought she'd skilfully evaded the question and decided to go for the direct approach. 'He said you two used to go out together.'

A smile tweaked Carol's lips and she seemed to concentrate harder on what she was doing. 'Yeah, we did for a while. I was still at school, then I went to uni in London and we decided a long distance relationship wasn't working. We always kept in touch, though and he was so supportive when I was having a hard time in Turkey.'

Carol moved the conversation on then, and Jess was left with an uneasy feeling there might be unfinished business between the two of them.

She'd been wondering about this since they'd moved into the new house. First with the kiss and the bum-slapping incident, and then yesterday evening she'd noticed Ben and Carol huddled together in the garden, deep in conversation, his arm round her shoulders. It was hard to say anything about it, though, because it would sound like she'd been spying on them, rather than just glancing out of the bedroom window while she was putting things away.

It was natural that Ben was in and out of Rob's house, sorting out the garages and planning their next bike ride. But was he really going round to see Carol? Was that part of the attraction that seemed to pull him next door so often? She caught her wandering thoughts, told herself not to be stupid and brought her mind back to her main concern about not seeing her son.

Ben always came back with news about Toby and what he'd been doing. Reassuring Jess that he was having a great time with Mo. What could she say? Toby was enjoying himself, and wasn't this what the summer holidays were all about?

'Enjoy a bit of free time,' he said to her when she voiced her disappointment that Toby was staying next door for another night. He stroked her hair away from her face and tucked it behind her ear. 'There's nothing to worry about. Carol is perfectly competent. And isn't that the whole point of being here?'

Jess sighed, laying her head on his chest. His arms encircled her, pulling her close. 'It's just that I want to do these things with Toby. I organised with work to take the summer holidays off, and now it feels like it's been for nothing. It's like she's taken him away from me. Stealing all the little trips that should be in his memories with me, not the next-door neighbour.'

She felt Ben's breath ruffle her hair. 'She's a bit more than a neighbour, love. She's going to be Toby's stepmother in the not-too-distant future, so it's good that he's getting to spend some quality time with her.' He pulled away, gave her a quizzical look. 'And we've all been friends up to now, so I'm not sure what's changed.'

He was right, they *had* all been friends. Was it Jess's fault, this falling-out? She'd thought about it so much, she was no longer sure.

'There's a week of the holidays left,' he continued. 'I've got a couple of jobs to do today and tomorrow for Mrs Watterson, but after that, I can take a bit of time off and we can do some family things if you like.' He grinned at her. 'Make it special. Play some games or sort out a couple of movies everyone might enjoy.'

She was grateful that he was willing to make such an effort. Being self-employed was a tricky balancing act, and she knew he had a list of customers all wanting him to do jobs for them. But the fact that he was putting his family first made her heart swell. Rob had always prioritised work, saying he was doing it for the family so they could be financially secure. But it had always felt like he was fobbing her off, his ego needing him to push on, achieve more, get promotions, prove that he was the best at his job.

She hugged Ben, gave him a kiss. 'That's a great idea.' Her mind was already working through possible meals, and she'd brought a new board game home from the library that Toby might enjoy.

'I'm picking Ruby up later, so it'll be a proper family event. All of us together for once.'

She tried to smile, act like she was pleased, but the thought of Ruby coming back had her shoulder muscles bunching like they were preparing for a fight.

'You will talk to her before she comes home, won't you? About the horrible tricks she's been playing on me.'

He gave her shoulder a reassuring rub. 'Course I will. I haven't forgotten. Now I'd better get off to sort out Mrs Watterson.' He winked at her. 'See you tonight.'

Jess went to make herself a cup of tea. She brought it back into the lounge and hugged it to her chest as she gazed out of the window. Ben's van was still in the drive, and she could see he was on the phone. He looked annoyed, his fist thumping the dashboard, a frown etching lines on his forehead. What the heck was that all about? Ben wasn't a man who was easily angered, taking most things in his stride. He was the voice of reason in their household, so it must have been something serious to get him so riled.

He reversed out of the drive, faster than she would have liked, and screeched off down the road, stopping at the junction with the main road, where he turned right. Mrs Watterson lived in the opposite direction, next door but one to Jess's mum.

Where's he going in such a hurry?

She sipped at her tea, thinking he hadn't really been himself since they'd moved in. A little jumpy, distracted, often not listening when she'd been trying to talk to him about things. Was there something going on that he wasn't telling her? An image appeared of him chatting to Carol, animated and laughing, her kissing him, the slap on the bottom. His arm round her shoulders in the garden, heads almost touching.

She shook herself out of that train of thought. It was ridiculous. Hadn't he been the one wanting to sort out the wedding, keen to commit? She was reading far too much into things. It was probably an issue with a customer that he had to go and sort out. An emergency that was going to mess up his plans for the day. Nothing to worry about. But that look on his face... He didn't tend to get emotionally involved with work issues, using his charm to resolve problems. No, that expression had told her this was something else entirely.

It was probably something to do with Ruby. His daughter definitely had the capacity to get him riled up. And Darcey lived in the direction he'd gone. Jess nodded to herself. Maybe he'd been talking to her about all the mischief she'd been up to.

Or she'd fallen out with her mother and wanted to come home early. It wasn't unheard of. She checked her phone to see if he'd sent her a message. Nothing.

She finished her tea and went back into the kitchen, deflated, and at a bit of a loss. A whole day to herself, and instead of it being a welcome treat, it felt like she'd been deserted, pushed to one side. She messaged a couple of friends to see if anyone was available for a coffee, but everyone already had plans, making her feel even more dejected.

She hoovered the house, did a bit of dusting, cleaned the bathrooms, then decided to go and do a grocery shop. Ben had got some bits and pieces, but she needed to stock up on essentials. It was her least favourite job, but it had to be done, and she could plan a special meal for the evening when everyone would be home again.

With a shopping list tucked in her back pocket, she went in search of her handbag. She could have sworn she'd hung it over the back of a chair in the kitchen. That was its usual place, but she couldn't find it anywhere. The hairs on the back of her neck started to prickle. Was this some kind of joke? Somebody messing with her again?

She'd pinned it all on Ruby, but now she was wondering if there might be a different culprit. Frustrated, she went to get her phone to ring Ben, but that was missing too. It had definitely been on the kitchen worktop where she usually left it. Unease swirled in her stomach. Had someone been in the house and stolen her things while she'd been hoovering? She wouldn't have heard them, would she?

She stood still and listened. Silence. Absolute silence. Usually she could hear something – birdsong, voices from neighbouring houses, cars. She noticed the kitchen window was shut, when she'd been sure she'd opened it earlier to let in some fresh air. She pushed at it, but it was locked. No sign of the key, which she always hung on the rack. In fact, the key rack was completely empty.

A sudden beeping made her jump, until she remembered it was her new washing machine telling her it had finished the cycle. She turned it off and the silence settled around her again. Oppressive in its totality.

Desperate for fresh air, she went to open the patio doors. They too were locked. As was the back door and the front door. And all the downstairs windows.

Someone had locked her in.

CHAPTER NINETEEN

Jess curled up on the sofa and waited. It was all she could think of to do, her mind going over and over the events of the past few days, trying to work out who could be playing these spiteful tricks on her. Thankfully Ben came home at lunch to pick up some tools he needed.

'Hi, honey, I'm home!' he called as he walked in the door, the smell of fish and chips wafting in with him.

She jumped up and ran to him, throwing herself at him before bursting into relieved tears, the whole sorry tale stuttering out of her before he had a chance to speak.

'Hold on a minute...' He looked thoroughly confused. 'Is this what you're looking for?' He held up her handbag.

She pulled away from him, her mouth dropping open, her words a hoarse whisper when she finally managed to speak. 'Where did you find it?'

'I saw it on the car seat as I walked past. Figured you must have been out and maybe had your hands full bringing stuff in. I thought I'd save you a trip going back out for it.' He frowned. 'Your phone was there as well, and the car keys.'

'I... I don't understand,' she stammered.

'Well neither do I, because the front door wasn't locked when I came in just now.'

'But... but it was. It was locked. And all the windows.'

He shook his head. 'Honestly, love, I have no idea what's going on. But I turned the door handle and it opened. Definitely not locked.' He took her hand and led her into the kitchen. 'I got us some lunch. Let's eat and then you might feel a bit better.' He was giving her a strange look, and as she sat at the kitchen table, she was certain of one thing and one thing only.

He doesn't believe me.

Feeling unsettled, the afternoon stretched interminably, and she tried to distract herself with a grocery shop and an afternoon of baking and cooking. She made a caramel cheesecake, Toby's favourite. Baked some biscuits for Mo. Stocked up with fruit for Ruby, who was watching her weight and would often turn her nose up at ordinary meals but happily eat a bowl of fruit and yoghurt. A ragu was bubbling on the stove, rich with red wine, just how Ben liked it. Toby would live on pasta given the opportunity, so she figured she had all bases covered.

Ben arrived back first, Ruby bursting through the door holding several carrier bags from her shopping trip with her mum.

'Looks like you had a fun time,' Jess said, a big smile on her face, feeling guilty that she'd accused Ruby of any wrongdoing, when it now seemed that wasn't the case. Ruby looked at her like she'd crawled out from under a stone, before clomping up the stairs, and Jess wondered if Ben had said something to her. When they'd discussed things over lunch, he'd suggested that Jess was 'a little stressed', his way of explaining away her assertion that someone had taken her phone, bag and keys and locked her in the house. Who could blame him for not believing her when he'd come home to find the door open, the missing items on the car seat and all the keys back on the rack? She had been locked in, though. Her things had been taken. She knew that, even if he didn't.

Ben followed Ruby in, carrying her overnight bag, which he dumped in the hall.

Jess scowled. 'You know, we need to talk about Ruby at some point.'

'What about Ruby?'

'She's so rude sometimes. Honestly, she just ignored me then and I was only trying to be nice.' She couldn't hide the hurt in her voice. 'Did you say anything to her about... you know?'

'No, I didn't say anything, not now you're saying maybe it wasn't her. And her behaviour...' He gave an eye-roll. 'We've all been there, haven't we?'

'I wouldn't have dared be that rude to an adult when I was her age. I would have had a clout round the ear.'

'Yes, well they banned corporal punishment, remember?' There was an edge to his voice, and she decided not to push it. She'd made her point and didn't want to spoil the evening.

'How was your afternoon?' she asked, relaxing into his hug. His heart was thudding, not the usual steady beat. She pushed back, scanned his face. 'Everything okay?'

He gave her his lazy smile, but it didn't quite reach his eyes. 'Yep. Mrs Watterson is well and truly sorted.' His eyes slid away from hers. 'What's for tea? Something smells delicious.'

She followed him into the kitchen, unease stirring inside her. Should she say something? Mention that she'd seen him go in the opposite direction? Or would that seem like she'd been monitoring his movements?

The door opened then and Toby tumbled in, followed by Mo, both of them dashing up the stairs before she could say anything.

Carol stood in the doorway, beaming. 'They've had a

wonderful day. I hope you don't mind, but we're doing movie night. And there's a game they wanted to play, one of Toby's.' She glanced up to where the boys had disappeared. 'They've gone to get it.'

Jess stared at her. 'But he's back here tonight. That's what we agreed.'

Carol shook her head. 'Oh no. That's not right. Ben, didn't you tell her?'

'Tell me what?'

'I asked this morning if he could stay longer, and Ben said it would be fine.'

'What?' Jess looked at Ben, who was scrolling through his phone, clearly not listening.

'I've just got to make a call,' he said, frowning as he walked towards the kitchen. 'It's a work thing.'

Her teeth clamped together.

'I'm sorry, Carol, but—' She was interrupted by a spine-chilling scream, followed by crashing sounds from upstairs.

'Oh my God, what's happening?' The colour had drained from Carol's face. She pushed past Jess and took the stairs two at a time.

Jess followed, heart thundering in her chest. The noise was coming from Ruby's room, and she stopped in the doorway, aghast. Ruby was hurling things at the wall above her dressing table, Toby and Mo crouched underneath. She was soaking wet, water dripping down her face, make-up smeared on the new white top she was wearing.

'What is going on?' Jess shouted. Ruby froze, her hand clutching a table lamp that she'd been about to throw at the boys. 'Put that down, now!'

'You don't tell me what to do,' Ruby snarled.

'I do when you're in my house,' Jess said, trying to keep her voice even. 'Now put it down and tell me what the heck is going on.'

Ruby hesitated for a moment, then threw the lamp onto the bed. 'They've ruined my new clothes.' Her voice hitched as she turned so Jess could see the full extent of the damage. 'Look at them.'

'It's only water,' Carol said before Jess could reply. 'I think I know what happened. The boys have water pistols. I bought them so they could play on the beach.' She laughed. 'It's just a bit of fun. No harm done.'

She went over to the boys and picked up Mo, sitting him on her hip before taking Toby's hand and leading him towards the door. 'I'll... um... leave you to sort this out,' she said over her shoulder before heading downstairs.

'I hate you, Ruby!' Toby shouted as he left the room.

'I hate you more!' Ruby shouted back, picking up the lamp and throwing it at the wall where the boys had been.

Jess was too shocked by the violence to know what to do for the best. Run after Carol and retrieve her son, or give Ruby a talking-to? She couldn't have her thinking it was okay to smash the place up, especially if it was only a bit of water on her new clothes.

'Ben!' she shouted. 'Ben, can you come up here, please?'

No response.

Ruby sneered. 'That's right, get Dad. He won't do anything. You know he won't. And you're not my mum, so you can't do anything either. I hate your stupid boy-child. I'm not going to live in the same house as him. I told Dad. And Mum. They said they'd talk to you about it.'

'What?'

She nodded. 'Yeah, that's right. You heard.' She flounced to the door. 'I'm going to tell Dad what happened. He'll believe me.'

Jess sank onto the bed, her head in her hands. This was not how the evening was supposed to go. And there'd been a gleam of satisfaction in Carol's eye that made her wonder. Had she given the boys water pistols knowing that they might cause trouble with Ruby? Was she deliberately stirring things up, trying to make a difficult situation worse?

CHAPTER TWENTY

Her planned family evening had turned into something resembling a NATO negotiation. Ruby refused to speak to her and locked herself in her room, shouting insults through the door when Jess tried to make peace.

'I don't know what to do for the best,' she sighed as she flopped down beside Ben on the sofa. 'She won't even talk to me, and we can't just leave things like this, can we?'

'I'm sorry, love. But I can see her point of view. She was so excited about her new outfits.' He sounded as downhearted as he looked. 'Darcey said she tried on hundreds of things before she made her choice. She'd been saving up her birthday money and weekly allowance so she could get exactly what she wanted.' His lips pressed together, a thin line of annoyance. 'It was really important to her to get the right look. And that top is silk. She says the make-up won't come off. I'll have to buy her a new one.'

'No, *I'll* buy her a new one. Honestly, I want to make this right. I know it wasn't my fault, but I do feel responsible given that Toby sprayed her with water.'

Ben took her hand in his. 'Look, I know this is all new, us

living together, but we've got to get some ground rules sorted out.'

At last! 'Yes, that's exactly what I was thinking. We can't have things carrying on like this, can we?'

His hand squeezed hers. 'No, we can't. So you'll have a word with Toby? Ask him to stop these practical jokes?'

She bristled, snatching her hand away. 'What? You can't pin all this on Toby. He only plays practical jokes in revenge for the hurtful things Ruby says to him. She calls him all sorts of horrible names. I've told you, but you don't seem to listen.'

His eyes widened. 'So it's my fault now?'

'No, no, that's not what I'm saying.' She folded her arms across her chest, wondering how they'd managed to get into yet another fight but determined to stand her ground.

'So what *are* you saying? I know boys will be boys, but Toby needs a bit of guidance in terms of what is acceptable behaviour.'

She huffed, incredulous. 'I think we could say the same about Ruby. She's so rude and disrespectful. And I really do think it was her who defaced my divorce documents. I mean, who else had access to those papers? Did you ask her about that?' He said nothing. 'I thought not. Why should I have to put up with that in my own home? And why should Toby? It's his home too.'

Ben slumped back on the sofa, eyes on the ceiling. 'This is doing my head in.' He sighed, his gaze dropping to meet hers. 'I thought Toby might be better here. It's the same as in the other house, though, isn't it? The kids always fighting. I thought they just needed their own space, but maybe...'

'Maybe what?'

'Maybe that's just the type of kid Toby is.'

Jess felt her mouth drop open. How could he blame Toby for everything when Ruby was clearly the antagonistic force? There was never any trouble when she wasn't there. But she couldn't say that. Not to Ben, who saw a very different side to his daughter.

She stood, unable to imagine how they could get through this impasse. 'I'm going to see how the boys are.' Perhaps a bit of space would help calm things down, she thought as she stomped next door and rang the bell.

Rob opened the door, pulling it wide to let her in.

'Hey, are you okay?' He studied her face, concern in his eyes, then rubbed her shoulder, just like he always used to do when she was upset. She very nearly burst into tears, but somehow managed to hold it together. Instead, she flapped a hand, wafting his concern away, pinning a bright smile to her face.

'Teenagers.' Her laugh sounded brittle, false, her voice higher than usual. 'I just came to check that the boys are all right.'

'Nothing to worry about. Carol has calmed everything down. She's such a great mum, never gets flustered.' He beamed, pride lighting up his face. 'Anyway, they're tucking into some food in front of a movie.'

Jess tried to blink back her tears again, but not fast enough.

'Hey, don't get upset.' Rob gathered her into a hug, so familiar it was like pulling on a favourite jumper. She rested her head on his chest, closing her eyes. 'It's not your fault, is it? I think it'll be fine. But we do need to talk to the kids, see what we can do to stop this happening again.'

Jess nodded and pulled away. 'I know. I just said that to Ben, but his daughter can do no wrong in his eyes.'

'Do you want me to have a word with him?'

She felt herself sag with relief. 'Would you? He might listen if it came from you.'

'I've already spoken to the boys about playing jokes on people.' He grimaced. 'Poor Toby was quite upset. And I can see his point. When you're bullied like that, it's the injustice, isn't it? That's what hurts.'

Jess nodded, her sympathies completely with her son. Her throat clogged with emotion, and the two of them stood in silence for a moment until the sound of footsteps coming down the stairs made her look up.

Carol froze when she saw her, a look of alarm on her face.

Rob turned. 'It's okay. Jess was just leaving.' But Carol had already run back upstairs.

Jess frowned, confused. 'Have I done something to upset her?'

'It's okay, don't worry about it. She's just very protective of Mo and was concerned that Ruby could have hurt him. I know it's not your fault, but...' He tailed off, his meaning clear. Carol blamed her for what had happened. After all, Jess was the one who had brought Ben and Ruby into their lives. 'Look, I was going to come round and talk to you about this, but for the time being, Carol thinks it's best if Mo doesn't come to your house. Not when Ruby is around anyway. And I'm sorry to say I agree.'

Jess glanced up the stairs, then lowered her voice. 'Don't you think Carol is overreacting a bit? The children have had fights before, and she's always been the one to say "kids will be kids" and brush it off as part of growing up. You've never seemed to be too worried either. So what's changed?'

'What do you mean?'

'She just seems to be behaving a little... out of character. Very protective all of a sudden.'

Rob gave her a quizzical look. 'I'm not sure I know what you mean. She's always had Mo's best interests at heart. Maybe the difference before was that she was in our house, whereas this is hers. She makes the rules as far as Mo is concerned, and that's fine with me.'

Jess hesitated, wondering how far to go with the conversation. 'She seems very jumpy. You must have noticed.' She hesitated. 'Are you sure this thing with the person from work has been resolved?'

Rob's eyes narrowed. 'Why do you ask?'

'Well, if he's still bothering her, that's enough to make anyone jumpy.' She thought back to the conversation she'd overheard. 'He didn't make threats, did he?'

Rob gave a frustrated sigh, glanced towards the front door, and Jess had the impression he was going to ask her to leave. His voice had a familiar patronising edge to it when he replied, like she didn't know what she was talking about. 'I did speak to her about it the other day after I'd been over to see you and Ben. You know I was worried about her, but she says she hasn't heard from him for weeks now, so it seems moving to a new job has done the trick.' He gave her the ghost of a smile, his eyes on the door again, and she decided it was time to take the hint.

'Well that's good to know. I'm glad it's sorted out.' She gave a quick smile. 'I think we've all been jumpy these last few days, with the move and everything.'

'You never did like change, did you?' She couldn't help feeling he was suggesting that she was the one who was being jumpy. And maybe she was. But someone had locked her in her house earlier today. She hadn't imagined that, or any of the other things. It had been easy to blame Ruby, but she was sure now that somebody else was playing games with her. Games that would make anyone uneasy.

'From what I can see,' Rob continued, 'Carol has been having a wonderful time with the boys. I've never seen her so happy. And you really can't blame her for being upset about the incident this evening.' He paused. 'I know Ruby's not your daughter, but you and Ben really need to have a proper conversation with her about this behaviour. It can't go on.'

Jess nodded, distracted. 'I've just said the same thing to Ben.' She moved towards the door. 'I'll expect Toby back after he's watched the movie, shall I?'

He flashed her a smile. 'I'll bring him round when he's ready.'

She opened the door and scuttled back to her own house, wondering how everything had suddenly become so difficult. One thing she knew for sure, though, Carol wasn't being honest with Rob. And if that was the case, were there other things she wasn't being honest about as well?

CHAPTER TWENTY-ONE

That evening, Ben managed to smooth things over with Ruby, and peace was restored. There was now a rule in place that forbade Toby from going into Ruby's room, and vice versa. There was even a notice on Ruby's door saying *No boys allowed* as a reminder. At least it was clear, one lot of boundaries sorted out, and Toby seemed okay with the arrangement.

Later, when he was having his bath, he called to Jess that there was no towel on the rail. She'd been busy tidying clothes off his bedroom floor, no longer allowed in the bathroom with him. He was at an age when he was increasingly private about his body, and she liked to respect his space. She grabbed a towel and opened the door. He was already out of the bath, his back to her, and she noticed them straight away. Bruises, purple dots on the back of both upper arms. She inched inside for a closer look, appalled to see they were the shape of fingerprints, like he'd been held tightly.

'How did you get those bruises?' she said, handing him the towel, which he wrapped round his waist.

'What bruises?'

She realised he wouldn't be able to see them and moved him

over to the mirror, lifting his arms so he could get a proper view. 'These ones.'

He pulled a face, squinting to see better. Shook his head, looking worried. 'I don't know.'

She frowned, unconvinced. 'Has someone been hurting you?'

He shook his head again, still peering at his reflection. He touched a bruise, wincing as he did so. 'I wondered why my arms were sore.'

She sat on the edge of the bath, determined to get a proper answer, making her voice as gentle as possible so he couldn't hear the anger bubbling up inside.

'Did Ruby do this to you?'

He thought for a moment. 'No, not Ruby.' He seemed very definite, and she had to believe him.

'Who then?'

His eyes filled with tears. 'I don't know.' He grabbed his pyjamas from the towel rail and pulled them on, as if that would make the problem go away.

'It's okay, love,' she said, putting an arm round his shoulders, stroking his hair. 'It's okay. Maybe you'll remember later and then you can tell me.'

He snuffled into her chest and she held him close until his tears subsided. Her jaw hardened. If it wasn't Ruby who'd hurt him, could it be Carol? Some sort of weird revenge for supposedly talking to her son about his dead father? Surely not. But Toby had been with Carol for the last couple of days. Did she have a side to her that none of them had been aware of? Since they'd moved, she did seem to have a bit of a temper, snapping at Jess on a few occasions now. Jess shivered at the thought. When she considered it, Mo was a timid child, full of anxieties. Could that be down to his mother's behaviour?

The thoughts went round in her head, making her increasingly on edge as she finished settling Toby in bed.

'What do you make of Carol?' she asked Ben when she joined him in the lounge.

He was sitting on the sofa, back towards her. He quickly turned off his phone and shoved it in his pocket. Picked up a glass of wine and passed it to her, a pretend smile on his face.

'Why do you ask?' he said with a forced nonchalance.

He definitely had the look of a guilty person, and she wondered what he'd been doing that he felt was wrong. Messaging somebody? Her heart gave a stutter. Carol, maybe? They were exes, after all. But she shook the thought from her head, telling herself not to be silly.

When did I get so suspicious? It wasn't a nice feeling, eating into her thoughts, making her second-guess every move of the people around her. But since they'd moved to the house, she was aware that things had changed. Someone was trying to make her feel uneasy. Scared even. And the dynamic was different. She appeared to be on the outside looking in. Was that the message she was being given when she was locked in the house? That she was separate, not part of the family?

'Jess, are you okay? You've gone blank.'

She brought herself back to the present, her question and his answer. 'She's being really off with me. Ever since we moved here, she's either avoiding me or challenging me. It feels... awkward.'

Ben patted the seat beside him. 'Come and sit down, love. I think you've just got to give her a bit of time. It can't be easy for her moving in next door to her partner's ex. It's not the same for me because me and Rob are mates and I've heard both sides of the story, so I know how things are between you. But Carol... well I don't suppose you two have spent much time together, have you?'

Jess took a sip of her wine. He was right, that was probably it. But still, Carol had been with Rob for almost a year, so surely by now she'd worked out how things stood. And Rob had asked her to marry him once the divorce had come through, so that should put her mind at rest. *Perhaps I just need to tell her how it is myself?*

Her eyes met Ben's. 'I think she's hiding something. And she's been monopolising Toby ever since we moved in, keeping Mo away from me after that incident about his allegedly dead father.'

'Allegedly?' He frowned.

She sighed. 'I'm not convinced he *is* dead.'

Ben whistled through his teeth. 'That's a big leap on the basis of a five-year-old child's view of reality.'

'It's not just that. I told you about the conversation I overheard.'

'Oh, that was Gary. You know, the guy who's been a bit creepy with her. She told me he's popped up again, seems to have found out where she's working and got her phone number. God knows how. Anyway, she doesn't want to tell Rob because he gets all protective and she's worried he'll go round and cause trouble.'

'Oh...' Jess felt wrong-footed, Ben's explanation so matter-of-fact it seemed to take all the perceived threat away. 'I didn't know that.'

It appeared there was a lot that Jess didn't know about Carol. But how was it that Ben seemed to know everything?

'See, you're making mysteries out of nothing.' He put an arm round her shoulders. 'I think you need to chill out a bit, stop looking for trouble where there isn't any.'

She decided he was probably right and remembered then why she'd asked the question in the first place. 'Toby has bruises on his arms. Right here.' She tapped her upper arm. 'Like someone had grabbed him really hard.'

He looked thoughtful for a moment. 'It could have been when he's been playing with Mo. You know they like to have a wrestle. Pretend they're WWE characters.'

She shook her head. 'Nope. The marks were too big for that. Mo's hands are tiny. These looked like adult fingerprints.' Or a teenager's. Could Ruby have done it? Toby had said not, but then he'd got all upset, so maybe he was covering up for her after all the previous upset, not wanting to cause more trouble.

Ben looked startled. 'You think it could be Carol?'

'Well, Toby has been with her for the last few days.'

'Or Rob?'

She gave a derisive snort. 'Don't be daft. You know Rob treats Toby like some precious ornament. He won't even let him come out for bike rides with you. And he's never done the rough-and-tumble stuff with him.'

'Well it wasn't me,' Ben said, withdrawing his arm and standing up. 'Before you ask.'

Jess stared at him. She hadn't thought about Ben. Had he been alone with Toby over the past few days? She wouldn't know if he had, because it would have happened next door. And by so quickly ruling himself out, in Jess's mind he'd just ruled himself in.

Her brain made a leap that halted her breath. Carol and Ben. Was there something going on between them? Could Toby have seen something and Ben had grabbed him, sworn him to secrecy or else?

She was appalled at the places her thoughts were taking her, dark places she hadn't known existed before they'd moved here. Ben stared at her, his eyes boring into her as though he was searching her mind, seeing what she'd been thinking. A blush travelled up her neck, burning her cheeks. Did he know she was questioning him? She hoped not, but his body language told a different story.

'I'm just nipping next door,' he said, an edge to his voice. 'I think the atmosphere will be warmer there.'

She watched him leave, wondering what she'd just done. Her and her stupid mouth, throwing accusations around.

What's happening to me?

She felt like she was floating, dissociated from reality. Had she really been locked in the house? Because everything had been normal when Ben had come home. Everything that had happened could be explained away, except the lipstick writing on the divorce papers. That was real. And if that was real, perhaps everything else was as well. She went to check.

After sorting through every drawer in the desk where she'd left them, the documents were nowhere to be found.

CHAPTER TWENTY-TWO

It was after midnight when Ben returned home. Jess had been in bed for a while, sleep proving elusive. Her mind was far too busy going over everything that had happened since the move, trying to find alternative explanations but always coming back to the same conclusion. Someone was trying to scare her, make her think she was going mad and alienate her from the rest of the family. Now Toby was caught up in the whole nasty scheme and it had to stop before it escalated even further.

The problem was how to persuade Ben and Rob that Carol was causing these problems. Both of them seemed to have been bewitched by her, and Jess knew she was going to have to tread carefully.

Ben flopped into bed without saying a word. He smelt of beer.

'I'm sorry,' she murmured, reaching for him, but he didn't respond to her touch. 'I'm sorry you thought I was accusing you of hurting Toby. I really wasn't.' She rolled onto her side, head propped in her hand, so she could see him. His eyes were closed.

'I'm too tired for this now. Tomorrow is another day.' His

voice was slurred, weary, and she knew it would be better to wait, but she couldn't help herself.

'I can't bear it when we fight,' she said, needing him to forgive her. 'I love you, Ben, I love you so much and I want all this nonsense to stop.'

'So do I,' he sighed. 'Please stop, then we can all just get on with our lives.'

Her breath caught in her throat. 'What? It's not me.'

'It sounds like you. I've had a long chat with Rob and Carol, and we're all worried about you. I'm going to take Ruby away for a few days, give you a break for the rest of the week, then you can have some quality time with Toby before he goes back to school.' He let out another big sigh. 'Hopefully absence will make the heart grow fonder, and we can reset and start again.'

'But... we had plans to do family things.'

'Yeah, but that's not gonna work right now, is it?'

She lay back down, unable to think of a reply, the shock that they'd been talking about her behind her back rendering her speechless. It was a horrible feeling, knowing she'd been the topic of conversation, a cause for concern. *Poor Jess, overwrought, stressed, needs to chill.* She could almost hear what they'd been saying. She was the victim here, so why was she feeling like the perpetrator?

'Oh, and I told Rob about the divorce paperwork being defaced, and he says he'll ask his solicitor to get a new set sent over tomorrow.'

She didn't dare ask if he'd tackled Ruby about that, but wasn't the fact that he'd spoken to Rob a tacit admission of her guilt? Perhaps it was one mystery solved at least.

The next morning, Ben responded to her in monosyllables and Ruby ignored her completely as they packed up ready for their holiday. They were going to Ireland on a bit of a road trip and it was a rush to get organised. Jess waved them off feeling empty inside. Was this situation of her own making? Everyone but her seemed to think so.

She rang her mum and explained what had happened, expecting her to say, 'I told you so.' But she didn't. Instead, she arranged time off work, and came over and mothered Jess for a few days, which turned out to be lovely. Toby was delighted to have so much time with his gran, and the chessboard was constantly busy with their games.

Jess had to admit that Ben had been right. Having a bit of space to reset had probably been the best idea, and nothing peculiar happened. Not one single incident, which sort of confirmed that Ruby might have been behind some of the tricks being played on her. Hopefully Ben would persuade her to stop, and if things started to happen again once she was home, well, that would be Jess's proof.

Perhaps that's the end of it, she allowed herself to think as she waved her mum off on the last day of the school holidays, looking forward to welcoming Ben and Ruby home.

Everything was calm for the next two weeks. The children were back at school, the adults back at work, and everyone kept themselves to themselves pretty much, apart from Toby going round to play with Mo and having a couple of sleepovers a week.

There was a bit of a change in Toby, though. Especially on the first day of school.

'George isn't going to be there,' he'd mumbled when Jess had asked him what was wrong. 'It's not going to be the same without him.'

George was Toby's best friend, and his family had moved to the UK over the summer. She'd known it would be a big blow to him, because they'd been friends since they were toddlers.

'But everyone else will be there, and he's not your only friend, is he?'

Toby considered that. 'No, I don't suppose he is. I do sometimes play with Madison.'

'Well then. Perhaps this is a chance to get to know her a bit better. And there might be new children you could make friends with.'

He'd cheered up a bit then, but she noticed he was still more subdued than usual, and was glad that he at least had Mo to play with.

It was Jess's day off, and she was getting on with the housework when she heard the doorbell ring. She opened the door to find a plump young woman with a frizz of unfeasibly red hair and a face full of freckles standing there.

'Hello. Mrs Baker, is it?' She seemed a little nervous, peering over Jess's shoulder into the house.

Jess smiled, puzzled. 'That's right.'

'I'm Deborah Quirk. Social Services. May I come in?'

Social Services? How odd. She frowned. 'Are you sure you've got the right address?'

The woman looked at a notebook in her hand. 'If you're Jessica Baker, mother of Toby Baker?'

'That's me.'

She smiled. 'Then I'm in the right place.'

Jess led her into the lounge, curious to know what the visit could be about, her palms slick with sweat for some reason. 'Have a seat.' She pointed to the armchair. 'Can I get you a drink? Tea? Coffee? Water?'

Deborah shook her head. 'I'm fine, thanks. I'd rather we got down to business.' She checked her watch. 'I've got rather a full day.'

Jess nodded, glad that it appeared this wouldn't take long. She perched on the edge of the sofa, her hands clasped between her knees.

Deborah cleared her throat and looked her straight in the eye. 'I'm here because we had a call from a... let's call it a concerned member of the public. They've seen bruises on your son and are a little worried about his welfare.'

Jess couldn't speak, her mouth hanging open.

Deborah's gaze didn't waver. 'I have some pictures and I have to say they do look rather nasty. Like someone has grabbed him. Roughly.'

Jess swallowed, fury flaring in her chest. Who on earth would be looking for bruises on her son? Then it dawned on her. This could only have come from one person: Carol.

What's she playing at? How could she do something so spiteful?

She gathered her thoughts, determined to fight back. 'Yes, I have to say I was worried about those too. They appeared after he'd spent some time with my husband's partner.' She was aware that sounded odd. 'They live next door and my son stayed there for two days over the holidays. I noticed the bruises when he came home.'

Deborah's eyebrows twitched towards her hairline.

Jess carried on, 'I know it might seem unconventional, but we felt it would be easiest for our son if we lived close by when we separated, so he could come and go between our houses. We both have new partners who have children and we've been trying to accommodate all their needs.' She was waffling, but couldn't seem to stop. 'My son and the son of my husband's new partner are very close, and it's good for them to be able to spend time together when they want. And Toby can go and see his dad whenever he feels like it.'

Deborah's mouth settled into a tight line. 'I see.' She scribbled some notes on the pad on her lap. 'But let's get back to the bruises. You suspect they happened while Toby was with his father and his new partner?' Jess nodded. 'And did you do anything about it? Have you spoken to them?'

'Well, no.' She'd hardly seen them since the trouble started, and once she knew they'd been talking about her, she'd kept away. 'My son said he didn't know how it happened, and—'

'You didn't talk to your husband's partner about it?'

'Toby didn't want to make a fuss.' Did that sound bad? That she hadn't followed it up?

'So you don't know exactly when the bruises appeared?'

Jess frowned. She couldn't say for sure now that Toby had decided he was old enough to bath and get ready for bed on his own. 'I hadn't noticed them before.'

'It's hard to date a bruise, isn't it?' Deborah was looking at her in a way that told her she was weighing up her answers, assessing whether she was telling the truth. She swallowed, suddenly hot. 'Could they have been there before he stayed with his father?'

'Well, yes, I suppose they could.' *No, no, I shouldn't have said that.* But it did make her think. Could it have been Ruby? That was a possibility she couldn't ignore. Or Ben?

Deborah's voice became sympathetic. 'I understand you've been under a lot of stress recently.'

'That's right. Moving house, making the separation from my husband formal, all of that.' Jess sighed. 'My partner's daughter can be a bit difficult, and...' She tailed off, thinking she was not playing this right at all.

'I've been in touch with Toby's school, and they did say they felt his behaviour was a cause for concern. That he was quieter than usual. And they'd noticed the bruises too, when he went back to school. They felt he wasn't being completely honest when he said he didn't know how he'd got them.'

'I know he's not as happy at school as he was. His best friend has moved to the UK and I think he's feeling a little lost without him.' She gave Deborah a tight smile. 'But I think he's finding his feet now.' She broadened her smile. 'I really don't think there's anything to worry about.'

'That's good to hear. I just want you to know that I'll keep the file open, and if you need us to help in any way at all... if you feel you're not really coping, then I want you to know you can give us a call any time.'

Jess bristled. What on earth had this 'concerned member of the public' been saying about her? 'I'm coping very well, thank you. I don't think that will be necessary.'

Deborah was studying her face, the silence almost unbearable. 'It's procedure, and I wouldn't be doing my job properly if I didn't follow up reported concerns thoroughly. Especially when the school have noticed a change in behaviour. I'll give you a call, arrange to come and see Toby, then we'll take it from there.'

She checked her watch, put her notebook in her bag and stood. 'It was lovely to meet you, Mrs Baker, and like I said, any concerns at all, please do get in touch.' She held out a card, which Jess took and stuffed in her back pocket, feeling dazed and confused. Angry that someone had reported her in the first place, and uneasy at the idea someone had been talking to Social Services about her and saying she wasn't coping.

As she said goodbye to the social worker and watched her walk down the drive, another thought popped into her head. Had Carol deliberately hurt Toby to use it against her?

It was shocking, but a possibility she knew she had to consider.

CHAPTER TWENTY-THREE

Did Carol have a dark side? On the outside, a gentle, vulnerable widow, and on the inside, someone who was consumed by a hidden anger, who wanted to steal Jess's family and discredit her in the process. She huffed out a frustrated breath. *For goodness' sake, listen to yourself. Carol's not like that.*

It might have been some do-gooder seeing the bruises and poking their nose in. At the swimming pool, on the beach... It was definitely a possibility she had to factor in. But the fact that the school had been concerned was a worry. And even more of a worry was the social worker focusing on Jess.

I should have said something to Carol at the time. Her mouth twisted from side to side. *I should.* But Toby had been so upset, not wanting to talk about it, and she couldn't be sure what had happened. *Should I have said something to Rob?* That was another yes.

Rob's car was in the drive, so he must be working from home. His office operated on a flexible basis and was happy for staff to be at home some of the time. As long as they were in the office on Monday morning for the weekly team meeting and they hit their targets, the boss didn't mind where they worked.

She hurried across the drive and rang the bell, her weight shifting from foot to foot as she waited, unsure how she was going to start this conversation.

'Jess.' He looked flustered, glanced over his shoulder. 'I'm just... I'm in the middle of something. Is it urgent, or can I come round when I've finished?'

'It's about Toby.' She wasn't going to be fobbed off. Surely his son's well-being was more important than anything else.

His eyes widened. 'Oh, right. Well come in. I'll, er... I'll just finish this call. Would you like to go and make us a coffee? I'll be down in a minute.'

He ran up the stairs and she walked through to the kitchen, filled the kettle and turned it on. She opened cupboard doors until she found the mugs, picked the one she always used to use when she'd considered these mugs to be hers and another for Rob. It was like she'd stepped into a time warp.

She found the coffee, the brand Rob always liked her to buy, even though it was a little bitter for her taste. Made the drinks and took them over to the dining table. So familiar and yet a million miles away from where her life had taken her.

Ben's face swam into her thoughts. *Should I have talked to him first? Told him what's happened? Maybe I should.* Quickly she tapped out a message, giving the bare basics of the social worker's visit, telling him she'd gone to speak to Rob. She could discuss it all with him that evening when he came home, see what his thoughts were, but at least he was in the loop.

The sound of footsteps thudding down the stairs made her turn off her phone, put it on the table. Once she had Rob's attention, she didn't want to be interrupted.

'Sorry about that,' he said, an apologetic smile on his face. 'I've been trying to speak to the guy for a couple of weeks, so I didn't want to have to ring back.'

Jess nodded. Sipped her coffee. Same old, same old.

However much he said it wouldn't, work always came first for Rob.

He sat down opposite her, reached for his coffee. 'So what's the problem, love? I thought Toby was doing okay.' He grinned at her. 'I think this new living arrangement is really working well for him, don't you?'

Jess sighed, wondering where to begin. 'I had someone from Social Services round this morning.'

He was about to take a sip of his coffee, but stopped, put his mug back on the table. 'Social Services?' He looked alarmed. 'What on earth did they want?'

'They haven't spoken to you, then?'

'No. Why would they?' That confirmed her impression someone had clearly pointed the finger at her alone.

She puffed out her cheeks, not sure how he was going to take what she was about to say. He was so protective of his partner, as she'd experienced in recent weeks.

'Look... you're not going to like this, but I think Carol is trying to cause trouble for me.'

He looked even more alarmed now, his gaze directed over her right shoulder.

She turned her head. Saw Carol standing in the doorway of the utility room, a basket of washing in her hands, a shocked look on her face.

Rob's mouth opened in a silent 'O', a flash of something that looked like panic in his eyes. 'Don't be silly. Of course she's not making trouble for you, are you, sweetheart?'

'I don't know what you're talking about,' Carol said. She was clearly in no mood to join in the conversation, her lips pressed so tightly together they had all but disappeared. She walked through the kitchen and opened the patio doors, closing them behind her with a bang. Jess could see her starting to hang up the washing outside, her movements staccato and angry.

Oh God, what have I done?

She glanced at Rob, wondering if she'd imagined that look in his eyes. There was nothing but concern there now. 'I'm sure it's all a misunderstanding,' he said, watching Carol as she flicked the creases out of each garment with a quick snap before hanging it up.

Jess decided to press on. Now she'd started, she might as well finish, and Rob needed to know the full story, otherwise he was likely to brush off her concerns. 'Toby had bruises on his arms.' She gestured to her own arm. 'Here... Like someone had grabbed him really hard. You could see the fingerprints.'

His face froze, the news clearly a shock. 'Oh my God, is he okay? Why didn't you tell me before?'

Yes, Jess, why didn't you?

She looked down at her hands, started picking at a bit of egg yolk stuck to the surface of the table. She had no logical answer; she'd just hoped that it had been nothing untoward and the problem would fade with the bruises. Taking the easy way out? She was ashamed to say that was the truth of it. She'd just wanted to smooth over the fractious atmosphere with her neighbours.

She glanced up to find Rob scowling at her, and gathered her defence. 'He said he didn't know how he got them. And when I pressed him, he got all upset.' Her jaw hardened, her gaze defiant now. She wasn't at fault here. It wasn't her who'd caused the injuries. 'It was when he came back from staying with you for a few days,' she said pointedly, maintaining eye contact as she waited for the implications to register.

Rob rubbed his hands down his face like he wanted to wash away the thought of his son being handled roughly.

'But... you can't go accusing Carol. That's just a leap too far. I mean, it could be when he was playing with Mo, or at the swimming pool. Carol said they were messing around with some older boys. It could have been when they had that fight with Ruby. Or... and I hate to say this, but it could have been

Ben. He's been here, playing with him, and I didn't think to keep an eye on them both a hundred per cent of the time.' His eyes were wild, his stare so intense she had to look away.

'They were adult fingerprints, not a child's. And I've asked Ben and he said it wasn't him. So that leaves you and Carol.' It was the first time she'd included Rob in her list of potential culprits, but for the sake of fairness, he had to be in there, didn't he?

'Bloody hell, Jess. What has got into you?' He leant towards her. 'Has he ever had bruises like that before?'

She shook her head, feeling guilty for even suggesting it.

'No, that's right, he hasn't.' Rob's voice was guttural, his jaw clenched tight. He was *seething*. 'Have you ever heard me raise my voice to our child? Get cross with him in any way?'

She shook her head again. 'Like I said, Carol is the most logical culprit.' She glanced out of the window at her neighbour, still hanging up washing outside. 'She's being really off with me. And who else would stir up trouble with Social Services?'

'You've got it all wrong,' he snapped, his face quite red now. She could honestly say she'd never seen him this angry. 'No way would Carol do that. Not after what she went through with her husband.'

She waited, hoping he would elaborate, but Carol came back in before he could speak. She walked over to the table, and Jess could see that she was shaking, a tremor in her voice when she finally spoke.

'Don't you dare accuse me of things I didn't do. Why would I want to cause trouble for you?' Her voice was high and screechy. 'The problem with you, Jess, is you think everything should be about *you*. Well it isn't. I have more important things to think about than you and your imaginary worries.'

With that, she stalked out of the kitchen. The front door slammed. A few moments later, there was the roar of a car engine.

'Oh God. What have you done?' Rob pressed his hands to his temples.

Jess wondered that herself, shaken by the venom in Carol's words.

'She shouldn't be driving when she's upset. That's how she had the accident the other week, and I can't risk—'

'You could have told me she was here,' she snapped. 'You know, when I came in, you could have told me.'

'I thought you knew. I mean, the car was in the drive.' Anger had given way to panic now.

Jess was confused. 'Not *her* car, though.'

'No, because it's at the garage. It wasn't right after she went off the road. They had to order a new part and she's using my car in the meantime.'

She rubbed at her forehead, not sure what to do for the best. Rob still wasn't taking her seriously about Carol. *Perhaps I should tell him about all the other things? Or will he think I'm going mad, like Ben?* Perhaps Ben had already told him. Hadn't he said they'd had a long conversation and were worried about her?

Rob stood and went to the lounge window, peering outside. He came back a minute later, hand raking through his hair. 'It's okay.' He sounded like he was trying to convince himself. 'She'll calm down. Give it a day or two, then you can apologise and we'll get back on track.'

Jess felt a surge of annoyance. Carol being upset was not the main worry here.

'You're missing the point, Rob. Somebody hurt our child, and somebody reported me to Social Services. It might be the same person, or two completely different people, but it's not a great situation.' Saying it out loud stirred a flutter of panic in her chest, her throat squeezing closed so she was struggling to breathe. 'And then... and then the social worker suggested I wasn't coping, so who put *that* idea in their head? And what if—'

'Sweetheart, you need to calm down.' His expression said he didn't have time for her hysterics, his mind on Carol rather than her. The last thing she felt like doing was calming down. She felt like screaming and shouting until he bloody listened to what she was saying. He just didn't seem to be hearing the words coming out of her mouth.

He put a hand on her shoulder and looked her in the eye. 'If you feel you're not coping, you just need to say.'

She smacked his hand away. 'I'm coping fine!' she shouted, shocking herself into silence.

He took a step back. 'Look, it's probably just a misunderstanding, like I said before. It'll blow over.' He reached out and patted her. A patronising gesture that fired her anger up another notch.

She gritted her teeth, her hands curled into fists by her sides. 'Aren't you worried that someone hurt Toby?'

He gave her that look again, his voice filled with forced patience. 'Kids play games. Boys will be boys. It could have happened in the playground.' He shook his head, his voice gentle. 'You can't go around accusing people of things when you have no evidence. That's just going to cause bad feeling, isn't it? I was always covered with bruises as a child, and if you'd asked me where they came from, I wouldn't have been able to tell you.'

She let his words wash over her, knowing that she'd been the same as a kid. Maybe he was right. The thought seemed to take all the fight out of her. *Am I overreacting?* Could this just be a young, zealous social worker, egged on by a highly vigilant school? She wished the school had spoken to her first, then remembered that it wasn't the school that had raised the issue with Social Services. It was the other way round.

Someone had wanted Social Services to believe she was

abusing her child. There was no getting away from that fact, even if the bruises had been acquired innocently.

And if the bruises had been an aggressive act by an adult, then whatever Rob said, however much he was in denial, Carol was the only person in the frame.

CHAPTER TWENTY-FOUR

Having managed to upset everyone apart from her mother, Jess decided the best thing would be to keep quiet and observe. Get on with her life as best she could and hope that now Carol knew she suspected her, all the nonsense would stop. And it did, for a time.

Four whole weeks passed in relative calm, and she started to believe that she didn't need to be on high alert all the time. Ruby was being reclusive, refusing to speak to Toby or eat meals with the family. Ben said they should give her a bit of space, which Jess was happy to do for the time being. Her mum had started picking the boys up from school every day, changing her work hours to do so, and Toby had got over his friend leaving and had taken a new boy under his wing. Helen had even started doing bits of shopping for her and making meals ready for when she and Ben got home.

The main niggle, though, was the fact that Mo was not allowed to come round and play at their house. True to her word, Carol was refusing to allow Jess to look after him, so Toby spent a lot of time next door instead. Something she was not happy with, given that Carol was the prime suspect for Toby's bruises.

One evening, the fourth in a row that Toby had spent at his father's, she burst into tears while she and Ben were watching a film, and all her worries and misgivings came flooding out in one long torrent of words.

'Hey, sweetheart,' Ben said, 'don't get yourself so upset. I'm sure we can sort something out.'

'But Carol won't speak to me any more and Rob's being all huffy, hardly giving me the time of day, always ready with an excuse to rush off.'

He handed her the box of tissues, waiting while she blew her nose and wiped her eyes.

'What about reinstating our Friday-evening meal?' She glanced up at him. That was the last thing she'd been expecting. 'I was saying to Rob and Carol just yesterday how much I missed our get-togethers, and I got the impression from the way they looked at each other that they want to go back to how we were but aren't sure how to do it.'

The idea of them all sitting round the same table was frankly horrifying. After the upset, the accusations she'd thrown around and her lingering suspicions, it seemed like the worst idea she could imagine.

'What harm can it do?' he said, tucking her hair behind her ear. 'Now we're all settled in and the stress of the move is over, maybe things will be all right.'

'You don't think it'll feel awkward?' How could it not?

He laughed. 'It's bound to be at first, but I'll make sure it's okay.' He smiled at her. 'Trust me on this one. I think it's what we all need. Then we can hopefully negotiate a truce with Carol, she'll let Mo come round, and we can get back to seeing more of Toby.'

Wasn't that exactly what she wanted? Be brave, she told

herself. Who dares wins and all that. But she sent Ben round to do the inviting, just in case.

Admittedly, conversation was a little stilted at the start of the evening.

'You look lovely,' Carol said to Jess when she came in. 'That yellow dress really suits you. I look like I've got liver problems if I wear anything close to that colour.' She pulled a face, pretending to hide her glass of wine behind her back. Then took a surreptitious gulp before pretending to hide it again, giving an exaggerated smile and a loud hiccup. 'Obviously that's not the case.'

The men laughed and Jess couldn't suppress her own smile. Carol did this so well, this clowning around, and she allowed herself to relax a little, hoping that the evening might continue in this vein, all animosity forgotten.

'You're so lucky with your hair colour,' Carol continued, clearly trying her hardest to be nice. 'And you've such a gorgeous tan as well.' She held up a pale arm. 'I look like I've just come out of the deep freeze, don't I?'

Another burst of laughter, and this time, Jess couldn't stop herself from joining in, glad she'd decided on a little secret forti-fication from the wine bottle before the evening proper had begun. It's going to be okay, she allowed herself to think as she started bringing the food to the table.

She watched Carol, trying to work out if something had changed, but she appeared more relaxed as the evening wore on and slipped into her easy banter with Ben. She was always self-deprecating, never aiming her quick wit at anyone else, and Jess couldn't help but admire that aspect of her personality.

Could we be friends? she wondered. Or is this all an act?

She'd seen another side to her, hadn't she? And Rob had suggested all might not be well in Carol's world. She couldn't forget the overheard conversation and the fact Carol had been so upset she'd driven off the road. And she couldn't discount her from being the person who'd hurt Toby and reported her to Social Services. Whatever the truth of the matter, she knew in her heart that she didn't trust her.

All the more reason to get to know her a bit better, she decided, resolving to make an effort to catch her on her own so they could have a proper chat.

Her chance came after they'd finished the meal. Rob was clearing up, Ben had gone out to the wine cellar, aka the garage, to get another bottle, and Carol went upstairs to use the loo. Jess waited a moment, then followed her up.

As she passed the bathroom door, on her way to her bedroom to wait, she heard the murmur of conversation. She couldn't help herself and moved closer to listen. Still Carol's voice was too indistinct for her to hear what was being said. She pressed her ear against the door. Now she could hear. Carol sounded angry, her voice shrill. 'Don't you dare threaten me. I've told you before—'

'What are you doing?' Jess's heart leapt up her throat and she turned to see Ruby staring at her. She jumped back from the door, her face on fire.

'Nothing, I was just wanting the loo and was checking there was nobody in there.'

'Oh yeah,' Ruby sneered. 'I'll tell whoever's in there that you were listening to them having a pee.'

Jess clenched her jaw. 'Don't you—'

The bathroom door opened and she spun round, finding herself face to face with an alarmed-looking Carol. Jess stepped back, so flustered now she couldn't think of anything to say.

'She was listening at the door,' Ruby said, delighted to be able to cause trouble.

'I was not.' Jess could feel her face getting hotter.

'Liar,' Ruby said gleefully. 'She's a weirdo,' she added to Carol before closing her bedroom door. The lock clicked.

The two women looked at each other, Jess so hot now she knew her discomfort must be clear. She tried an apologetic smile. 'Honestly, I wasn't listening at the door. I just came up to use the loo and didn't realise there was anyone in there.' Even to her own ears, the excuse didn't sound convincing.

Carol's eyes narrowed. 'You *were* listening, weren't you?'

Jess shook her head, panic making her breathless. 'No, no, really I wasn't.'

'Ruby's right. You're a liar. It's written all over your face.'

'I'm sorry you think that.' She looked at her feet, blew out a breath, deciding to press on with her initial mission. 'The thing is... I think we've got off on the wrong foot since we moved in. I hate to think there's any bad feeling between us and... well, I'm really sorry I've upset you.'

Carol's hands gravitated to her hips and she leant forward, her face inches from Jess's. 'You accuse me of hurting Toby and think I won't be upset?'

Jess grimaced. 'I'm sorry it came out like that, but I was beside myself with worry after Social Services came round. I wasn't thinking straight.'

'Damn right you weren't. You don't see what's right in front of your eyes, do you? And do you know why that is?'

Carol glared at her, waiting for an answer, but Jess had no idea what she was supposed to say.

'It's because your head is way too far up your own arse.'

With that, she swept past and hurried down the stairs, while Jess stumbled to her bedroom and sank onto the bed.

That really hadn't gone according to plan. She was ashamed to have been caught listening at the door, something Ruby would be happy to broadcast far and wide. But Carol was hiding something, she knew that for sure now. Someone was threatening her. But who?

CHAPTER TWENTY-FIVE

By the time Jess had psyched herself up to face her guests again, ready with more apologies, they'd already gone. Toby was watching his favourite astronomy programme on TV, completely engrossed. Ben was sitting alone at the kitchen table, staring into a mug of tea. He looked up when she came in, his expression grim.

'What the heck is going on, Jess?'

Her mouth moved, trying to form words, but nothing came out. She didn't know herself what was going on, so how on earth could she explain to Ben?

'I thought you were going to apologise to Carol for the last upset, try and make peace with her, but instead you've done the opposite.' He shook his head. 'She was fuming. Said you were impossible. Grabbed Mo and went home. Poor Rob's gone to see if he can calm things down. Again.'

Jess sank into a chair opposite him, annoyed with herself for not listening to her own voice of reason. The one that had told her it was wrong to eavesdrop on Carol's conversation.

Ben raised an eyebrow, jerked his head towards the ceiling. 'What happened up there?'

For a moment she was too ashamed to talk about it. Her eyes dropped to her lap, unable to bear the accusation in his eyes, and she busied herself picking imaginary fluff off her dress. But then she remembered Ruby's role in the whole episode, and knew she had no choice. Ruby wouldn't hesitate to tell her father what she'd seen.

Ben listened as she told him what had happened, his expression growing increasingly dark. A nervous tic twitched at the corner of his eye, something she'd never noticed before.

'So... who was she talking to?'

Jess shook her head. 'I don't know, I didn't hear much, but I have a feeling it's the same person she was speaking to the other week.'

'You mean the last time you were listening in on one of Carol's private conversations?'

Jess cringed inside. It sounded so bad. *What sort of person have I turned into?*

Ben gave a frustrated huff. 'Everyone's got their secrets. Things they want to keep to themselves. Why should you know everything about Carol's life? It's her choice what she tells other people, and she's not going to tell you anything if you're constantly snooping on her. You've got to try and earn her respect. Then she might open up. But the way you're going now, you're just turning her into an enemy, and to be honest, it's making things awkward for all of us.'

'I know, I know,' Jess sighed. She glanced up at him, and decided it was time he started to listen to her concerns, rather than always taking sides with Carol. 'But it happened by accident. It's not like I deliberately went up there to listen in on a secret conversation.'

'You need to stop being so suspicious of everyone.' She could tell by the forced patience in his voice that he was fuming.

'That's all right for you to say. You're not the one who's had someone terrorising them for weeks, or been accused of hurting their son and is now being watched over by Social Services.'

'Ah, Social Services. I forgot to mention that. A woman called round yesterday wanting to speak to you.'

Her mouth dropped open. 'Yesterday,' she squeaked, panic strangling her vocal cords.

'That's right. You were late getting home from work, remember?'

She did remember. Carol was picking up the kids from school for a change, and Helen had wanted her to help choose an outfit for a friend's wedding.

'Why didn't you say anything? Can you imagine how bad it looks that I haven't got back to her?' He looked away, took a swig of his tea. 'So... what happened?'

'Nice enough woman. She asked if she could have a look around. Toby showed her his room and they had quite a chat.'

'Was Ruby here?' Why did that thought make her nervous?

'She was at cheerleader practice.'

Jess breathed a sigh of relief. 'And... er, did the woman say anything?'

'Just that it had been a very informative chat and she'd be in touch.'

'Did she talk to you about... you know, Toby's bruises?'

There was a hard glint in Ben's eye. 'You mean was she sussing me out to see if I was a child abuser?'

Her heart skipped. 'No, no, that's not what I meant.' Her denial sounded over-effusive, false.

'So... what did you mean exactly?' His voice was low and calm, but it held an accusation all the same. She recognised that he hadn't answered her question, batting it away with one of his own.

She felt flustered, unable to extract herself from the hole she'd dug herself into.

'Please, let's not argue. I *know* you're not a child abuser, but when she came to see me the first time, it seemed like all of us would be on her radar. I didn't mean to imply anything, honestly I didn't.' Her eyes met his and she gave him an apologetic smile. 'I just want to know what she said, see if I can work out what she's thinking.' She reached across the table for his hand, noticing his lack of response. 'Hopefully Toby has reassured her that nothing untoward is happening.'

Ben shrugged, took his hand back. 'You know I consider Toby to be my own. The son I always hoped for. You've seen how I make a point of sitting down with him in the evenings, having a chat about whatever he wants. I love him, Jess. There's no way I'd hurt him. No way.' His jaw worked from side to side, his anger barely contained. 'And I don't know what he said to her.' He stood then, took his mug to the sink and rinsed it out, put it on the drainer. 'I'm off out on the bike. I need a bit of fresh air.'

'But it's dark,' she called after his retreating back. 'And raining.'

The door slammed behind him. She'd never known him to go out cycling as much as he had since they'd moved. Which made her wonder whether he was actually cycling or whether it was just an excuse to get out of the house. Perhaps he only went as far as the pub.

As she sat with her head in her hands, wondering how everything had started to fall apart so quickly, Toby came in.

'Mummy, what's the matter?'

He only called her that when he was anxious, and she sat up, pinned a smile to her face and gathered him in her arms.

'I'm just a bit tired, sweetheart. It's been so busy since we moved.'

He wriggled onto her lap and they sat for a moment enjoying a cuddle. It didn't happen as often these days, and she relished the warmth of his body against hers, knowing she would do anything for this child. He was the centre of her world, and if someone had been hurting him, she would do her utmost to get to the bottom of it.

'Ben told me that the lady from Social Services came round,' she said. Toby snuggled his head into her neck, his breath warm against her skin, but he didn't reply. 'Deborah. He said you had quite a chat.'

She felt his head move, like he was nodding, but still no reply.

'Was it okay? She wasn't bothering you, was she?'

'I liked her,' he said. 'She knows all the constellations and she was saying how lucky we are on the Isle of Man because we have dark skies and can see all the stars but people in England aren't as lucky because they have too many street lights.' He looked at her then. 'Can you imagine not being able to see stars?'

She laughed, relieved that Deborah's visit didn't seem to have made him anxious. 'No, I can't imagine that.' She stroked his hair, kissed the end of his nose. 'How are you doing? Is everything okay?'

He snuggled back into her. 'I wish we could go back to our old house.'

Her heart sank. 'Why's that, sweetheart? If we lived in our old house, you wouldn't be able to play with Mo all the time, would you?'

'I liked it better before Ben and Ruby came to live with us.'

She hid her sigh, thought for a moment before she spoke. She knew he didn't get on with Ruby, but hopefully her belligerence was just teenage hormones that would pass.

'I thought you liked Ben?'

He murmured something she couldn't quite make out.

'Say that again, darling, I can't hear you.'

He wriggled off her knee and shook his head, took her hand. 'No more questions, Mummy.' He yawned and rubbed his eyes.

'Can we do some reading before bed? I want to read some more of the encyclopedia you got me from the library.'

'Okay, but just a couple of pages. I hadn't realised how late it is. Let's go and get ready.' She stood and walked upstairs with him, worry worming its way into her brain. She'd thought he said 'he's too rough' when she asked about Ben, but she couldn't be sure.

'You've got to wait until I've got my pyjamas on,' he told her, stopping outside his bedroom door. 'I'm not little, like Mo. I don't need any help.'

'I know. But I'll just come in and tidy up a bit while you get ready.' That way she had an excuse to check and make sure he had no new bruises.

He shut the bedroom door in her face before she could get inside, though, and she wondered where this had come from, this insistence on privacy. Had someone been making fun of his body at school? She'd have to have a word with his teacher, she decided, because it was a recent development, and since Toby was her only child, she had nothing to compare his behaviour with. Or was it because someone was hurting him and he didn't want her to see the evidence? The thought took her breath away. Everything else paled into insignificance compared to this. She could almost cope with a stroppy stepdaughter, a tricky relationship with her ex-husband's partner, and someone who was out to cause trouble. But the thought of someone hurting her son... that couldn't be allowed to continue.

She decided she'd try again tomorrow, be more insistent about checking, but for tonight, she didn't want to unsettle Toby any further.

CHAPTER TWENTY-SIX

Jess was at work the next day when her phone rang. Unknown number. She was putting books back on the shelves and the library was pretty empty, so she walked through to the corridor and answered it.

'Ah, Mrs Baker? It's Deborah Quirk here, Social Services. Is this a good time to talk?'

Her heart dropped like a stone. What now? She looked around to check she was alone, then ducked into the public toilet and locked the door. 'Is there a problem?'

'I'm afraid there is.' Deborah's voice was all business. 'Can we meet? I think it's better we speak face to face. Could I come and see you at lunchtime?'

Jess's heart was racing. This was not good. Not good at all. She swallowed, tried to sound calm. 'What sort of problem?'

'I'd rather not discuss it over the phone, but shall we say one o'clock?'

Jess agreed, then disconnected, a feeling of foreboding heavy in her chest. She sat on the loo, not sure her legs would hold steady. There was no point trying to second-guess things, she told herself, as her heart raced with panic. She'd just have to wait, deal with it once she knew what was happening. She checked her watch. A little over an hour and a half to go.

The waiting was torture, her eyes drawn to the clock every few minutes.

Deborah arrived five minutes early, and Jess whisked her off to the small meeting room at the back of the library, desperate to know what was wrong.

'We'll sit here, shall we?' She indicated the two easy chairs in the corner, separated by a small coffee table. Much less formal than the meeting table on the other side of the room.

'Perfect.' Deborah sat, setting her bag on her knee and reaching inside for her notebook and a sheaf of papers.

Jess could feel herself shaking, and clasped her hands together in her lap so it wouldn't be quite so obvious.

Deborah put her bag on the floor, pen in hand, notebook at the ready. She gave Jess a smile before her forehead crumpled into a frown. 'Thank you for agreeing to meet at such short notice, but I'm afraid things have escalated somewhat and I do feel we need to make some decisions.'

'Escalated?' Jess's voice rose an octave. 'What do you mean? What's happened?' A sheen of sweat coated her palms, making them slide together as her grasp tightened. 'Is Toby okay? He was fine this—'

Deborah leant across the coffee table, put a hand on her arm. 'Please calm down, Mrs Baker. Toby is safe. But we need to discuss how best to keep him that way.'

Jess's eyes widened, her voice a frightened squeak. 'What do you mean? Why wouldn't he be safe?'

'The school have been in touch with me. A couple of times, actually. Once last week and again today. More bruises, which concerned them.'

'More bruises?' Jess cursed herself for not pushing to check the previous evening.

'You hadn't noticed?' Deborah raised an eyebrow.

She shook her head. 'He's at an age where he wants his privacy. I was wondering about it last night actually, whether someone at school has been making fun of him. You know, body-shaming or something. It was just chance that I noticed the fingerprints on his arms a few weeks ago.'

'Yes, fingerprints.' Deborah nodded. 'That's what the new bruises look like as well. First on his shoulders, like someone has grabbed him and given him a good shake. Then under his ribcage, like he's been picked up.' She paused. 'You can see why the school are concerned.'

Tears pricked Jess's eyes, the thought of someone hurting her son unbearable. 'You spoke to him the other day, didn't you? Did he tell you who's doing this to him?'

'Not exactly.' Deborah hesitated, straightened the paper-work into a neat pile. 'But my strong feeling is... it relates to your household.'

Jess's mouth fell open, her world in free fall. 'How can you say that?'

Deborah's mouth twisted to one side and she appeared to be considering something before she spoke. 'My interview with him led me to believe that he sometimes doesn't feel safe in his own house.'

'What?' Jess's heart flipped in her chest. She stared at the woman, unable to believe what she was hearing.

'He's not keen on your partner's daughter, is he? In fact I'd go so far as to say he's frightened of her.'

'Well they don't get along, but everything has been fine between them the past few weeks. I know it'll take a little while for them to get used to living in the same house, but I'm pretty sure she's not responsible for his bruises.'

'Then there's your partner.'

Her heart did another flip, her breath hitching in her throat. She remembered Toby's muttered words. Had he said that Ben was too rough? Could it be him? Impossible. He'd always been so gentle with Toby when she'd seen them together. Ben was a nurturer, not an abuser. He was too laid-back to get angry enough to give someone a shake or grab them roughly. He was the sort who walked away from conflict. *No, it can't be Ben.* She sat up straight, ready to fight his corner. 'What about him?'

'Toby says he liked it better when you didn't live with him.'

'Well, it'll take a while for him to get used to the new living arrangements, but he does have access to his father any time he wants.'

Deborah considered that for a moment. 'Can I ask... Does your partner like Toby?'

'Of course he does. He's always wanted a son.'

'I got the feeling there was something Toby didn't want to tell me about their relationship.' She paused, choosing her words carefully. 'Do you think Ben might be the one hurting him?'

'No,' Jess snapped, wishing that she'd pressed Toby for a clear answer the night before.

Deborah stared at her for a long moment. The only person in the household she hadn't accused of hurting Toby was Jess herself. *Is she coming to me next?* The social worker tapped her notebook with her pen, her voice clipped. 'Well it's a mystery then, who's hurting him. But until we get to the bottom of it, I think it would be safest for him to live with his father for a while.'

Jess gasped, her hand flying to her chest. 'What? You can't do that.'

'I'm afraid I can. The school have concerns. A member of the public has concerns. We really have to act on it. Especially with all these recent cases in the news where Social Services have been involved and children have gone on to be harmed. We've made a policy decision in the department that it's better to be cautious than see that sort of outcome. If we upset people in the process, so be it, but the safety of the child is our priority.'

She took a breath, her voice more conciliatory. 'It's clear that Toby is unsettled. His behaviour has changed at school, there's evidence of potential physical abuse, and several people are concerned, including his father and stepmother.'

Jess sat back in her chair, feeling as though everyone else's views held weight but hers were ignored. 'What? You've spoken to them? And can I just point out that Carol is not his stepmother. Not yet.'

'I'm sorry, but I don't think it's time to be pedantic about titles. You're all involved in Toby's care, so yes, I have spoken to them. And they're concerned as well. I've suggested the temporary change in living arrangements and they're more than happy to comply. I have the signed paperwork here. We can review it in a few months, see how things are then.'

Tears were rolling down Jess's face now. She gulped, struggling to speak. 'Someone is framing me. I'm sure of it. I've had all sorts of weird things happen since we moved into the new house. It's just me who's been targeted, and then this trouble started with Toby. Someone clearly wants me to be blamed.'

Deborah's eyes narrowed, and Jess realised how unhinged she sounded. Without tangible evidence, who would believe her?

'I don't know what's going on,' she pleaded. 'But nobody in my house is hurting him.'

Deborah closed her notebook. 'Can you say that for sure?'

Jess could hardly breathe. *I don't think I can.*

CHAPTER TWENTY-SEVEN

Jess got home to find her mum already there, sitting at the kitchen table with an empty mug in front of her.

'Oh, Mum, am I glad to see you. I can't get hold of anyone. Ben isn't answering. Neither is Rob.' Her mum got up to give her a hug and Jess clung to her, all the trauma of the day forcing its way out in an enormous sob. Helen held her, rubbing her back until she could speak. 'I haven't a clue what's going on.'

When she pulled away, she could see that her mum had been crying too. 'I know, love. We're all at a loss. Poor Rob is furious. The social worker rang him and he was straight on the phone to me.'

'You spoke to him? I couldn't get an answer, it just went to voicemail all the time. That's why I rang you in the end.'

'I've spoken to everyone. Rob, Carol, that social worker, the school. I went in and asked to see the head teacher so I could hear it from the horse's mouth, as it were.'

'You did?'

'I cancelled my appointments for this afternoon. I mean, I wasn't going to be doing anyone any favours trying to cut hair in this state. You know nobody is more important to me than Toby.'

Jess sighed, wishing she could have done the same, but she'd been on her own at the library, Pam having called in sick that morning, and she couldn't leave. She sank into a chair, dropped her bag on the floor. 'So what did the head say?'

'Apparently Toby's form teacher noticed the bruises when they were doing PE and felt Toby was worried about something. He said he's been unusually quiet since they started back after the summer and was evasive when anyone asked him what had happened.'

'That's exactly how he was with me. I feel so bad that I didn't know about these latest bruises, but he's insistent that he should do everything himself at the moment, won't even let me in the room when he's getting ready for bed.' Tears welled again and she tried to sniff them away. 'I should have sensed something was wrong, shouldn't I? What am I going to do?'

She felt her mum's hand on her shoulder. A gentle squeeze. 'I'll make us a cuppa.' Jess watched as she filled the kettle. 'Toby's fine, though, that's the good news. A bit upset about all the fuss. And he won't talk to me about the bruising either. You know what he's like. Once he's made up his mind about something, there's no changing it, is there? So I thought it best not to press.' She opened cupboards, got out two mugs. 'We arrived home just as Mo came back from the dentist with Carol, and he cheered up then. Especially when she told him she was cooking his favourite meal for tea. And she'd got them a new game for the Xbox.'

Jess swiped at her tears, furious that Carol was the one comforting her son.

'Carol's so thoughtful, isn't she?' Helen said as she made the tea.

'Huh,' Jess scoffed. 'You think so?' Anger burned in her chest. 'I'm pretty sure all this trouble comes back to her.'

Helen brought the mugs to the table, sitting across from her, a frown ruffling her forehead. 'I don't know what's got into you, love. Rob told me about you blaming her for Toby's bruises, but I honestly can't see it. She's so careful with Mo, isn't she? Such a caring mum. She'd do anything for that child.'

'For her child, yes, but what about mine? Does she really care, or is it just for show?' Jess gritted her teeth. 'I think she's using him to get at me.' Her mum stopped stirring sugar into her tea, looked startled. 'I don't think she wants us living next door,' Jess continued. 'I think that's what this is all about. She wants me out of their lives and she wants my son. Then they'd be the perfect family, wouldn't they?'

Helen's mouth fell open. 'You can't really believe that?'

'There weren't any problems until we moved here. Now she's gone all weird on me. In fact, not just weird. Downright nasty at times. And she's hiding something. I've overheard two conversations she's had with someone, and—'

Helen held up a hand to stop the flow. 'Hang on a minute, you're not making sense.'

'I am. I'm making perfect sense, but nobody will listen to me.'

'That's because you sound... well, you sound bitter.'

'What?'

Helen sighed, continued stirring her tea. 'Jealous, even.' She caught Jess's eye, her voice softer now. 'Do you think the problem might be that Carol has got what you want? Are you having second thoughts about separating from Rob?'

The question caught Jess unawares, and suddenly all her uncertainties came flooding back. Her eyes slid away from her mum's, unable to bear the scrutiny.

She picked up an elastic band from the table, started twisting it round her finger. 'I'll admit it wasn't an easy decision. And now with all this business with Toby, I can't help blaming myself.' She looked up, caught the concern in her mum's eyes. 'Is it my fault this is happening?'

'The grass is always greener,' Helen said, taking a sip of tea. 'Perhaps it was something you had to get out of your system. You were so young when you and Rob got together. But maybe you can see now that what you had is actually what you want.'

Jess blinked. *Is it what I want?* Her heart said no, emphatically no. But her head reasoned that life had been so much easier before. Had it really been so bad? 'There's no going back, though, is there?'

Her mum's eyes sparkled with a glimmer of hope. 'Do you want to? I'm sure Rob still loves you. In fact, the other day he said to me, "I'll always love Jess."'

Jess frowned. 'Oh, Mum, that doesn't mean anything. I'll always love him too. Just... not like that. Not romantically.' She twisted the elastic band tighter. 'We're still friends, I think we'll always be friends. I just can't live with him any more.' She sighed, thinking she sounded petty, juvenile. 'But I'm always second-guessing myself about it. Wondering if I've just created a whole mass of problems. If I could just have been satisfied with what I had, I wouldn't be facing this situation.'

Her mum patted her hand. 'Personally I think you drew the short straw with Ruby. She's not easy to get along with, is she? And Ben doesn't have the focus on work that Rob has. I mean, self-employment isn't really secure.' She took another sip of tea. 'I'm not sure what you see in him, really. Well, obviously he's a looker. And charming. But I'm not convinced he's a keeper. I've heard all sorts about him when he was young. Caused a whole heap of trouble for his gran.' She looked at Jess over the rim of her mug. 'I don't believe a leopard changes its spots. He's got an eye for the ladies, that one.'

Jess squirmed in her chair, uncomfortable with how the conversation had developed.

'I love Ben.' She knew without a doubt that this was true.

'And I know he loves me. You see, Mum, he actually wants to spend time with me and Toby. Wants us to be a family and do things together. With Rob, it's all about work and ambition, and yes, that means he earns good money, but it's not enough. It's not what I want.'

Her mum gave her a hard stare. 'It's not all about what *you* want, though, is it? You've got a child to think about. Somebody is hurting him, and at the moment, Social Services think that someone lives in this house. Which leaves us either Ruby or Ben.' She finished her tea, put her mug back on the table. 'The truth is, if you want what's best for your son, getting over this nonsense with Ben and asking Rob to take you back is your best option.'

Jess couldn't believe her mum would suggest such a thing.

'It's not.' She shook her head. 'I know that's what you want, but it's not what Rob wants. He loves Carol, not me. And Carol doesn't want me anywhere near her child, or their life. *That* is the issue.' Her voice was rising with frustration. 'You don't want to hear it, but *she's* the one causing problems. And now Toby is going to be living with her.' She pulled at her hair. 'I can't bear it.'

'Oh for Goodness' sake,' her mum snapped. 'I know you've got it in for that woman, but she's always struck me as a lovely person. And I consider myself a pretty good judge of character.' Her words rattled through Jess's head like a round of bullets. 'I think you're jealous. And... actually, I suppose if you can make Rob believe that Carol is hurting your child, he'll kick her out. Then there's a chance you two can get back together.' She tapped a finger to her temple. 'That's what's going on in your head, isn't it?'

Jess stared at her, incredulous. 'Nothing like that is going on in my head, I can assure you.'

A strained silence settled between them, broken by a loud tut from her mum. She stood and put her cup on the side before picking up her bag. 'I'm really sorry, love, but I've got to go. I said I'd do haircuts over at the nursing home this evening. We'll talk tomorrow when you've had time to think things over, shall we?' She bent and gave Jess a kiss on the cheek, started walking towards the front door.

Jess stood. 'Wait, Mum.' As she followed her into the hall, she was startled to hear feet running up the stairs. A flash of pink disappeared out of sight down the landing. Ruby. Was she listening? There was the clunk of a door shutting.

Helen's gaze followed Jess's. 'She's trouble, that one.' With an emphatic nod, she pulled the door open and left.

CHAPTER TWENTY-EIGHT

Jess wandered around the house, restless. She couldn't bear to look out of the back windows in case she saw Toby enjoying himself without her now she'd been excluded from his life. Deborah had told her that for the next month, nobody from her household was allowed to be alone with her son. After that, they would see how things were going and think about a plan going forwards. The thought of being apart from him, away from his bright-eyed chatter, his endless curiosity, his sloppy kisses, brought a deep ache to her heart.

Her mind was so numb with the horror of her situation that she couldn't think beyond the practicalities. How was this supposed to work when they had a shared garden? It was impossible. Ridiculous. Apparently there would be supervised access visits at a centre run by Social Services. Her skin crawled at the thought.

It's not right. None of it.

Her fists balled at her sides, her body twitching with the need to do something to change her situation as she paced like a caged animal. Unfortunately, it appeared that the social worker had the law on her side and there was nothing Jess *could* do for the time being. What she had to focus on was changing Deborah's mind. She rubbed at her forehead, trying to work out how she was going to convince the woman that her household had done nothing wrong. That Carol was the one who needed looking at more closely.

Maybe it's Carol I need to focus on.

She chewed at a nail, constantly checking her phone. Surely Ben would have seen her messages by now. The sound of muffled voices from next door caught her attention, louder than usual. An argument? That was strange. Rob wasn't one to argue.

She paused to listen, but couldn't make out what was being said. Then she heard shouts in the garden, Carol calling Mo. He must be outside playing with Toby. She walked to the window to look, but stopped herself before she got there. If she saw her son, she knew she'd want to go to him, hold him in her arms and refuse to let him go.

This is too cruel. Her heart kept skipping beats, her breath fast and ragged. An overwhelming feeling of panic filled her chest, leaving little room for air. Her hand grabbed at her throat as she gasped like a fish out of water, sure she was suffocating.

With clumsy fingers, she tried ringing Ben again. Straight to voicemail. She'd already left half a dozen messages and was starting to wonder what he was doing. But she couldn't think about that now, not when she was on the verge of a panic attack.

She needed to get away, be on her own; that way she might be able to calm down. *I need some space to think.*

She went upstairs, knocked on Ruby's door. No answer. She tried the handle. Locked. 'I'm going out, Ruby.' Her voice was raspy, her throat raw with the effort of drawing breath. 'I'll only be an hour or so, okay?'

Still no reply. Well, she'd be safe enough locked in her room until Ben got home. And she was fourteen, old enough to be left alone for a short time.

She hurried back downstairs, grabbed her keys and got into

the car, not daring to look behind her lest she should see her son. The thought ripped her heart in two and she tasted salt as silent tears rolled down her cheeks. How could anyone think she could be hurting him? They don't, she reminded herself. Not explicitly. Someone in her household, they'd said. Ruby or Ben?

Obviously Ruby was a distinct possibility; her animosity towards Toby had clearly ramped up several notches since they'd all moved in together. It was understandable in a way, given Toby's penchant for practical jokes, which Jess would admit could go a little too far at times. On the other hand, Ruby was a bit of a prima donna, having been an only child all her life, and her father opting for the path of least resistance. She ran to him whenever there was a problem with Toby, setting Jess and Ben against each other at every opportunity.

Ben. She'd kept trying to dismiss the idea, but she really had to face up to the fact that it could be him. She knew the strength of his hands, many years of working with wood and tools making the muscles in his arms as taut as steel cable. She felt it sometimes when they were making love, the firmness of his grip making her gasp. She'd had bruises too, hadn't she?

Accidental, she stressed to herself. Always accidental.

Her mind chattered on until the blare of a car horn brought her back to her senses and she swerved out of the path of an oncoming car. She stomped on her brakes, heart thundering in her chest as she realised how close she'd come to having a crash. The last thing she'd been aware of was backing out of the drive at her house, no idea how she'd come to be on this narrow back road with its blind corners.

Unnerved, she drove on at a snail's pace, recognising where she was. Completely on autopilot, she'd made her way up to Archallagan Plantation, a forest just a few miles away from Peel with myriad paths snaking off into the trees, leading to hidden ponds and silent glades. Dark avenues of spruce stood tall in their regimented rows, the ground a mossy green carpet dotted with ferns, paths edged with heather and bilberry bushes. It was easy to get lost in here if you weren't familiar with the place. But this was where she always came when something was troubling her. The shush of the wind in the trees was soothing, and when you were in the heart of the forest, you could believe you were the only person in existence. Here she could think without being disturbed.

She pulled on her walking boots and grabbed her coat from the back seat, fastening it against the chill of the breeze. The forest was at the top of a rise and always caught the wind, the bonus being glimpses of the hills and valleys of the island as you walked round the perimeter path. But her goal was to head to the dark heart, where there was a pond. Striped dragonflies flitted over the surface of the water, bright blue damselflies busy in the reed beds at the edges. She often came here with Toby, bringing a fishing net so they could do a bit of pond dipping.

A sob erupted from her chest. It was one of her favourite things that they did together, loving the excitement when Toby found a new bit of wildlife he'd never seen before. There was a play area as well, with tree stumps as stepping stones and an obstacle course that they raced each other round. She could hear the ghost of his laughter, see him skipping through the trees. A child without a care in the world. At least he had been.

She made her way to a picnic bench, lost in thought. How would she explain the situation with the supervised visits? Or the fact that they couldn't spend time together in either of the houses? It didn't bear thinking about, but at some point he'd have to be told.

Not yet. Not if I can find out who has been hurting him.

The idea of talking to Ben about it without it seeming to be an accusation made her heart lurch. He'd been so sensitive to her thoughts the other evening, she couldn't imagine it was going to be straightforward. Had she already undermined the trust in their relationship?

It could be Ruby, and Toby was too scared of whatever she'd threatened him with to tell. But again, how would she get a confession without making things with Ben impossible?

Her thoughts brought her full circle back to Carol. She still seemed the most likely culprit. When Jess thought about all the other things that had happened, Carol was the only person who could have engineered them... and she had a solid motive. Whatever her mum, Rob and Ben said, Jess knew there was a side to Carol that she didn't want other people to see. A part of her life that she was keeping secret. Perhaps if she could find out what it was, she could talk to Rob again. Get him to see that Carol wasn't fit to be Toby's stepmother. That it was her causing all the trouble. The problem was getting anyone to believe her.

What if they don't ever let Toby live with me again?

Her heart rate picked up once more and she shivered. The thought was horrifying. Could that happen? She had no idea, but she needed to find out. There was so much she didn't know.

The ringing of her phone brought her back to the present. She looked at the screen, Ruby. She hesitated for a moment then answered. But it wasn't Ruby calling her.

'Ben! Where the hell have you been? Why haven't you been answering?'

'I managed to smash my phone at work. Dropped a bloody drill on it.' He sounded distracted, not himself at all.

She was half relieved, half annoyed at his explanation. It wasn't the first time he'd wrecked a phone at work.

'I just got home. Ruby said there's been some trouble with Social Services.'

'That's right.' She had no idea where to start, her throat clogging with emotion at the thought of it.

'What a mess,' he sighed. 'I'm so sorry it's come to this, but... Where are you?'

She wasn't sure she wanted to tell him, not ready to go home and face reality just yet. 'I had to find a bit of space to think.'

'Mo's not with you, is he?' She realised Ben sounded agitated.

'What?' It seemed like an odd question, a diversion from the most important thing that had ever happened to her. 'Why would he be with me? You know Carol won't let me anywhere near him.'

'It's just... he's gone missing.'

CHAPTER TWENTY-NINE

Jess stared at her phone in disbelief before putting it back to her ear. 'Sorry, say that again. I don't think I heard you properly.'

'You need to come home. Mo's disappeared. Carol's hysterical.' Ben sounded like he was panicking himself. 'We need you here.'

The words slammed into Jess's brain. 'You're kidding me?' But she knew it was real. This was happening. Mo, a defenceless five-year-old boy who she loved like her own son, had gone missing. She was already hurrying back to the car as she spoke.

'The police are here.' Ben's voice didn't sound like him at all, and she wondered if the officers were standing next to him.

She disconnected and started jogging, the uneven ground jolting her knees, making her stumble, but she kept going, her breath rasping in her throat as she splashed through puddles, skidded on the muddy path.

Mo had disappeared. She was finding it hard to believe. He was quite a clingy little boy who really didn't like being alone. She couldn't think that he'd wander off on his own accord. Which brought a whole raft of terrible scenarios crashing into her head.

She sped out of the car park, hoping she'd get back to find out it was a false alarm and he'd turned up safe and well. But when she pulled into the drive, her stomach writhing with nerves, a police car was parked in front of the house.

Two police officers, a woman and a man, were sitting in the lounge. Ben was pacing the floor.

'Thank God you're back,' he said, his face sagging with relief. His complexion was grey, worry etched in every furrow of his brow. But he didn't come and give her a hug, his eyes holding an accusation, like she'd done something wrong.

'I only went out for a walk,' she said, her voice defensive. 'Just to clear my head.' That wasn't a crime, was it?

The female officer stood, and Jess could see that she was twice the age of the young man and clearly the one in charge. She had short grey hair, a hawkish face. She tugged at her black protective vest, adorned with various bits of equipment. 'I'm Sergeant Rosemary Quayle, and this is my colleague, PC Jason Kelly.' The PC gave a tight smile, his hair slicked back on top, shorn at the sides. 'I think you know why we're here?'

Jess nodded. 'Mo's missing. That's what Ben said.'

'That's correct. Have you seen him today at all?'

She had to think. 'I'm not sure that I actually have. I might have heard him earlier when I got home from work.' She frowned. Had she? Or was that yesterday? 'But I really can't be definite.' She was frustrated that her memory was so cloudy. 'I've been a bit distracted.'

'And what time would that have been?' The sergeant's eyes bored into hers, making her fidget. She sank onto the edge of the armchair by the window, her hands clasping her knees to try and stop the shaking that ran through her body.

'It was about half five, I think. I didn't check the time, but I left Douglas just after five, so it must have been around then.'

PC Kelly was busy scribbling in his notebook while she

spoke. There was a grim expression on his face, judgement in his eyes, like he might not believe her.

'My mum was here.' Yes, her mum would probably be more use than Jess. 'She saw Mo when he got home from school. Have you spoken to her?'

The sergeant nodded. 'Yes, we have, but we think she left your house a while before he disappeared. Your neighbour remembers seeing her walk down the road back towards her own house.'

Jess grimaced, feeling completely helpless. 'I'm not sure I can really tell you anything else.'

The sergeant gazed at her, the silence oppressive. 'I believe you and your neighbour have had a few differences recently.'

A sudden heat flooded her cheeks as she understood where this line of questioning might be going. 'Well, yes, I suppose we have.'

'She seems to think you might have taken her son as an act of revenge.'

Jess's breath stuck in her throat, her body frozen as if paralysed. How could Carol shift the blame onto her? This was really going too far now.

'That's ridiculous,' Ben said, jumping in to help her. She felt the sting of tears, her body shaking so much now she couldn't hide it. 'I'm sorry, but Jess isn't like that. She's very fond of Mo, aren't you, love?'

She blinked, wiped at her eyes, finally finding her voice. 'I think of him as part of the family, I really do. This is so out of character. I can't think that he'd wander off.'

'So what do you think has happened?'

She thought for a moment, considered the conversations she'd overheard. The perception of a threat. Could that threat have been aimed towards Mo rather than Carol herself? Should she mention it? There was no decision to make if it would help in any way to find the missing child.

'I have a feeling there's something going on in Carol's life that she's not telling anyone about.' The sergeant raised an eyebrow. Jess continued, because there was no going back now that she'd started. 'I overheard her arguing with someone. Well, pleading with them actually. And she sounded frightened.' That was right; Carol had told the caller not to come near her. Or was it Mo she didn't want them near?

The sergeant glanced at her PC. 'Interesting. And when was this?'

'The first time was a couple of months back, and then I heard her on the phone again a few days ago. She's been acting a bit odd since we moved in. Very protective of Mo.' The PC wrote it all down and the sergeant nodded her encouragement. 'I don't know if she's told you, but she had trouble with a work colleague who became a bit of a stalker. She changed jobs, but it seems the guy has found her again. She told Rob that it was all sorted, but I don't think it is. I wonder if he's been threatening her. Or Mo.'

She knew she had little evidence, but if Carol could throw around baseless accusations, then she should be able to put her own theories in the mix. There had been some sort of threat in those phone conversations, and her conclusions weren't outside the realm of possibility.

'That's all very helpful,' the sergeant said. She glanced at the PC. 'We'll follow it up. I think we're done here for now, but we're organising a search party if you'd like to help.'

Jess leapt to her feet. 'Of course we would, wouldn't we, Ben?'

'Absolutely.'

The sergeant checked her watch. 'Everyone is meeting at the school in half an hour. We'll split you up into teams and try and get the whole town covered that way.' She gave Jess another of her long stares. 'If you think of anything else that might help, please give us a call. As I'm sure you're aware, time is of the essence in missing children cases.'

Jess swallowed, not wanting to dwell on the possibilities, none of which were good.

CHAPTER THIRTY

The search finished when darkness began to draw in, no sign of Mo anywhere. Even Ruby had come out to help, and she seemed genuinely concerned that the young boy was missing.

They were walking up the road to their house when a police car drew up next door. The sergeant got out and opened the back door, and Rob clambered out, a floppy Mo in his arms. Jess gulped, feeling a surge of relief that he'd been found. But the little boy looked limp, lifeless, and her joy that he'd been found fizzled. *Is he all right?* She wrapped her arms around her chest, holding herself tight, unable to move, hoping for the best while her mind was thinking the worst.

The PC opened the door on the other side, and Carol appeared, her face streaked with mascara. She took Mo from Rob's arms while he opened their front door. Now there was movement from the child, his arms and legs wrapping round his mother like a koala, his head burying against her neck. Carol was smothering him with kisses, her shoulders shaking as she sobbed.

Jess still couldn't move, Ben beside her, his arm finding its way round her waist, holding her close. It didn't feel real, like she was watching a movie.

The sergeant walked up the driveway behind Carol and Rob, casting a glance in Jess's direction. 'I'll be over to speak to you in a minute, Mrs Baker,' she called before following their neighbours into the house, the PC close on her heels.

'Thank God he's safe,' Jess gasped.

'Why's that police officer coming to talk to you?' Ruby asked. She peered at Jess over the top of her glasses, which had slid down her nose. 'What did you do?'

'Nothing, I didn't do anything.' The relief that Mo had been found evaporated as Ruby's words hit home. Why *did* the sergeant want to talk to her? She couldn't think of a reason, unless it was just to let them know what had happened, reassure them that everything was okay. *Do the police do that?* She didn't think they did. Not usually.

Ruby pointed to her eyes and back at Jess. I'm watching you, she was saying, in a way her father could not hear.

Ben shivered. 'Come on, let's get inside. It turns cold once the sun's gone down at this time of year.' He steered Jess up the driveway, his arm still around her waist, Ruby clinging to his other arm, not wanting to be left out.

He took Ruby into the kitchen to sort out snacks while Jess went upstairs to get a jumper. She was coming downstairs when the doorbell rang. The police officers were standing on the doorstep.

She gave a nervous smile, their blank expressions telling her this was not a courtesy visit.

'Is he okay?' she asked, desperate for reassurance. 'He looked very floppy when he came out of the car.'

'He's going to be fine,' the sergeant said as she followed her into the lounge, Ben coming in from the kitchen to join them.

'Where was he?' Jess moved towards Ben for moral support, her hand finding his.

'That's the strange part,' the sergeant said, turning to her. 'He was up at Archallagan Plantation. A mountain biker found him by the pond. He was lying on the ground like he'd fallen asleep next to one of the trails. The man tried to wake him up, but it was clear the lad was barely conscious, so he called the emergency services.'

Jess tightened her grip on Ben's hand, her heart fluttering in her chest. 'But that's where I was. That's where I went for a walk.' Icy fingers of fear walked down her spine.

The sergeant raised an eyebrow. 'Quite a coincidence.'

Jess glanced at Ben, who was looking very confused. It was a hell of a coincidence, there was no getting away from that. A wave of nausea flowed through her, and Ben let go of her hand, started rubbing at his chin, a clear sign that he was feeling anxious.

'What's going on, Jess?' he asked.

She didn't like the look on his face, the accusation in his eyes.

'He wasn't there when I was,' she said, her voice plaintive. 'I would have seen him.' What else could she say to convince everyone she was telling the truth?

The sergeant fixed her with that piercing gaze, the one that made her feel like searchlights were illuminating every stray thought in her mind. 'Now, Mrs Baker, are you sure he didn't go up to Archallagan with you? Perhaps you didn't mean to leave him there.'

'What?' Jess's brain froze, the shock of this suggestion so great all the strength went out of her legs. She clutched at the mantelpiece for support, a strange buzzing in her ears. 'No! That's not what happened. It isn't.' She looked around the room, four pairs of eyes staring at her. Her heart was racing now, sweat coating the palms of her hands. She felt trapped, cornered. For the second time that day, she was being accused of something she hadn't done.

'It's Carol, isn't it? She's the one blaming me.' She huffed in frustration. 'Can't you see this is a set-up?'

'I can't see how she set you up,' the sergeant said, with forced patience. 'You're going to have to explain how that works.'

Her radio crackled and she looked at the PC. 'I'd like you to stay here with Mrs Baker, while I go and speak to a colleague. I won't be long. Perhaps someone could make a cup of tea?' She flicked a glance towards Ben before looking directly at Jess. 'You've gone very pale.'

The PC sat reading through his notes while Ben took the hint and went and put the kettle on. Jess could see the sergeant outside, speaking to another officer. He was holding up a phone, showing her something.

Ben came back into the lounge bearing mugs of tea, which he handed round, and Jess clasped hers to her chest, grateful for the warmth. Ruby went upstairs to her room, obviously bored of proceedings.

The minutes dragged by, nobody speaking. Ben's phone rang and he checked the screen, held it up. 'Work,' he said, a definite note of relief in his voice. 'I'll just go up to the office and take this.' He meant the corner of their bedroom where they had a desk, laptop and filing cabinet. He was often up there sorting out work schedules for the weeks ahead, ordering materials or preparing invoices.

Now that Jess was alone with the young police officer, she felt vulnerable in her own home, his eyes watching her every move. She perched on the edge of the armchair, sipped at her tea. 'Can I offer you a biscuit or anything?'

He shook his head. 'No thanks.' Silence settled around them and she was aware of every sound, every tick of the clock on the wall, every slurp of his tea.

An awkward ten minutes later, the sergeant returned.

'Okay, Mrs Baker. Some new information has come to light, and I think we'd be better off having a chat down at the station.'

'You're arresting me?'

'No, we just want you to help us with our enquiries. We need to get this wrapped up as quickly as possible, and I need to give something to the tech people, so it sort of kills two birds with one stone, if you like.'

'Is it really necessary?' Jess glanced towards the stairs, willing Ben to come back down. 'I've told you all I can.'

'Like I say, some new evidence has come to light, and we'd really like to talk to you about it.'

'Can't we do it here?' Her voice was shrill, panic swelling in her chest.

'No,' the sergeant insisted.

PC Kelly was already on his feet, towering over her as she was ushered towards the door.

'I need to tell Ben where I'm going.'

'I'll tell him,' the sergeant said, looking up the stairs. She nodded at the PC. 'If you could show Mrs Baker to the car, I'll be down in a minute.'

With that, she was clumping up the stairs and Jess was being led out to the car and bundled into the back seat, the door closed firmly behind her.

This couldn't be happening. It felt like her body wasn't her own, a disconcerting sensation, like she was dreaming. She put a hand on the glass, could feel the coolness against her palm, the steam from her breath fogging the window. She wiped a circle clean.

The lights were on in the bedroom. She could see the outline of the sergeant, then Ben, as he walked towards the window and stared straight at her.

CHAPTER THIRTY-ONE

She was taken to the central police station in Douglas and led to a small, stuffy interview room.

'I just need to go and speak to a colleague. I'll be back shortly,' the sergeant said.

Jess was left alone. Her eyes scanned the room, taking in the recording machine at the end of the table, the four plastic chairs. Bare walls apart from the mirror. She'd heard the door click shut. *Am I locked in?* She wasn't sure but didn't dare check in case they thought she was making a run for it.

She sighed, studied her fingernails, pushing down the cuticles, tidying them up one at a time, just for something to do.

How did Mo get to Archallagan? It wasn't like he could have walked there. Somebody must have taken him. *Not me.* But how could she prove that? How do you prove that you *didn't* do something? Only by proving you were doing something else, she supposed. But she'd been there on her own, nobody else around. No alibi whatsoever.

I'm being set up. She was adamant about that. Was it the same person who'd been playing tricks on her? Was this an escalation of their activities? In which case, were they coming to the finale or was this just the start of it?

Welcome to your nightmare. How true that had proved to be. It was certainly feeling like the worst nightmare she'd ever had. And with this incident close on the heels of the Social Services episode and Toby's mysterious bruises, she was being painted in a very bad light.

Her mind could only consider one thing. *This is Carol's doing.* The question was why. If she could get a clear view of what the woman had to gain, then maybe she could persuade the police to consider it as a line of enquiry.

Carol wants to step into my shoes. That was the only rational explanation. Now she had Rob to herself in the house, she wanted to cut Jess out of the picture altogether. Perhaps she wasn't as comfortable with their blended family project as she'd seemed to be. Perhaps that was a front for Rob's benefit.

Her head was throbbing and she rubbed at her temples. Just get through this, she told herself. Then she could talk it over with Ben. She hadn't even had a chance to speak to him about the Social Services decision that Toby couldn't live with them, and she was desperate to get his view on things. He always thought outside the box and could often see a new way forward when her thoughts had hit a brick wall.

She was sweating, damp patches on her T-shirt. She wiped her hands over her face, willing the ordeal to be over.

The click of the door opening made her look up. The sergeant and PC came in, sat on the other side of the table, their faces blank masks.

'Sorry to keep you waiting, Mrs Baker.'

She tried a smile, but it was over before it had begun, dread stirring up the contents of her stomach.

'I had to speak to our tech people. And I had to get a warrant.'

'A warrant?' Jess's voice was no more than a whisper.

'We need to search your car.'

'What?'

The sergeant's elbows were on the table, and she steepled her fingers, resting the tips against her lips as she gave Jess that steady stare. 'I'm afraid a serious allegation has been made against you.'

'But I haven't done anything.' Jess's eyes flicked from the sergeant to the PC and back again. There was no response in their eyes, no recognition that she might be speaking the truth.

'Mo's mother believes you drugged her son, took him to Archallagan and left him there.'

'Drugged him?' She shook her head, appalled. 'No. I didn't.' Her voice was filled with panic. 'I didn't do any of that. Why would I?'

'She believes it was a revenge attack.'

Jess was aghast, her hand pressed to her chest to try and calm the mad fluttering of her heart. 'I wouldn't do that.'

The officers stared at her, waiting for more.

'Honestly, revenge is not something I ever think about.' They didn't look convinced. 'I'm not that sort of person,' she pleaded.

'Apparently relations between you have... got out of control.' The PC nodded along as his colleague spoke. It was obvious he'd already made up his mind who was telling the truth.

The muscles tightened at the back of Jess's neck, pulling at her shoulders. What could she say to persuade them when there was a strong element of truth in that last statement? Her mouth flapped open and shut, no words coming out.

'The bad feeling has escalated,' the sergeant continued. 'And Social Services have said your son has to live with your ex-husband on the basis that they believe a member of your household has been harming him.'

Her summary was enough to fire up Jess's brain, and the

words came out in a forceful rush. 'But that's not even true. Social Services have got it wrong.' She gasped with frustration. 'Nobody in my household is harming him. This is her doing. It's Carol.'

The sergeant's mouth twisted to the side. 'Well she definitely thinks you blame her, even though she denies any wrongdoing.' She looked Jess in the eye. 'She also thinks taking her son was your way of getting back at her.'

'It's rubbish. She's talking rubbish. Surely you can see that.' Jess could feel herself being backed into a corner. 'I'm a librarian, not a kidnapper.' She gave a strangled laugh, the whole idea ridiculous.

'I don't think kidnappers have any specific profession,' the sergeant countered, deadpan. 'And anyway, we have evidence that suggests otherwise.'

Jess's eyes widened. Oh God, this sounded bad. 'What evidence.'

'Her son always has a phone on him so she knows where he is.'

'Does he?' She hadn't known that, had never seen Mo with a phone. Maybe it was a new thing Carol had started recently.

'The phone had been switched off, so it didn't work as a locator when we were looking for him.' The sergeant leant forward. 'But now that it's back on again, it clearly shows that he made the exact same journey that you did. At the exact same time.' There was a gleam of satisfaction in her eyes. 'Now the thing is, we don't believe in coincidences like that, do we, PC Kelly?'

Jess felt the colour drain from her face.

'I'd like a solicitor,' she said.

CHAPTER THIRTY-TWO

Her solicitor turned up within the hour. Stella Corlett had been a family friend for as long as Jess could remember, a little dynamo of a woman with short wavy hair that had been black when she was young but was now a classy shade of platinum. She'd gone to school with Jess's mum and had established herself as one of the top criminal advocates on the island.

Jess thought she might faint with relief when she saw her. 'Thank God you're here,' she said when she appeared in the doorway.

Stella put her bag on the table, pulled out a yellow legal pad and a pen and sat opposite, studying Jess's face.

'This is all a bit of a mess, isn't it? You know, when your mum told me what was happening with you and Rob, I had a really bad feeling about it. Honestly, I've never seen a divorce that was truly amicable. Let alone moving in next door to each other.' She tutted. 'All this blended family nonsense. It's never easy mixing parents and children. Never.'

Jess sighed. She didn't want a lecture. She wanted to get out of this police station and go home. Try and pick up the pieces of her shattered life. Goodness knows what Ben was thinking about everything.

Stella held up a hand. 'I'm sorry. You don't need to hear that. Let's see what we can do to get you out of here. You'd better go through the whole series of events with me. In as much detail as you can remember. Okay?'

'Are they going to keep me here?'

'Until they've searched your car. And looked through your phone. Then they'll probably have more questions.' Stella's lips pressed together, an apology in her eyes. 'I'm afraid it's going to be a long night. But I'll do my best to fight your corner for you.'

Jess reached across the table and grabbed one of her hands. Gave it a grateful squeeze. 'Thank you.'

Stella caught her eye. 'I have to ask you this... Did you take the boy?'

Jess snatched her hand back, appalled that she'd asked. 'No I did not,' she snapped.

Stella gave a satisfied nod. 'Right then. Let's get to work.'

Jess finally got out of the station at 6.30 the following morning. She hadn't been charged but had been released pending further enquiries and under strict instructions that she wasn't to leave the island.

She felt the weight of suspicion pressing down on her as she left, Stella guiding her to her car. 'I don't think they've discovered any evidence on your phone for us to be concerned about. We'll have to wait for forensics to come back on the hair samples they found in your car.'

'But I told you. Mo's in my car all the time. I've taken the boys out together loads of times, so finding a few of his hairs there doesn't prove a thing.'

Stella opened the car door and Jess slid into the passenger seat, adrenaline still coursing round her veins, heart pumping like she'd just run a marathon. She was dog-tired but wired with all the caffeine she'd drunk to keep her awake for the questioning. Round and round the same story, trying to catch her out.

'I know.' Stella patted her knee. 'I really don't think they've got anything conclusive. It's all circumstantial. I don't want you to worry about it.'

'But how can I not worry? It's just another thing Social Services have against me. They're not going to let me have Toby back with this hanging over my head, are they?'

Stella sighed. 'Probably not. But I'm going to do everything I can to get this sorted out quickly. If you're absolved of all guilt, we can draw a line under it.'

'People don't forget, though, do they? Once an accusation's been thrown at you, it doesn't go away. Some of it sticks.' Jess gave a huff. '"No smoke without fire." I overhear people saying that all the time in the library when they're sitting there gossiping.' Angry tears sprang to her eyes. 'That's what they'll be saying about me.'

'Well, none of this is public knowledge.' Stella sounded upbeat, in a forced sort of way. 'Hopefully we'll be able to keep it quiet.'

Jess turned to her, unable to believe that was what she really thought. 'You're joking, aren't you? We're talking the Isle of Man here. Everyone knows everything. You can't keep things secret. If someone coughs in Ramsey, they know about it in Douglas. You of all people must realise that.'

Stella was quiet as she started the engine, pulled out of the parking space and into the road, heading back towards Peel. 'Oh, Jess,' she sighed. 'I don't know what to say that'll make you feel better.'

Jess turned to look out of the window. There was nothing she could say. Nothing at all. Life as she knew it would never be the same again.

CHAPTER THIRTY-THREE

The bedroom light was on when she got home. She crept inside, aware that Ruby would still be asleep, put her bag on the hall table and trudged up the stairs, stopping at the top while she gathered herself. How the heck was she going to start this conversation? More to the point, what sort of reception was she likely to get?

Their bedroom door was ajar, and she could hear Ben's voice.

'I don't know, mate,' he was saying with a sigh. 'Everything has gone tits-up since we moved, it's just one thing after another. Talk about Armageddon... I seem to be living in the middle of it. God knows what's got into Jess. She's morphed into someone I don't even recognise.'

She tensed, shocked by his comment. *Have I changed?* She didn't feel like she had; more that everything around her had shifted.

'Sorry to hear that.' A man's voice. She peeked through the gap in the door, saw Ben sitting at his desk, his laptop open in front of him, his back towards her. He was on a Zoom call, but she couldn't make out who he was talking to. She held her breath, listening. 'Even more reason to take up my offer now, don't you think? I really could use you here. You'd have a gang of lads to manage. Your own projects. My right-hand man, as it were.'

'It sounds very tempting.' Ben was doodling on his notepad with one hand, the other rubbing at the back of his neck.

'There's a lot of money to be made. Fabulous place to live. Honestly, mate, you'll love it here. And the women... don't get me started on the women.'

Ben laughed. 'I'm almost there. I've been trying to move things forward, you know, doing my best, but it's not really gone to plan. It's all got a bit... tricky.' He gave a little snort, like that was an understatement. 'So... how long have I got?'

'There's a project I need to get going on. I've been stalling the guy, but he's growing impatient and wants us to get started. The sooner the better.' The man broke off to speak to someone in the background before turning his attention back to Ben. 'I just want to stress that everything that happened before, you know, that's all water under the bridge. You did me a favour in the end, running off with my girlfriend. I've got a lovely new wife, a baby on the way, couldn't be happier.' He laughed. 'Come on, what do you say? Got to be worth giving it a go. Doesn't have to be for ever.'

Ben stopped his doodling. 'Give me a deadline. Otherwise, you know me... it'll never happen.'

'Look, seriously now, I've got to have a manager in place to make this business work efficiently, and if it's not you, I need to get someone else. I've been talking to a couple of other lads who are keen, but I know I promised you first refusal. And no doubt about it, you are my first choice.' The man sighed. 'I mean, I asked you before, didn't I? Before all that... trouble. But let's not get into that. The thing is, I trust your work ethic, mate. We go way back, don't we? So I'd rather it was you. And I've given you a while to think about this now. I really need an answer by the end of the day.'

Ben whistled through his teeth. 'Okay, okay, I understand where you're coming from.' He scratched his head with the end of the pen. 'I'm sorry I've kept you hanging.' He wrote something on the pad. 'I keep forgetting... how far ahead are you there? Tell me in UK time when I need to call you by.'

'We're four hours ahead at the moment. I need to know by four p.m. your time at the very latest. That gives you the best part of a day to get your ducks in a row and square it with the missus, if that's what you need to do. You'd love it here, mate. You really would.' The man was silent for a moment. 'If it would make things easier, I'm happy for you to come over for three months and give it a try before you fully commit. But it's a long-term offer if you want it. What I need is someone to help me develop the business.'

Ben wrote something in the notebook, underlined it. 'I hear ya. Look, I'd better go. Jess will be back soon. She messaged me from the station to say she's on her way.'

'Okay, take care, and I know you'll make the right decision. This job's got your name written all over it.'

'Yeah, yeah. Thanks, mate. Talk later.'

Ben shut his laptop, the pen still in his hand. He tapped it against the notebook, lost in thought.

A hand landed on Jess's shoulder, and she reared back, startled. A voice whispered in her ear. 'Caught you snooping again, haven't I?'

She spun round and Ruby put a finger to her lips, shushing her, then beckoned for her to follow to her own bedroom. Not sure she had any choice, Jess crept after her. Once she was inside, Ruby closed the door silently behind them, clearly not wanting to alert her father.

'Looks like you're in a whole load of trouble,' she whispered. 'Beating up your son, drugging and kidnapping little kids, telling your mum you've changed your mind about being with Dad. And now you're listening to his private conversations.' She shook her head, eyes wide in mock horror, her finger wagging from side to side. 'That is not going to go down well.'

Jess was appalled by the list Ruby had just reeled off. Put like that, it was pretty damning. She opened her mouth to speak, then closed it again. Reasoning with Ruby was a challenge at the best of times, but after a night with no sleep, she wasn't mentally prepared. 'It's not what you think,' she hissed. 'None of that is true.'

Ruby picked up her phone, flicked through it, then tapped. Jess could hear her own voice, then her mum's. It was a recording of their conversation the previous day. But it had been edited to make it sound like she was saying she had doubts about being with Ben.

She gasped. 'That's not what I said. You've taken out half the conversation. Spliced bits together to make it mean something different.'

Ruby grinned at her. 'I know. Cool, yeah? Amazing what editing apps can do these days.'

'Don't you dare play that to your dad.' Jess tried to sound authoritative, like she was in charge, but there was a note of fear in her voice. Something Ruby picked up on straight away. A triumphant gleam shone in her eyes.

'Yes, that wouldn't be good, would it? Not on top of everything else.'

Jess folded her arms across her chest, glared at the girl. 'What is it you want?'

'See, I knew you were clever.' Ruby's patronising tone grated on Jess's nerves. She clamped her teeth together lest she say something that would tip this situation the wrong way. Waited. Ruby was clearly enjoying herself, dragging things out like a cat playing with a mouse.

'What I want. What I really, really want.' Ruby gave a silent giggle. 'If I'm going to get anywhere as an influencer, I need clothes and props and lots of cool stuff.' She leant against the wall, phone in her hand, the languid pose of someone who knew they had the upper hand. 'Cash is what I want. A lump sum to get me started. Let's say five hundred pounds. Then fifty quid a week.'

Jess gasped. 'Don't be ridiculous. That's an outrageous amount.'

Ruby shrugged, pushed herself off the wall, pointing the phone in Jess's direction as she made for the door. 'I'll just have to tell him then. Let him have a listen.'

Jess reached out and grabbed her shoulder, spun her round, anger burning in her chest.

'Don't you dare,' she hissed.

Ruby grinned. 'Or what? What you going to do about it?'

Jess swallowed. What could she do? She bit her lip, determined not to cry. The best thing she could do was buy herself some time.

'Okay,' she said eventually. 'Okay, you win.'

'Five hundred quid up front, weekly payments every Friday.'

Not a hope in hell, she thought to herself, but nodded all the same, before escaping from the room.

CHAPTER THIRTY-FOUR

She leant against the wall in the hallway, her heart pounding as she tried to grasp these new developments. Ruby was trying to blackmail her, and Ben was talking about working away some- where. It sounded from the conversation like it had been in the offing for a while. Why hadn't he spoken to her about it? Was he worried that she wouldn't want him to go? And what about Ruby, where did she come into his plans?

She took a deep breath. There was no point trying to second-guess things. It was time for a proper conversation. It was ages since they'd had a decent chat about how they felt, tiptoeing around the sensitive subjects so they wouldn't start a row. Well, they were way past the point of no return now. If their relationship was to have a future, they needed to confront the issues head on, even if it did get a bit heated.

She pushed off the wall and walked into the bedroom, finding Ben still sitting at the desk, staring into space.

He spun round in his chair when he heard her come in, gave her a weary smile. 'Hello, love.' He got up and wrapped her in a hug, stroking her hair. 'Are you okay? Last night must

THE WIFE NEXT DOOR   191

have been awful.' He kissed her. 'I love you so much, sweetheart. We'll get through this, I promise.'

She clung to him. 'I love you too,' she mumbled into his chest.

He kissed her hair, laid his cheek on the top of her head, and they stayed like that for a few minutes, neither of them seeming to want to let go. It felt to her like the end of something, and if she let go of him then everything they had, all her dreams for the future, would start crumbling in front of her eyes. She couldn't face that, not on top of everything else. Couldn't risk telling him that she'd overheard his conversation. I'll wait for him to say something, she decided. If he had to make a commitment by the end of the day, surely he'd say something to her.

Eventually she pulled away from him, her eyes meeting his. He bent to kiss her again, but she dodged him, shook her head. It was no good. She couldn't pretend she hadn't heard. It was time to get everything out in the open.

'What's wrong?' he asked, concern in his eyes as he brushed her hair away from her face.

'What's wrong?' She flopped onto the bed. 'You mean apart from Social Services taking my only child away from me, and the police thinking I drugged and kidnapped Mo?'

He grimaced. 'I'm sorry, love. That was a stupid question.'

'You seem preoccupied,' she said, a determined set to her jaw. 'Is there something you want to talk to me about? I mean, there's been all this stuff with Toby, and it just seems to have gone right over your head.'

Before she could follow that train of thought any further, Ben started to speak. He sat beside her, taking her hand. 'There is something, actually.'

She turned so she could see his face, waited for him to carry on.

'I've been offered a job in Dubai.'

'Dubai?' she squeaked. She'd been trying to convince

herself that she'd misheard the conversation, that Ben couldn't possibly be thinking about moving abroad.

'Ian, a workmate from way back, moved over there a few years ago. He's done really well for himself, got a good business going, but his foreman has just left. I'd forgotten about him really. He asked me to go over before, probably four or five years ago when he was just setting up, but then... well, let's just say we had a falling-out. Anyway, he messaged me out of the blue and we got talking. All is forgiven, and he offered me the job.'

Jess swallowed, hardly able to ask the question because she didn't want to know his reply. 'You... you want to take it?'

He looked down at their hands, twined his fingers with hers, let out a big sigh. 'Honestly? I'm tempted. I find self-employment hard. I'm not really cut out to run my own business. I hate all the admin stuff and doing quotes and chasing money. I'm better on site, organising the work.'

He'd complained before about the paperwork side of things and she'd brushed it away as just something you had to get on with, like it or not. She hadn't realised it had been such a barrier for him. 'I can help with the admin. You only had to ask. Honestly, it's not a big deal.' She gave a laugh, relieved there was a simple solution. 'You don't have to go all that way just to avoid a bit of paperwork.'

His eyes met hers then slid away. 'It's not just the paperwork. It's... well, I guess I feel a bit... jaded.' He swallowed. 'I don't know how to explain it. I've always travelled. Before Gran was ill anyway, and then I came back to look after her. At the same time, I started looking after Ruby more and I realised how much I'd been missing not spending time with my daughter. So I stayed.' She watched his Adam's apple bob up and down. 'Thing is... I've always got a buzz out of moving about, living in different places. New cultures, different climates, meeting all sorts of people.' His eyes lit up as he was talking, and she saw a different man to the one she knew. A man who could see a future he wanted. A future he needed. One that he didn't currently have. The thought crushed her.

'What about me?' she whispered, unsure if she was anywhere in his plans. 'Why go along with buying this house and talking about getting married if you're not going to stay?'

He pulled a face. 'Technically I didn't buy the house, did I? Rob did.'

'Yes, but that was only till you sold your gran's house and we could put down a deposit and get a mortgage to buy it off him.'

He was quiet for a moment. 'Ah, yes, well there's been a change of plan there.'

'What do you mean?' Her heart was racing now, her dreams of their future evaporating. How could he change plans without talking to her first? They were a team, weren't they?

He was still staring at their hands, and she willed him to look at her so she could get some measure of how he was feeling. 'I'm not selling Gran's house just yet. Darcey's landlord is selling up, and you know what it's like finding a rental at the moment. They're as rare as hen's teeth. So she's a bit stuck. And given the animosity between Toby and Ruby, we thought it would be better if Ruby lived with her full-time. Darcey's got a new job on the district nurse team in Peel, so she'll be doing nine to five. It just seemed like the right thing to do. It's not for ever, but it could be a while before a better option comes up for them.'

Jess gasped, her voice shrill. 'And when exactly were you going to tell me?'

'I've told you now.'

'After the decision has been made. Weren't you going to discuss it with me first?'

He looked a bit nonplussed. 'But it's about my family, not yours. And Ruby was adamant she'd rather live in Gran's house with her mum.' He gave another shrug. 'Obviously Darcey will pay rent. I'm not giving it to her for free or anything. And it'll be a bit more income for us. It seemed like a no-brainer.'

His actions defied words. How on earth could he think this arrangement was okay? She was so incensed she was struggling to know where to start, how to articulate exactly what she was feeling. 'So we're not buying this house after all?' She pulled her hand away from his. 'Does Rob know?'

'I only sorted all this out with Darcey last night, so I haven't had a chance to talk to him yet. But whatever happens, it's a good investment for him. Plenty of people would be happy renting it.'

She gritted her teeth, aware that he'd avoided her original question. 'What about me, Ben? Where do I come into these plans of yours?'

His expression softened. 'I want you to come with me. That's partly why I want us to get married sooner rather than later. The culture in Dubai... it's better if we're married.'

She stared at him. 'How long have you been planning this?' Realisation was dawning that this was not a spur-of-the-moment thing but a long-held ambition. 'And is that the only reason you want to marry me? Because of the culture in Dubai?' She couldn't keep the incredulity from her voice. Or stop the tears from sliding down her cheeks.

His face coloured, his hand raking through his hair. 'No, no, you've got it wrong. I shouldn't have said it like that. I'm sorry, I messed that up big-time.' He snaked an arm round her waist, but she stood, anger burning in her chest. 'Sweetheart, I love you.' He reached for her, but she moved back a step. 'Please believe me.'

'I'm not sure what to believe any more,' she snapped, unable to look at him, her mind spinning with everything she'd learned. How could he imagine that she'd go with him when Toby was here?

Christ, she needed to talk to someone about all this. Get a

different perspective before her head exploded. Ben was not being straight with her. She didn't trust Ruby as far as she could throw her. She sure as hell didn't trust Carol, and she wasn't even sure about her mum any more, not after their last conversation when she'd urged her to go back to Rob. Just thinking about Rob, she had an overwhelming urge to lay all her troubles out for him like she always used to do. He was so good at picking through the bones of a problem and working out what really mattered, seeing a way through. That was exactly what she needed. Not sympathy, not tea and cake. She needed solutions. But Rob was no longer hers, and she was going to have to sort this out for herself.

She felt Ben's hands on her shoulders and raised her eyes to meet his. She stepped away from him. 'You've not been straight with me, Ben. You've known about this job for a while, haven't you?'

'Today,' he protested. 'He called this morning.'

She huffed. 'Don't be ridiculous. That's not true and you know it.'

His brow creased in frustration. 'Are you saying I'm a liar?'

'I know you bloody are. I heard him say—'

His expression changed and she realised what she'd said, heat rising through her body.

'You heard?' Accusation glinted in his eyes. 'You were listening?'

Her mind froze. *Oh God, what have I done?*

CHAPTER THIRTY-FIVE

Their eyes locked. Sweat beaded on her brow. It was time, she realised, to get everything out in the open.

'Okay, I did overhear your conversation. It wasn't intentional. I got back from the police station, and when I came upstairs you were talking to that guy. I was going to just come in, but then he started talking about offering you a job and I was so shocked I couldn't move.' It all came out in a rush, leaving her a little breathless.

Ben didn't say a word, just stared at her.

'You lied to me just now,' she said, her voice wavering as the reality hit home.

Still he said nothing.

Her heart was hammering so hard her body was shaking. *How do you deal with silence?* She kept on talking. 'Ben, what's happening to us? This place was supposed to be the start of our future, a new beginning, but I don't think it ever was that to you, was it?'

He ran his tongue round his lips before answering. 'It was. Really it was. But... well, things changed.'

'Like what?'

'Well, Toby and Ruby having that major fight. They can't be in the same house, so that needed addressing.'

Her mind questioned again whether those fingerprints could be Ben's. Was that his way of 'addressing' the problem? If she asked him straight and he denied it, would she believe him? She didn't think she would.

'And living next door to your ex... I thought I'd be fine with it, but really, I don't think I am. I think I'd prefer us to have our own space. A proper new start.'

'But what about Toby? Where does he come into all of this?'

Ben sighed. 'I know. It's a problem.'

Her breath caught in her throat. 'He's my son,' she hissed. 'Not a problem.'

He rolled his eyes. 'I didn't mean it like that. You're twisting my words now.'

'I'm not twisting anything.' They squared up to each other like boxers before a fight.

He grunted. Glared at her. 'We can't seem to have a sensible conversation at the moment, can we? Honestly, I don't know what's got into you.'

'Nothing has got into me,' she shouted, angry that he was laying all their problems at her door. 'I think it's perfectly reasonable for me to be upset at being lied to.'

'It wasn't a lie as such.' He threw up his hands. 'Well okay, it might have been a little bit of one. But I just need time to think about things. You sort of ambushed me. I wasn't ready.'

Her hands gravitated to her hips. 'So if you're not ready to tell me the truth, it's okay to lie to me?'

'That's not what I said.'

'It's exactly what you said.'

He closed his eyes, rubbed a hand down his face and took a few deep breaths. 'Right, so... I've got a job to do today. I have to go. I don't want to leave you like this on an argument. I'm not running away, I genuinely have to go, okay?' He came towards her. 'Can we call a truce and talk about this later?'

'Your friend wants a decision by four o'clock,' she said, appalled that he was going to walk out on her now.

He nodded. 'I know. I know exactly what he said, but I can't talk about it now.' He looked at his watch. 'I've really got to get going.' He reached out a hand, caressed her shoulder. 'Sweetheart, I hate it when we fight. Let's give ourselves some time to think about things, and I'll come home at lunchtime.' He gathered his jacket, picked up his van keys and left.

Well, that didn't go well, she thought as she watched him walk down the drive and get into his van. Their rows were getting worse and she could feel herself shaking. But now that she'd caught him out in one lie, she wondered what else he might have been lying about.

Suddenly she was too tired to stand, the lack of sleep muddying her thoughts, making it impossible to see a way forward. She flopped onto the bed, her eyes closing, willing sleep to come. But she couldn't blot out that expression on his face. The anger in his eyes. This wasn't the Ben she'd fallen in love with. He was funny and kind and she would trust him with her life. Seemed she hadn't known him at all. Hadn't realised he could turn on her like this.

Maybe I'm overreacting, she thought as she finally drifted off to sleep.

She woke just before one in the afternoon, the house quiet, hunger gnawing at her belly. Light infused the room, sneaking round the corners of the curtains, telling her it was a sunny day outside. Her mouth was dry, her head throbbing, and she clambered out of bed and went to the en suite in search of painkillers.

God, I look rough, she thought as she caught her reflection

in the mirrored cabinet over the sink. Dark rings circled her eyes, the lines at the corners of her mouth deeper than usual, her forehead creased against the pain of the headache.

She found the painkillers and downed a couple, ran herself a glass of water and turned on the shower. Even though it was the last thing she felt like doing, it was time to face the world. Time to address everything that had happened and work out what the hell to do about it. There had to be a way to get her life back on track. There had to be a way to make sense of the last few weeks.

Feeling a bit more human once she was washed and dressed, she checked her phone. Several missed calls from her work colleague, Pam.

She cringed. *I've got to tell her what's happening.* She owed her that, as she'd been such a support over the last couple of years, always ready to listen and help with advice.

'Pam,' she said, when her friend answered. 'I'm sorry I didn't pick up before.'

'Are you okay? Lisa said you wouldn't be in today. She asked if I could cover your shift.' Pam was whispering, and Jess could imagine her at the desk in the middle of the library, not wanting to leave her post. Pam was a stickler for that. 'She said you had some things to sort out, and it got me worried. It's not like you to miss work, unless you're half dead.'

'It's a long story,' Jess said, rubbing at her forehead, trying to ease the throbbing. 'Basically, I ended up at the police station last night. Mo went missing and they're trying to pin it on me. And Social Services seem to have it in for me at the moment as well.' She sighed, feeling like the weight of the world was on her shoulders. 'It's all a bit of a mess.' She quickly ran through the details.

'Flipping heck, love, that sounds horrendous. How long are you going to be off?'

'Oh, just today. I didn't get home until six thirty this morning, so I needed some sleep.'

'Are you sure? I mean, it's not that I want you to be off work, but... what about child safeguarding procedures?'

Jess's brain screeched to a halt. She hadn't thought about that, not even considered the effect that events in her private life might have on her work. 'Oh my God, you're right. They won't let me work, will they, with this hanging over me?'

She did a lot of work with children, had reading time with mums and toddlers, ran the after-school club three days a week. None of that could happen with a possible charge of kidnapping hanging over her. All the energy sapped out of her. If she couldn't work, how would she manage financially?

'I'd better ring Lisa, see what she says.' Speaking to her manager was the last thing she wanted to do, but she had to tackle her problems head-on if she was going to find a way through this mire. They said their goodbyes and she dialled Lisa before she could procrastinate.

'Jess, thank you so much for calling,' Lisa said when she picked up. 'You were on my list for this afternoon, but I didn't want to disturb you. How are you?' She had one of those voices that was perfect for sympathy, all soft and gentle and apt to bring tears to Jess's eyes if she was feeling under the weather. It was happening now, her eyes brimming. She sniffed, sat up straighter.

'I'm okay, thanks. It's just Pam said... and I hadn't thought about this, but she thinks there might be an issue with the child protection procedures.'

'Ah yes. That's *exactly* what I needed to talk to you about.'

Jess felt her chest tighten, apprehension gripping the back of her neck. *I can't lose my job.* It was her only bit of independence, her only source of income, and besides that, she loved it.

'I'm afraid we're going to have to ask you to take leave until the police investigation is completed at the very least.'

'At the very least?'

'Human resources are looking into it, but it seems the problems with Social Services, just because of the nature of the case, and the police having questions about child abduction... well, we can't ignore those things.'

Jess swallowed. 'Am I... am I going to lose my job?'

'Let's not get too far ahead of ourselves. I'm sure it'll all get sorted out and I don't want you to worry about it. But in the meantime, you have a nice rest and I'll keep in touch, okay?' She made it sound like she was doing Jess a favour rather than threatening to take away her livelihood.

Jess disconnected. On top of everything else, her career was now in ruins.

CHAPTER THIRTY-SIX

Jess was in the kitchen, trying to work out if she could face eating anything, when she heard the front door slam.

'I'm in here, Ben,' she called, thankful he'd been true to his word and come home for lunch.

She stood still, waiting for his reply, or for him to appear, but instead she heard footsteps running up the stairs. Ruby? She must have forgotten something she needed for school. A few minutes later, she heard her running back down and waited to hear the door slam again, Ruby's usual mode of exit. But it didn't. Instead, she appeared at the kitchen door, brandishing her phone, a scowl on her face.

'We had a deal,' she said. 'I just checked, and you haven't put that money into my account.'

'No, and I won't be doing either. I haven't got money like that to spare, and now it looks like I might be losing my job, I can't give you what you want, I'm afraid.'

It felt good to stand up to her. She fully intended to talk to Ben about the recorded conversation when he got home. Clear the air between them so there were no nasty surprises and they could be honest with each other about what they wanted going forwards.

Ruby's eye's narrowed, her face pinched. 'But I need that money. There are things I have to order.'

Jess folded her arms across her chest, determined not to be bullied.

'I doubt there's anything essential. You have a lovely bedroom with new furnishings. Your mum has just spent a fortune on you in Liverpool. I can't see what else you could possibly need.'

'Yeah, well you wouldn't understand, would you?' Ruby's voice was thick with emotion, and Jess noticed she was looking quite distressed. For once, the hard front she usually wore had slipped, her vulnerability clear to see.

'Maybe not.' Jess softened, her maternal instincts coming to the fore. Was there something else going on here? However difficult Ruby could be, she was still a child. She frowned. 'Are you in some sort of trouble? Is that why you need the money?'

'My life is none of your business,' Ruby said, enunciating each word. 'We have a deal.' She jabbed a finger at Jess. 'If the money isn't in my account by the time I get back from school, I'm giving that recording to Dad.'

She waited for Jess to say something, but there was nothing she *could* say. She didn't have the money and that was that. She'd just have to get to Ben first, make sure he heard her version.

But Ben didn't come home for lunch, messaging to say he had to stay and get the job finished; that it was proving trickier than he'd thought. He finally arrived home just after six, smelling of sawdust and leaving a trail of it behind him. There was no doubting he'd been to work, so he'd been telling the truth about that, at least. She caught the thought, appalled that she was doubting everything he said. It was funny how one lie could undermine the foundations of what she'd considered to be a rock-steady relationship.

What else has he been lying about? The question kept popping into her head, and she couldn't shake it free.

She gave him a tight smile, nervous now about the conversation she knew they were about to have. He didn't meet her eye, his movements slow and deliberate, like he was weary to the core.

'Sorry I'm late. Ruby went to a friend's house after school and asked if I'd pick her up on my way home. I was talking to her about the Dubai job, telling her we'd be getting married before we moved over there, and she went ballistic.' He sighed. 'It's taken me the best part of an hour to calm her down. She told me I was making a mistake. That you didn't really love me.'

He put a hand in his pocket, pulled out a shiny pink phone. Ruby's. A weight landed in Jess's stomach, taking away any appetite she might have had. *He's heard the recording.*

She swallowed her panic, held a hand up to pre-empt him. 'Look, I know what you're going to say, but I've got to tell you that recording of Ruby's has been heavily edited. She's determined to make me look bad.'

His voice was gruff. 'You would say that, wouldn't you? Why should I trust you over my daughter?' The pain in his eyes was real. 'When she played me this, I understood what she was so upset about.'

Jess very much doubted that he did understand. And there was something going on with Ruby, she was sure of it. Why else would she need all that money?

'That conversation has been pulled apart and put together again with some editing app. I've heard it. She tried to blackmail me with it.'

His eyes narrowed. 'Don't be ridiculous. Why would she do that?'

'Well, for starters, she doesn't like me. And she really doesn't like Toby. But I genuinely think she's in some kind of trouble and needs money.'

His frown deepened. 'What would she need money for?'

'I don't know. But it was a large amount, and she was distraught when I made it clear I wasn't going to pay her. I'm wondering if it's something to do with Instagram, maybe pictures she doesn't want people seeing. Something like that?'

'You mean... someone's blackmailing her?' There was a note of panic in his voice.

Spoken out loud, it sounded far-fetched, but hadn't she read a couple of articles recently about this behaviour being rife amongst teenagers? She grimaced. 'I'm just guessing here, but her Insta profile seems to be the most important thing in her life.'

He sagged a little, the fight wiped out of him by concern for his daughter. As he pocketed the phone, his eyes met hers. 'I've got to ask you... Did you mean it? That you were having second thoughts?'

The directness of his question caught her off guard. She took a deep breath. *The truth. It's time for the truth.*

'I... Well, not exactly. But I'm worried you lied to me.'

He looked at the floor, scuffed his toe in a little pile of sawdust that had fallen off his boots. 'Yeah, I'm sorry about that. I knew a move to Dubai would be a big thing for you, and I just felt cornered. Didn't know what to say.'

'So you lied. Which then makes me wonder what else you've lied to me about.'

His eyes found hers. 'Nothing, I swear to God. That's the only thing.'

He came closer, stroked her cheek with the back of his hand. 'Sweetheart, I love you.' The expression in his eyes told her he meant it. 'I want us to be married. Not just so we can go to Dubai, but because you are the best thing that's ever happened to me.'

She knew that was a lie too. His daughter very firmly held that accolade. Jess would always come second in his eyes; something Ruby was well aware of and would use to her advantage whenever possible. Was it the same with every parent? she wondered. Did their children always come first? She thought about Toby, how she would do anything for him. *Does Toby come before Ben in my heart?* In all honesty, she knew he did. But that was how it worked with any relationship, the compromise that had to be made. It was just a little bit harder to live with when it was someone else's child.

There was an important issue he was overlooking here, though. Had he asked her what she wanted? Had he even considered how she'd feel being so far away from her son, given that Social services wouldn't allow him to come with them? He's assuming I'll go with him, she thought, knowing that she never could.

'I can't leave Toby,' she whispered, wanting with all her heart for it to be possible to be with this man. This joyful soul who'd brought so much fun to her life.

'He could come for holidays. Think of that. He'd love it. I mean, loads of kids go away to school. It would be just like that. And he's got Rob and Carol here. And Mo.' He gave her a hopeful smile. 'I'm not even sure how much he'd miss us.'

His words were like an arrow to her heart.

She pulled away from him, hurt beyond words, beyond even tears. *Of course he'd miss me. He would.* She was Toby's rock, the one he came to when he was upset. He was only happy now because he was confident she was there whenever he needed her. Meanwhile, he was enjoying having Mo to play with all the time, like the younger sibling he'd always yearned for. In fact, of all of them, the new living arrangements probably suited Toby the best.

A sudden realisation hit her then, that the current situation suited someone else better. The fact that she wasn't allowed to be with her son. Someone had engineered events to fit their own agenda.

She studied Ben for a moment before she spoke, as if the answer to her question would be written on his face. 'Was it you?'

'What do you mean?'

'Hurting Toby. Was that you? So he couldn't live with us and then I'd have less excuse to say no to Dubai?' She nodded to herself, sure she was right. 'You don't actually want him living with us, do you?'

'Christ, Jess. Where the hell did that come from?' He glared at her, his face starting to redden as his anger rose.

Her resolve wavered, shocked that she'd just blurted it out like that. She wanted to retract her words, but they were out there now, and they'd landed on target. She could see the damage she'd done reflected in his eyes.

His jaw moved from side to side. 'It pains me to say this, but I think we're finished.'

The blood drained from her face. 'What? You don't mean that.'

'It's clear you don't trust me. And if you can accuse me of hurting Toby, then you don't know me at all.' He glowered at her. 'You've helped me make my decision. I asked Ian for a few extra hours so we could talk before I made a final commitment, but it's very clear now what I need to do.'

He spun on his heel and tramped up the stairs, leaving a trail of sawdust behind him.

She ran after him, desperate to stop him from doing something rash. 'I'm sorry, Ben. I didn't mean it.'

He turned and held up his hands. 'It's too late. It's over. We're going.' He walked along the landing to Ruby's room, opened the door. 'Pack your bags, we're leaving.'

Jess leant against the wall, horrified by what was happening.

I've ruined everything. Or, said the voice of reason, somebody has ruined it for you.

CHAPTER THIRTY-SEVEN

Later, she lay on her back on the lawn, looking at the night sky. The house was dark. Nobody home except her. Next door, she could see the glow of a night light in the boys' room. Tears had dried on her face, her eyes sore. Once Ben had left, she'd had a bit of a meltdown, throwing things, and shouting and screaming until her throat was sore. There was nobody to hear, so she just let it all out. All the sadness and anger and frustration that had built up over the last few weeks.

Here she was, supposed to be starting a new life with the man she loved, setting up the perfect blended family. Instead, she now had nothing. No partner, no son, possibly no job. Even the house wasn't hers. She only had a few days of annual leave left, and once those were used up, she'd wouldn't be getting paid. *How am I going to cope?* Not just financially, but living next door to a son she wasn't allowed to speak to, let alone hold. Someone had taken away her rights as a mother. And if that wasn't bad enough, she had a criminal case hanging over her unless she could work out exactly what had happened with Mo.

Of course, whatever Ben said, everything that had been

taken away from her would have suited his plans. A new start after all that trauma was exactly what she needed, right? And wouldn't Dubai be a great adventure? She gritted her teeth. Was it him engineering things to make her want to leave, to run away for a while? But then she remembered the expression on his face when she'd accused him of hurting Toby, and she just knew in her bones that he wasn't lying about that. She knew he'd been genuinely horrified that she'd even entertained the thought. Ben wasn't devious. He wasn't a schemer. He might bend the truth when cornered, but she didn't think he was the architect of her demise.

It had to be someone else.

Ruby couldn't be discounted, but Jess now suspected that Ruby had other things on her mind. She might be manipulative and spoilt, but she couldn't possibly have taken Mo. No, this was the work of an adult.

She got up off the grass and brushed herself down, went back inside and rang her mum.

'I'm coming round,' Helen said when Jess had told her everything that had happened. 'You can't be on your own at a time like this.'

She tried to protest that she was an adult and fine on her own, but to her mum she would always be a child who needed nurturing. And sometimes it was nice to be mothered, even as a parent herself.

Half an hour later, she heard a car draw up outside and went to the window to see Rob parking on her driveway, her mum in the passenger seat. She cringed, not wanting to have to explain to her almost-ex-husband what was going on with her domestic arrangements. Typical of her mum to ask him for a lift.

She opened the door and Helen breezed past. 'Rob very kindly picked me up,' she said, giving Jess a peck on the cheek

'Yes, I can see that.'

Rob gave her a wave as he went round to open the boot. He heaved an enormous suitcase onto the drive, then took out a holdall and a tote bag.

'Christ, Mum, it looks like you've brought everything but the kitchen sink.' Jess gave a brittle laugh. 'I was thinking about a sleepover. You know, a carrier bag would have done the job.'

Her mum chuckled. 'The weather's changeable this time of year. You have to be prepared. Layers, my dear, lots of layers.'

They watched Rob load himself up with all the bags and make his way carefully towards the door. Jess reached out to take the holdall and tote bag off him so he could focus on the beast of a suitcase.

'It's only one night, though,' she protested.

'Oh no, love. No, no, no.' Helen wagged a finger at her. 'This isn't a sticking-plaster visit. We're going to sort this out properly.'

Rob shot Jess a look over her mum's head, and she knew he was thinking the same as her. It was a comforting thought. She wasn't alone in this, was she? She smiled at him, hopeful that there was a way to sort things out regarding access to Toby.

'It was good of you to give Mum a lift,' she said. 'Though why she couldn't drive herself or ask me, I've no idea. I honestly thought she'd be walking round as usual.'

'Oh, I offered. You know she hates driving unless it's absolutely necessary. I dropped by her house earlier to sort out a bit of childcare for this week. You know, now that you...' Rob grimaced, gave a heartfelt sigh and placed a comforting hand on her shoulder. 'I'm so sorry about what's happened.' Propping the suitcase in the hallway, he flapped his arms at his sides, like he wanted to hug her but wasn't sure what the protocol was now they were formally separated.

Jess looked away, tears welling up, her throat too choked to speak.

'I know you wouldn't hurt Toby, and whatever happened to Mo, I know that wasn't you either. It would be completely out of character, and I have stressed all of this to the police.'

'Absolutely,' her mum chimed in. 'You can't even step on an ant or put slug pellets out, so how could anyone think you'd hurt either of those children?' She had a ferocious scowl on her face. 'It's ridiculous. And why the police are keeping you under suspicion, well, that's just laziness on their part.' She gave a nod. 'I told them. When they came to talk to me, I gave it to them straight.'

Jess gave her a hug, then Helen beckoned Rob to join them, and they stood there for a long moment, locked in a triumvirate of solidarity.

'We are family,' her mum said, her hand grasping Jess's shoulder tight. 'Whatever has happened, nobody can take that away from us. We'll fight this together, Jess. Don't you worry. You're not on your own.'

That was too much for Jess and the tears started to flow.

'Helen's right,' Rob said, his arm round her shoulders. 'You're not on your own.'

'But I feel like I am. I can't be with Toby, and now Ben's left me too.'

'Oh, love,' her mum said, 'don't go getting yourself all upset. We'll sort it out, won't we, Rob?'

'Of course we will. And it isn't just you. We're a blended family, right?'

Jess huffed. 'That's not what Carol thinks. She said there was no way I was parenting her child. But she's got mine, hasn't she?' The sobs started up again, the absence of her son a gaping hole in her heart.

Her mum moved away, and Jess clung to Rob like a limpet to a rock. She'd never felt so bereft in her life. How was she going to pick up the pieces and carry on?

Helen came back with a box of tissues. 'Here you are, love.' She rubbed her back as Jess wiped her face and blew her nose. 'This is why I've decided to come and stay for a while. In fact, I was wondering on the way over whether we might make this a more permanent thing now Ben's gone. I can help with the bills, it'll be cheaper for me than living on my own, and I'll be here to look after Toby and Mo whenever I'm needed.' She passed Jess another tissue. 'Couldn't have worked out better. Perhaps this is the silver lining, eh?'

'You'll blend in very nicely,' Rob said.

Helen laughed. 'I see what you did there. We can be a multigenerational blended family now, can't we?'

Jess froze, the implications of her mum's words starting to register. She loved her mum dearly, but living with her, well, that was something else entirely. Instead of feeling comforted, she felt her life was spinning further out of control.

Rob stayed and helped Helen sort out Ruby's bedroom, which was going to be hers for now, and she fussed around rearranging things so it suited her better. She was humming when she came downstairs, a happy smile on her face.

'I think this could work out just fine,' she said. 'That's a lovely big bedroom, and right next door to the bathroom.'

Jess forced a smile. 'I'm glad you like it. But I think I'll be fine on my own, you know, in a few days.'

'Nonsense. The more I think about it, the more I think the idea of me moving in would work best for both of us. I mean, financially you're going to struggle, aren't you?'

It was true. She would. Perhaps this was the only solution. For now.

She looked at her mum then, and the thought struck her that the way things had turned out suited her very well. Jess knew that Helen had been worried about money recently; she also knew that she wanted to spend more time with Toby, wasn't too keen on Ben and thought the sun shone out of Rob's backside. If the horrible turn of events benefited anyone, it was her mum.

She hardly dared think it, was appalled at the words in her head. *Was it Mum who engineered all of this?*

CHAPTER THIRTY-EIGHT

'Are you all right, love?' her mum asked later, when Rob had gone home and they were sitting watching an historical drama series that Helen was devoted to. 'You're ever so quiet.'

Jess had been staring into space, not interested in the television, her thoughts dominated by the idea that her mum might not be the benign presence she appeared to be. She kept telling herself it was just too fanciful, Helen wasn't like that, then her mind would go scurrying around looking for evidence to support the idea that perhaps she was.

Her mum had been an advocate of smacking when Jess had been a child, dishing out many a slap round the legs for playing up when they were out shopping. And Jess remembered being grabbed and shaken so her teeth rattled when she'd been messing about on the clifftop path and nearly gone over the edge. She'd had bruises on her arms then, and even now could remember how much they hurt, the shock of being grabbed so hard.

She's had the opportunity to give Toby those bruises. But then wouldn't he have been wary of her, acted differently when she was around? Jess had seen no sign of that, just unadulterated affection.

Now she looked at Helen, settled on the sofa next to her with a cup of tea in hand and a plate of biscuits by her side. She was loving this. She tried to tell herself that it didn't mean she'd done anything wrong, but still the suspicion lingered, souring her thoughts.

'I think I'm going to go and have a bath,' she said, getting up. 'It might help me relax.'

'Good idea, love. You're looking ever so peaky.' Helen gave a satisfied sigh. 'We're going to be fine, sweetheart. Don't you worry. Tomorrow, when you're feeling a bit fresher, we'll sit down and work out what we need to do to make all these problems go away.'

Jess thought what she needed was a miracle, and that was not likely to happen. 'Thanks, Mum,' she said wearily. 'I'll see you in the morning.'

'I'm working in the morning. But I'll be back to pick the boys up from school.' She beamed. 'I'll get us something nice for tea afterwards, then we can have a good old chat.'

She's got it all worked out, Jess thought as she climbed the stairs, every step an effort. Her mind was mush, no idea any more what might be real and what might be manipulation. She'd made such a mess of things; how could she trust her own judgement? She'd thought Ben was her future, and look what had happened there. It could still have been him, she reminded herself as she closed the bathroom door and turned on the taps.

As she lay in the bath, she wondered what would have to happen for her to get full access to her son again. If the injuries stopped, what did that prove? Not a lot really, nothing conclusive anyway, but how would Social Services interpret things? Would they say that it meant it was someone in her household who'd been doing it? That the new arrangement was working, so no need to change it? Then she'd never be able to be a proper mum to Toby again.

She squeezed her eyes shut, willing the thoughts to go away, to stop tormenting her. Then Mo's little face swam into her mind, and that took her in a whole new direction, trying to work out how she was going to convince the police she'd had nothing to do with his abduction. Apparently Mo couldn't remember anything, so he couldn't tell them who might have been involved. They had no real evidence, she reassured herself, or she would have been charged. Wasn't that what Stella had said? But she had no alibi either. And unless she could point the finger at someone else, she was clearly their number one suspect. After racking her brain until the water was cold, she still couldn't work out a solution.

There was a new piece to the puzzle. Although she would like to think Carol was behind all her troubles, she was struggling to lay Mo's abduction at her door, because she'd heard her shouting for her son. She was definitely next door when Jess had driven off. And Helen wouldn't have been able to get to Archallagan because she refused to drive on those back roads, ever since she'd had an accident years ago. Now she was only brave enough to go on the main roads, and that was only when she had no alternative, preferring to take the bus or get a lift.

She shivered and got out of the chilly water, glad that she'd managed to absolve her mum of suspicion. That felt better. Quickly she dried herself, threw on her dressing gown and made her way to her bedroom. It was going to feel strange sleeping in here on her own.

Her mum was sitting on the bed, smiling, a mug in her hand.

'I made us some hot chocolate. I thought it might help you sleep.'

Jess returned the smile, then grabbed her pyjamas from

under her pillow and went to the en suite to put them on. Already this was feeling claustrophobic.

It'll just take a bit of getting used to, she told herself. And really, given the sudden change in her personal circumstances, what choice did she have?

CHAPTER THIRTY-NINE

Despite her weariness, Jess couldn't sleep. She stood at the window, watching the occasional car passing. Then she noticed Rob getting in his car, driving away. She checked the time. It was after ten. Late for him to be going out.

Her phone pinged, and she dashed over to the bedside table, snatched it up, hoping it might be Ben. Because even though he'd walked out on her, she still hoped there was a way for them to make this right.

She checked her messages. Not Ben.

Can you ring me on this number please. Urgent!!! Carol

She frowned. The number wasn't the one she had saved for Carol on her phone. Odd. But then Carol *had* been behaving very oddly. Suspicious of things. Anxious. Snappy. They hadn't spoken for a while, so why did she want Jess to phone her now? Was it to berate her for supposedly kidnapping Mo?

What if something's happened to Toby?

She froze, panic making her heart race, then rang the number.

'Hello.' Carol sounded wary, her voice a whisper. 'Is that you, Jess?'

'It is.' She held her tongue, kept back everything she'd been wanting to say to Carol, letting her neighbour take the initiative.

'Look, we need to talk.'

'We do.'

'Tomorrow. Meet me at the back of Peel Castle. Half nine.'

It wasn't what Jess had been expecting. 'What? Why there?'

'It's a safe place to talk,' Carol hissed.

Jess pictured it in her mind. The ruins of the sandstone castle sat on a little rocky island attached to Peel Hill and the marina by a short tarmacked causeway. A concrete path ran all the way round it, much of it not visible from land. In her mind, she could hear the sea pounding the jagged rocks beneath the path, and wasn't sure she would feel safe there with someone who appeared to want to destroy her life. You're being melodramatic, she told herself. You can run away if it doesn't feel right.

'Okay,' she said carefully, thinking she'd put on trainers just in case.

The phone went dead and she stared at the screen. Weird. A different phone. A whispered conversation. It felt... clandestine. A secret arrangement. I'll tell Mum where I'm going, she decided, still unsure if she trusted Carol's motives.

She hadn't said what she wanted to talk about, had she?

It had to be Toby and Mo. Those two incidents were the things they had to discuss, no question about it. They were the common denominators in their lives, the things that connected them

Unless... It could be... She stopped herself trying to second-guess what Carol had in mind. There was no point. All she could do was show up and listen.

CHAPTER FORTY

The next day, she woke late. Her mum had already left for work when she got down to the kitchen, a note on the worktop to say she'd bring something home from M&S for tea. At least that was one less thing to think about.

She sat in the lounge, very aware of the quiet. She heard Rob leaving, calling out his goodbyes. He always did that, like he was going off on a long trip somewhere rather than just out to work for the day. She smiled to herself. He had so many funny little habits. She'd have to admit she sort of missed them now, even though they'd driven her mad when she was living with him.

Absence makes the heart grow fonder. Wasn't that the truth.

Speaking of hearts, she wondered if Ben would have a change of heart once he'd cooled down. But then, asking him if he'd hurt Toby had been the final straw; that and Ruby's editing of the conversation between Jess and her mum. She sighed and sipped at her coffee. What a mess she'd made of everything. So many bad decisions. *What was I thinking?*

Everything ran through her head like a movie, all the things that had led her to this place in her life. All the decision points.

She frowned as she realised that a lot of decisions had been made for her – her own choices pre-empted by those made by other people in her life. It was strange how that had happened. Almost as if she'd been shepherded to where she was now. She shivered, a weird sense that something in her mind had shifted, a connection made, but she couldn't quite grasp it.

You can't blame other people, she told herself. You've got to take responsibility. Wasn't that what her mum had always drummed into her?

She finished her coffee, checked her watch and slipped her trainers on. It was almost time to meet Carol. Nerves twisted in her stomach. Was this a showdown type of conversation? Was this going to be Carol giving her an earful of abuse? She had no idea. It was a strange place to meet when they lived next door to each other. But it would be private, and maybe that was what Carol was after. There would be nobody around at this time of day.

A chilly breeze was blowing off the sea as she stood next to the castle walls, trying to find some shelter. Seabirds wheeled on the thermals. Pigeons cooed above her head, perched in gaps between the stones. A seal popped its head out of the water, then dived back under. She folded her arms across her chest, thinking she should have put on a warmer jacket. Checked her phone. No messages. Carol was half an hour late now. Jess had called her several times, but she wasn't answering, and after leaving the first message, there didn't seem any point in leaving more.

Ten minutes later, she decided she'd waited long enough and set off back home, furious that she'd been led on a wild goose chase. Or had it been a diversionary tactic, getting her out of the way so Carol could set up one of her nasty tricks? Her heart sank at the thought, trepidation jangling her nerves.

I bet she's laughing her socks off, she thought as she stomped up the hill back to the estate, feeling stupid that she'd fallen for some sort of practical joke. She opened the front door carefully, not knowing what she might find. But all was quiet, everything in its place, just as she'd left it.

She was making a cup of coffee when her phone rang and she snatched it up, sure it must be Carol. But it wasn't.

'Hello, love.'

'Ben.' She sank into a chair. Just hearing his voice brought a rush of longing.

'Um... I'm sorry,' he mumbled. 'I just sort of... well, I lost it a bit, didn't I?'

She cleared her throat, her voice croaky and hoarse. 'It's okay. I shouldn't have said what I did.'

'And I should have believed you rather than Ruby. Darcey told me what she'd done with the editing. She gave her such a ticking-off when she found out. Silly girl was boasting about it, how she'd split us up and hadn't it worked out well?'

Jess clamped her jaw tight. There was nothing she could say, but she did know that she and Ruby would always struggle to be family. That much was clear at least. Had it been Ruby playing tricks on her all along? It seemed very likely. It could have been her behind Toby's bruises as well, and he'd been too frightened to say. Yes, that all made sense. The only thing that didn't make sense was Mo's kidnapping. That couldn't possibly have been Ruby.

'What's happening with Dubai?' she said, to change the subject and stop her mind spinning in circles.

She heard a big sigh, sending white noise into her ear. 'It's not happening.'

'What?'

'Seems like it was a hoax. I found out that the guy I was speaking to doesn't live in Dubai. There is no job.' His voice cracked, like he was close to tears. 'I can't even reach him now;

everything was done over Messenger and Zoom, and his accounts have disappeared.'

She gasped. Ben was one of those people who was always upbeat, even on a bad day. Shock stole her words; there was nothing she could think of to make him feel better. 'Wow,' was all she could manage.

'I know. I can't believe it. I've spent a fortune on flights and a hotel for the first week while he got accommodation sorted. It's all non-refundable because it was last-minute cheap deals.'

'But you said you knew him?'

Another sigh. She hadn't ever heard him so down before and couldn't help feeling sorry for him. 'I mean, it's years since we worked together. And I'll admit it was a surprise when he got back in touch because there'd been a bit of bad feeling when we parted company. Before that, though, we'd got on great. He said it was water under the bridge, that this was about work, not our personal lives, you know?'

'I... um... I don't know what to say.'

'Yeah, well, there's nothing *to* say. I should have known it was too good to be true. Should have worked out this was his way of getting back at me, though why he waited so long, I've no idea. Anyway... I just wanted to say sorry. That's all.'

'Apology accepted,' she murmured, blinking back tears.

'Um... I don't suppose I could come back, could I?'

She swallowed, torn between longing and hurt. He'd walked out on her for the promise of a new and wonderful life. An adventure. The lure of it had been more important to him than she was. If he'd done it once, he could do it again. Why should she trust him now? She squared her shoulders, took a deep breath.

'Mum's here. She's staying for a bit. I think... I'm not sure what I think.'

'Please, Jess. Can we give it another go? We've both made

mistakes, haven't we? Let's just put them behind us and try again.'

Jess wasn't exactly sure what *her* mistake had been. Was it her suspicion that he might have been the one hurting Toby? And if she'd thought that, what did it say about her trust in him as a parent? It would be so easy to believe they could wipe the slate clean. She yearned for him, to feel that love she'd thought they shared. He was her soulmate, wasn't he? Or had she glossed over his flaws to make him into the person she'd been looking for? 'Um... I need to think about it.'

'I've nowhere else to go. Darcey said I can sleep on the sofa for a couple of nights, but we've got a proper rental agreement and she won't let me stay there any longer.'

He was trying to put pressure on her now, and something clicked into place, sealing her decision. 'Look, Ben. I'm sorry to say this, but that's not my problem. You made your choice.'

She hung up before she could change her mind, dropping her phone on the table as if it was an unexploded hand grenade. It rang again, but she didn't answer, switching it off so she couldn't be swayed.

CHAPTER FORTY-ONE

With no job to go to, no children or partner to look after, she was completely lost as to what to do with herself. Despite the cool breeze, it was a lovely autumn day. She could go out in the garden, except she'd be seen from next door, and she couldn't bear that feeling of being watched. The police still had her car while they did forensic checks, so she couldn't go far.

She opened cupboards in the kitchen, making a mental list of things she needed, and decided to walk to the supermarket and stock up on a few essentials while she still had money in her account. It was a clear sign of desperation. Something to fill the empty hole where her life used to be, take her mind off her worries.

An hour later, she was home, all the shopping unpacked and no clue as to how she would fill the rest of her day. She was sure Stella, her solicitor, should have rung by now; she'd promised to keep her up to date, and Jess was keen to know how the police case was developing. Were they going to get her in for another interview? Had they found new evidence? Would they press charges? Stella had been non-committal the previous day when she'd rung her. Said they just had to wait, because things on the island had a pace of their own, and that pace tended to be slow.

She dug her phone out of her bag, remembering that she'd switched it off earlier. When she turned it back on again, a series of pings told her she had several missed calls. She scrolled through the list. Five from Ben. Well, he wasn't going to get a reply from her. Not yet. Two from her mum, probably wanting to know what ready meal she fancied for tea. And one from Carol on her new number.

Her finger hovered over the screen while she debated whether to ring her back. Her phone pinged again. A voicemail message. She was just about to listen to it when the front door burst open and Rob staggered in. It took her a moment to register what she was seeing. He was clutching his arm, his shirt red where his hand was clasped, blood dripping on the floor.

She jumped up, her brain paralysed with shock for a second. 'Oh my God,' she gasped. 'What happened?'

'Help me, Jess.' He looked very pale, like he might faint, and she guided him to a chair before dashing into the utility room, where they had a first aid kit. She was all fingers and thumbs as she tried to find some swabs and sterile dressings, fumbling to open the wound pack.

'She just went for me,' Rob gasped, his teeth gritted against the pain.

'Carol?' She eased his hand away from his shirt. There was a four-inch gash in his forearm, still oozing blood. 'She did this?' It was hard to believe that the woman she'd likened to a timid mouse when they first met had turned into something more akin to a sabre-toothed tiger.

He nodded, biting his lip as she dabbed at the wound with an antiseptic wipe.

'Sorry, I know it stings.' Carefully she cleaned away the blood, her heart pounding as her mind asked a barrage of questions that would have to wait. Her priority was to stop the bleeding.

'She... she grabbed a knife out of the block in the kitchen and... tried to *stab* me.' His voice sounded exactly the way Jess felt – incredulous.

'Christ! Why would she do that?' She stopped dabbing, glad to see that the cut wasn't as deep as she'd first thought. Rob's face crumpled, his chin quivering. Rob never cried. Not once in all their time together had she seen him like this.

'She's...' He shook his head, unable to speak for a moment. 'She's not been herself recently. Not since we moved in. It's jealousy. Pure and simple. She was talking about how you'd be out of her hair once you were charged with Mo's disappearance, and I was standing up for you, saying that you wouldn't hurt a child, and then... she just went ballistic.' His teeth clamped his lip as he grimaced against the pain, and Jess went back to tending to his wound, the bleeding almost stopped now.

She glanced towards the open front door, nervous now.

'Where is she? Is she still next door?'

'I... I think so. I just ran for my life.'

'We've got to call the emergency services.' Jess picked up her phone, her breath hitching in her throat when she saw another answerphone message from Carol. 'Oh my God...' Her eyes met Rob's. 'She rang me.'

Quickly she dialled up voicemail, all thoughts of ringing the police and an ambulance forgotten for now. She put it on speaker so they could both hear. Two new messages. She played the first one.

'Change of plan. I'll call you later.' Carol sounded a bit manic. Definitely not herself.

Jess shuddered, wondering what the woman might have had planned for her at the back of the castle. A quick push over the edge onto the rocks below when there was nobody around to see? She felt queasy at the thought. For some reason, Carol had decided it wasn't the right venue, and for that she was truly grateful.

She saved the message and played the second one. Carol's voice was fraught, staccato, not sounding like the earlier message at all.

'Archallagan. Meet me there. By the pond.'

'Why would she want to meet me there?' Jess glanced at Rob, who looked nonplussed. 'She knows I don't have a car at the moment. It's still with the police.'

'I told you... she's not thinking straight.' He considered for a moment, then came up with the only explanation that might make sense. 'Do you think it's because that's where Mo was found? And where you were on the day he went missing?'

She frowned. 'You're not... you don't really believe that I took him, do you?'

There was a moment's hesitation, a beat that told her whatever he was about to say wasn't what he was thinking.

He opened his mouth to speak, but she held up a hand, stopping him, hurt that even Rob, who knew her better than anyone, didn't believe her. 'Mo's kidnapping was nothing to do with me. I was set up.'

'Carol's adamant that it was you. In my heart... Look, I know you wouldn't hurt a child, but with the evidence from Mo's phone, it doesn't look good.'

'No, it does not look good. I'm well aware of that,' she snapped. 'And do you know why it doesn't look good?' She banged a fist on the table, making him jump. 'Because that's exactly what Carol intended.'

He pulled a face, looked like he hardly dared speak. 'I don't see how she could have set you up, though.'

'Well I've thought about this a lot, as you can imagine. The only thing I can think of is she hid Mo's phone in my car, so when I went out, it recorded him being exactly where I was at the same time. You know I'm slack about locking the car; she knows that too. It would have been easy for her to slip it in there and retrieve it later.' She had his full attention now, his eyes on stalks as she laid out her theory. 'Mo could have been taken to the forest after I'd gone.'

He took a moment to process what she'd said. 'Oh God, she did go out in the car looking for him. She said she was driving round the streets, but she could have gone up to Archallagan. Mo was drugged; she could have hidden him in the back and I wouldn't have thought to check.'

With that, Jess knew she was right, had been all along. She heaved a sigh. 'I have no way of proving it, though, that's the problem. I mean, the police have the car for forensic examination and they're going to find Mo's hairs all over it, aren't they? It's not like I clean my car out very often.'

They fell silent, both of them lost in thought.

'You've got a lawyer, haven't you?'

'I have. You know Stella. She's obviously on the ball, but the fact that Mo's phone could be tracked to the same place as me is a big concern. It's much too easy to pin it on me if there's nobody else in the frame. Especially with everything else that's been happening, and this bad feeling between me and Carol being played out for all to see.'

Rob nodded, lips pursed as he thought, then his eyes lit up. 'Wait, I've got an idea. What we need is a confession. If we can get Carol to admit that's what she did, even get her to tell us why, then you'd be in the clear.'

Jess huffed, disappointed. 'Yeah, like she's going to do that.' She couldn't help the sarcasm, her spirits having taken a nose-dive after talking everything through. 'I'm not going anywhere near her. The woman's deranged. Look what she did to you. We need to get you to hospital, get that wound stitched up.'

Rob studied his arm, where he'd been applying pressure with a dressing. 'It's stopped bleeding now. It's not too bad.'

'Hmm. I don't know. That's quite a cut.'

He rummaged in the first aid kit, pulled out a packet of Steri-Strips. 'These will do the job.'

Jess sighed, knowing better than to argue. Rob could be so stubborn, but it was his wound, so it was clearly his choice. 'Okay, if that's what you want, but you'll have to let me put them on. I think it's a two-handed job, and you're not really in a fit state, are you?'

He handed her the packet, and she pulled the edges of the wound together and applied strips until she was happy it would do. 'I'll just put a dressing over that, bandage on the top, and you're good to go.'

When she'd finished, he reached over and squeezed her hand. 'We always were a good team, weren't we?'

She gave him a tight smile. They'd had their moments, she'd have to admit, and in times of crisis they'd always managed to pull together and get through things.

'Right, well, I think I should go back in there,' Rob said, getting up. 'See if she's calmed down and I can get her to see reason.'

Jess looked at him like he'd grown a second head. 'What? No, don't be so stupid. Let's just ring the police.' She picked up her phone, ready to dial.

'I'm not sure about the police. I mean, what if she says it was self-defence?'

Jess stopped what she was doing, put her phone back on the table. 'Hmm, I see your point. They'd have to take that seriously. Then you'd be dragged in for questioning.'

Rob nodded. 'She'll find a way to blame it on me.' His jaw had a determined set to it, and she knew it was pointless trying to change his mind. 'I think we should at least try to talk to her. And if it's really not safe, if she's still manic and we can tell we're not going to get anywhere with her, then we call the police. But the best outcome would be to try and get some sort of explanation out of her that we can record to clear you of any wrongdoing.'

Jess sighed. He was probably right. In an ideal world, a confession would tie everything up very neatly and help to get her life back in some sort of order.

He put his hands on her shoulders, looked her straight in the eye. 'You're Toby's mum, and my best friend. I can't have you going to prison for something you didn't do. I've got to try.' He gave a nervous laugh. 'If you don't hear from me in... I don't know... half an hour, then you can ring the police.'

'Don't be daft,' she said. 'I'm coming with you, then she'll be outnumbered. Hopefully that'll make her see sense.' She swallowed her fear as she got to her feet. 'Let's go.'

CHAPTER FORTY-TWO

Jess went over to the knife block, pulled out the carver and the boning knife, passing the larger blade to Rob. 'There you go. We'll feel safer now.' For a moment she wondered how her life had become so surreal.

Rob looked at the knife in his hand, adjusting his grip. 'I'm not sure I'd even be able to use this. You know... if it came down to it.'

Jess glanced at her own weapon, the blade gleaming in the sun. 'I don't think any of us know what we're capable of until we're pushed to our limits.' Would she be able to use this in self-defence? She wasn't sure, but having it in her hand made her feel safer, even if it was more of a deterrent than anything else.

Rob paused by the patio door, his hand on the handle, like he was having second thoughts, then he pushed it open and they stepped outside. Jess glanced round furtively, glad that their gardens weren't overlooked, because it wouldn't look good if one of the neighbours saw them skulking across the lawn armed with knives.

They stopped in front of the neighbouring patio door. Rob peered inside, then turned and whispered, 'I can't see her.' Jess could feel her heart racing, her T-shirt damp with sweat. 'Just let me check something.' He crept round the side of the house, came back a few moments later looking mightily relieved. 'Her car's gone. It's not in the drive.'

Jess put a hand to her chest to try and still her jittery heart. 'Do you think she's gone up to Archallagan, then? Ready to meet me there, like she said in her message?' The thought sent a chill through her.

'I think that's the only logical conclusion. I mean, where else would she go? And why send you that message if she didn't mean it?'

He was right. And if they were going to get a confession out of her to clear Jess's name, it looked like they would have to follow her up there.

Rob seemed to read her mind. 'We'll go together. I'll drive, and I promise, whatever happens, I'll keep you safe. Any hint of danger and we're out of there and on the phone to the police, okay?'

She nodded.

'I'll just get my keys, then.'

He pushed open the patio door and they stepped inside, Jess feeling like she was tethered to him by an invisible cord, not wanting to be on her own.

'Oh my God,' she gasped when she saw the pool of blood on the kitchen floor. It seemed Rob had lost a lot more blood than she'd realised. 'Christ, you can't drive. You should be resting.'

She noticed he was sweating, beads of it glistening on his brow. He wiped a hand across his forehead. 'I'm okay. I mean, it's stopped now, hasn't it?'

'I know, but you could faint at the wheel or something. In fact, just sit down for a minute, will you?' She guided him to a chair, putting her knife on the table. 'I need to clear up before Mum brings the kids home. We can't have them coming back to a scene of bloody carnage. Honestly, they'll think someone's been murdered, you know what their imaginations are like.'

Rob pulled a face. 'Yes, you're right. No child needs to see something like that in their own home.'

She looked again at the pool of blood, feeling a bit queasy, not sure she was up to the task. What would drive someone to violence like that? Another thought wormed its way into her mind.

'Are you sure this fight was about me, or is there something else going on with Carol?'

Rob looked down at his hands, considered for a moment. 'Well... if I'm being totally honest, not all of it was about you.' He heaved a sigh before carrying on. 'She's gone all paranoid, you see. She's got this idea in her head that her ex is going to take Mo off her.'

'Do you know, I did wonder if he was still alive.' Suddenly the overheard conversations started to make sense. 'But why tell us he was dead?'

'That's what she wants everyone to think. And definitely what she wants Mo to think. She doesn't want him to remember his father.'

'What?' The idea seemed inconceivable.

'Apparently it was a difficult relationship. He was quite a bit older than her and very controlling. He didn't like her working or having her own money, so she had to ask for everything. And then he'd get drunk and hit her. Apparently it was all fine until Mo was born, then things went downhill very quickly. It took her almost two years to find a way to escape.'

Jess was shocked, not sure what to say. Carol had given no indication that she'd been through such an ordeal.

'The guy doted on Mo. It was Carol who couldn't do anything right, and he was furious when she took the boy away. Seems it's taken him until now to find her.' Rob winced, clearly in some pain. 'He's been ringing her, threatening all sorts if she doesn't send him money.'

'He's blackmailing her?' That wasn't what Jess had overheard. The conversation was more about not being in contact, wanting the caller to stay away.

'Trying to. The point is... she's scared of him. Believes he might come over here and kidnap Mo, take him back to Turkey. I said I'd pay him off if that would solve the problem.' He winced again, putting his knife down so he could adjust the dressing on his arm. 'She told me to butt out and let her do things her own way.'

'So when Mo disappeared, she thought it was her husband who'd taken him?'

'Yeah, that's right.' He blew out his cheeks. 'Major panic.'

She thought about it for a moment, and the more she went over it, the more confused she felt. 'But... how does that square with her taking Mo and leaving him up in the forest to frame me?'

Rob's eyes narrowed. 'I can't think. I guess maybe his threat of kidnapping gave her an idea about how she could get you out of our lives?' He stood, picking up his car keys from the worktop. 'There's no logic to anything she does. Believe me, I've looked for it.' He headed towards the front door. 'Come on, let's go and find out the truth, shall we?'

Jess followed him, her brain trying to find some sort of rationale for Carol's behaviour, but still none of it made sense. The only thing that did make sense was getting Carol to admit that she'd framed Jess so she had some evidence to take to the police.

CHAPTER FORTY-THREE

'I'll drive,' she said, holding out her hand for the keys, but Rob shook his head.

'No need. I'm fine.' He caught her quizzical look, glanced at the bloodstained bandage on his arm.

'It looks like it's started bleeding again,' she pointed out. 'It would be better if you let me drive this time.' Their eyes locked. 'Come on. I'm perfectly competent. I passed my test a year before you did, remember? And I've never had a crash.'

'I'm sorry, but you're not insured to drive my car any more.'

There was nothing she could say to that. The truth was, she needed him, not only to get her to Archallagan, but for moral support. If it had to be on his terms, then so be it.

Should we have just called the police? she wondered as they set off, one hand grasping the door handle, the other ready to grab the wheel if it looked like he was going to faint. He was driving faster than she would have liked, and her foot pressed on an imaginary brake pedal.

'What are you doing?' Rob asked, his voice sharp, the car swerving into the middle of the road as he looked at her rather than at where he was going.

She clung to the handle as he flung the car back into the right lane. 'I'm just not sure you're fit to drive.' Her mouth clamped shut. She'd said her piece and he was in no mood to listen. This was a bad idea. She wished it was Ben with her in the car. He'd be calm and reassuring, not all wound up like Rob seemed to be.

They were at St John's now, turning up the back road that led to the forest. She gazed out of the window, trying to work out what Carol might be planning. It wouldn't be easy to reason with her, she decided, because there was no logic to anything she was doing.

Five minutes later, they were pulling into the car park. There was only one other car there: Carol's. It was empty.

'So what's our plan?' Jess asked. Her palms were greasy with sweat, and she wiped them on her jeans, unsure if she really wanted to go any further. She wished they'd brought the knives with them, but they'd been left in the kitchen in their haste to get out of the house.

Rob opened his door. 'I think we head for the pond where Mo was found. That's where she said she was going to be, isn't it?'

Jess stayed put, not ready to leave the safety of the car. 'And then what?'

'Well, we'll have to play it by ear. It depends what sort of state she's in.'

She leant forward, looked at the dark entrance to the forest. It didn't look inviting any more. It looked like a place where someone could stalk you and you wouldn't have a clue they were there. It looked like a place where you could be ambushed, attacked and left to die, and nobody would find you for hours. Maybe days. She shuddered.

He put a hand on her shoulder. 'Look, I haven't mentioned this before, but she had an app on Mo's phone to log his whereabouts.'

'I know that.'

'Yes, but what you don't know is that she put it on your phone too. She told me when we were arguing. You'd been taking pictures, and you left your phone on the worktop when you went to get something from upstairs. She pretended to be scrolling through the photos and downloaded the app.'

Jess gasped. 'You're kidding me.'

'I didn't want to freak you out, but it's true. She did it to me too.' He held up his own phone. 'That's why I have a second phone she knows nothing about.'

'Wow. She really *is* paranoid.' She shook her head, finding it hard to believe someone would do that.

Rob put his phone back in his pocket. 'Leave yours in the car, then she'll know you're here but she won't be able to track us.'

Jess thought for a moment, then nodded. It sounded like a sensible idea. Wasn't it funny, she thought, how Rob and Carol's relationship had looked so perfect from the outside, but inside it was rotten to the core?

They got out, both of them scanning the car park, but there was no sign of anyone.

'This is really creepy,' Jess said as they set off up the path, wishing again that she'd brought the knife with her. 'She could be anywhere.'

'Yes, well two can play at the spying game. What she doesn't know is I put the app on her phone too, so we should be able to find her pretty easily.'

He fished his phone out of his pocket, found the app and studied the map that came up, then looked at the path ahead of them. 'Well, she's actually being true to her word. She's at the pond. Or her phone is anyway.'

His words were meant to reassure, but they had the opposite effect. Just because her phone was at the pond didn't mean

Carol was there too. She could be following them, knife in hand, ready to attack at any minute.

Jess glanced over her shoulder, heart racing. She didn't like this. Not one bit.

CHAPTER FORTY-FOUR

Rob put his phone back in his pocket and reached for her hand. 'It's okay, sweetheart. It'll all be okay.'

Jess turned to him then and he stopped walking, lacing their fingers together. It felt familiar, but strange as well. His eyes met hers, his face softening.

'I've been wanting to find the right moment to talk to you, but it's been impossible with everything...' He gave an exasperated huff. 'You know I still love you, don't you, Jess?'

She ran her tongue round dry lips, not sure she wanted to hear this. Unclear how she should respond.

His thumb stroked the back of her hand. 'We've always been such a strong team, you and me.'

She nodded, because that much was true. Except when she'd met Ben and understood everything that was wrong with her relationship with Rob. How safe and dull her life was, how she'd extinguished her hopes and dreams in exchange for reliability. How she'd ceased to be herself.

She drew her hand away. 'I love you too... as a friend. And we will always have Toby, and our past together,' she said, hoping he'd get the message.

He grabbed her hand back. 'But we can have a future too.'

She desperately wanted to move on, to get this conversation with Carol over with. But she could imagine that the turn of events had been a massive shock to him, his dreams for the future crumbling just as quickly as hers had done. However, that didn't mean they should take a step backwards. They could help each other move on from this trauma together. Just not as a couple.

'Can we talk about this later, Rob?' She tried to be gentle. 'I'm focused on Carol and finding her before she finds us. I can't really think about anything else.'

'I just want to know how you feel, darling.' He squeezed her hand, his eyes pleading with her. 'Please. Can we try again? Get back to how we were?'

She looked away, tried to wrestle her hand back and get moving again, but he was holding on tight. 'Later, Rob. Please.' It came out more snappily than she'd intended.

He opened his mouth to say something, then thought better of it and dropped her hand. 'Okay,' he muttered, marching ahead, clearly hurt.

As they made their way up the path, she thought she heard the snap of twigs, the scuffle of feet, and whipped her head round. Her heart was thundering in her chest, eyes raking the undergrowth as she spun in a circle. A rabbit bounded out of sight. A breath of wind sighed through the trees. The weather had changed, clouds scudding overhead, bringing an increasing gloom.

She caught up with Rob, not wanting to be too far away from him as they turned off the main track and onto one of the narrow paths that would lead them to the pond.

'I promise we'll talk about it later,' she said to his back.

He turned, scowling. 'You *know* we're meant to be together. You and me.' He looked up to the sky, then back at her. 'I don't understand why you can't see it.'

She gave a frustrated sigh, not wanting to get into it now, but also realising they weren't going to get any further until she addressed the issue.

Oh dear. How to respond? She didn't want to lie to him or lead him on, but she also needed him to be with her until they found Carol. She gave him a smile, let him take her hand, changed the subject.

'It's this way, isn't it?' She pointed to a fork in the path, indicating they should go left. 'Do you think you should check your phone? Make sure she's still there?'

He had another look at the app. 'Hmm. She doesn't seem to have moved.' He put his phone away again, his arms swinging by his sides as they walked. He was chattering about the future, and how her mum could stay on next door while Jess moved in with him and Toby. How happy they could be together. She let it wash over her, this fantasy world he was creating. Because that was all it was. She knew there was no going back to how they'd been.

She tugged at his arm, stopping him. 'It's just round this corner,' she whispered. 'I think we need to be quiet.' He nodded, his eyes lit with excitement, the opposite of the knot of fear in her belly. He was still living his dream, not present in their reality. And that worried her. Had the shock of his stabbing got to him? She couldn't have him off in fantasy land when they might be faced with real danger. 'Let's not get too far ahead of ourselves,' she murmured. 'We've got to get through this before plans can be made about anything else.'

He nodded, his smile replaced by a mask of concentration. 'Of course. Yes, you're right.' He gave her shoulder a squeeze as they crouched behind a dense thicket of willows growing at the edge of the pond. 'But we're going to be just fine.'

She would have liked to feel as confident as he sounded, but she was on high alert, ears straining, every sound making her twitch. The pond was only small, the size of a tennis court, surrounded by clumps of willow and reed beds, the forest pressing in all around. Gusts of wind shushed through the branches, bringing a chill to her skin.

Rob checked his app again. 'It's still saying she's around here somewhere.'

'Maybe I should just call out to her? She's only expecting me to be here, isn't she?'

He considered her suggestion. 'But then we lose the element of surprise. She might run away, and then we'll never get her confession and you'll still be in the picture for kidnapping Mo.' He crept forward, round the edge of the pond, getting closer to the picnic benches, which was where she was likely to be. *Unless she's hiding. Luring us into a trap.*

She wondered again about Carol's game plan. She already had Jess's husband and child, and was probably going to get her sent to prison, so she'd be well out of the way. There was nothing more Jess could give her. No reason for Carol to physically hurt her.

Why had the woman arranged a meeting in the first place? And why had she stood her up, changed locations? Jess thought about the two messages. One sounding strained and odd, the other one hissed like she didn't want to be overheard.

When she considered it, she only had one side of the story, and there were always two sides. The wound on Rob's arm. Had he goaded her? Had he started their fight?

Her doubts crept with her along the side of the pond, consuming her until she felt certain something was very off about this whole situation.

She stood up. 'Carol! Carol!'

Rob snapped his head round, eyes wide in alarm. 'What are you doing?' he hissed.

'I want to talk to her, not fight her.' Jess peered through the trees, trying to see if she could spot Carol anywhere. 'She wanted to meet me earlier today. Wanted to talk. So I'm going to try that first.'

He looked like he was going to argue with her, but then held up his hands. 'Okay. We'll do it your way.' His acquiescence was unnerving.

She pushed past him, calling Carol's name. No response. The picnic area was empty. She stood still, listening to every creak and swish and crackle. Then she heard an unfamiliar noise coming from the undergrowth further into the forest, where bilberry bushes and heather lined another path. She could see a patch of blue, a jumper, she thought, and headed towards it.

There on the ground was Carol, a red bloom across her stomach, her hands covered in blood.

CHAPTER FORTY-FIVE

Jess screamed and dropped down beside her. Carol's eyes were closed, her face deathly pale. Jess felt for a pulse on her wrist, but there was nothing, her skin icy cold.

Rob stood behind her, watching rather than helping. 'Is she dead?' His voice was a monotone, robotic, not sounding like him at all.

Jess was crying, tears streaming down her face. Yes, she and Carol had had their differences, but there was no way she wanted things to end like this. 'I... I think so.'

He gave a sigh that went on so long it must have emptied all the air out of his lungs. Then he tutted. 'Looks like we're too late.'

He crouched and felt in Carol's pockets, pulled out a folded piece of paper, soggy with blood. Opening it up carefully, he studied it for a moment. 'Oh God, no. She threatened it, but I didn't believe her.' Jess glanced at him, registered the horror on his face. 'She's killed herself,' he whispered, pointing to a bloody knife lying beside her on the ground.

He handed her the note, and she read the scrawled words.

I can't go on. Please look after Mo and tell him I love him.

Not much of an explanation for something so finite, she thought, something that had happened without any sort of warning signs. Poor Mo. Her heart was breaking for the child. How on earth did you explain this to a five-year-old?

Rob pulled out his phone. 'I'll call for an ambulance. Emergency services. That's what you do in these situations, isn't it?' He scratched his head, hesitating. 'Even though the person is already dead?' His voice was matter-of-fact while he dealt with the practicalities. Jess could see he hadn't processed the reality of the situation, wondered when it would hit him that the woman he'd thought he was going to marry was dead. He walked down the path a short way as he talked to the operator.

Jess stared at Carol's face, tears still streaming down her own. Then she blinked, not sure if she was imagining things. *Did she move?* She peered closer, saw a muscle twitch by Carol's lips.

She felt again for a pulse, trying her neck this time, and thought there was a flutter of something. She bent to see if she could feel a breath. Yes, there it was, a definite whisper of air against her cheek. Her heart flipped, relief washing through her.

Then she realised that Carol was trying to speak. 'Rob... did... this...' she whispered. 'Run.'

A chill seeped down Jess's spine, adrenaline spiking in her veins. *Rob stabbed her?* She was about to ask Carol what had happened when she saw Rob turn and make his way back to her. He had to keep believing that Carol was dead. Otherwise...

She sat back on her heels, looked at the stab wound inflicted by her husband. How could he? It was starting to make sense now. His behaviour when they'd found Carol, the woman he supposedly loved. He'd thought she was already dead because he believed he'd killed her, unaware that he hadn't finished her off.

Fight it, Carol, she silently urged as she stood, shifting her weight from foot to foot, wondering how long it would take for an ambulance to get there. Longer if they thought it was about recovering a dead body rather than saving a life, she decided. But Carol didn't have long. She needed immediate attention if she was to have any chance of survival. Jess could see now that her hands were pressed to the wound in an attempt to stem the blood.

Her mind flared to life. She had to ring the ambulance service back, make sure they knew it was an emergency so they got here as fast as they could. That gave her two options. She could go back to the car and retrieve her phone, or... get Rob's phone off him. That would be quicker.

She looked at him standing with his hands in his pockets.

If she grabbed the phone off him, he'd try and grab it back, and he was six inches taller and much stronger than she was. Could she slide it out of his pocket when he wasn't looking? That didn't seem to be an option either. He was watching her every move.

'Don't worry, sweetheart,' he said, reaching for her hand. 'I'm sure they'll be here soon.' She wondered then if he'd actually rung them at all. Or had he moved away just to pretend to be doing it? She could no longer trust anything he said, could she?

Revulsion curdled the contents of her stomach. She didn't want his hand anywhere near hers, but she couldn't slap him away without alerting him that something was wrong. She let him curl his fingers between her own, and swallowed down her distaste. Cleared her throat. 'What did you tell them?'

'Body in the woods, basically.'

The matter-of-fact way he said it made her stomach turn, and she had to fight hard not to be sick. How could he be so cold about someone he'd shared his life with?

'Can I borrow your phone to ring Mum?' she asked casually. 'Let her know we're going to be late?'

She felt him tense, his hand holding hers a little tighter. 'Oh,

I don't think we'll be that late. It's all self-explanatory, isn't it?'
He waved a hand towards Carol and Jess's gaze fell on the
knife, nestled in the moss. Could she use that to make him give
her his phone? No, she warned. She couldn't have her fingerprints on there, because then Rob could try and say she'd done
it. Goodness knows there was enough evidence of bad feeling
between her and Carol for the police to take *that* accusation
seriously.

She gritted her teeth. There had to be something she could
do. Every second counted. She saw Carol's eyelashes flicker,
and pulled at Rob's hand to distract him.

'Can we move away a bit. I'm sorry, but I can't look at her.
It's just too...' She buried her head in his chest as she inched
backwards down the path, angling the two of them so his back
was to the body, just in case Carol moved again and he saw it.
As she'd hoped, his arms circled her, pulling her close, his hands
stroking her hair. She wrapped her own arms round his back,
letting them slide lower.

The top edge of his phone was poking out of his back
pocket. She slid it out and ducked out of his embrace before he
even understood what was happening. Then she ran, weaving
through the trees, the low branches making it harder for Rob to
follow, her feet slipping and sliding on the muddy ground. This
was it, her one and only chance.

CHAPTER FORTY-SIX

The crack and snap of breaking twigs told her he was not far behind. Her heart pounded in her chest, breath rasping from her throat as she stumbled over the uneven ground, the phone shoved into the waistband of her jeans so she didn't drop it.

She knew this place from many a visit here with Toby, exploring the undergrowth, making dens out of fallen branches, and if she wasn't mistaken, just up ahead was a dense patch of forest with remnants of walls and ditches from when it was once farmland.

She sped up, snaking round patches of brambles, making sure she wasn't going in a straight line. Just as she'd thought, there was a stone wall in front of her, a bike track running alongside it. She threw herself over it, pressing herself against the mossy stones, the ground lower on this side.

Did he see me? Does he know I'm here?

She held her breath, her heart hammering so hard her body shook with each beat.

Silence.

Her skin prickled with sweat. Another minute passed, no sounds of footsteps, no scuffles, just the shushing of the wind.

She inched to her feet, peeped over the top of the wall. No sign of him. He must have taken the other path.

She let out a long breath, pulled the phone from her pocket and crouched back down while she dialled the emergency services, desperate to get the paramedics here as fast as possible to try and save Carol.

It might already be too late. That thought alone brought a silent howl to her throat.

The operator answered.

'Hello, I—' The moment she spoke, a hand reached over her shoulder and snatched the phone from her.

'Oh no you don't.' Rob grinned down at her, disconnecting the call. He looked so pleased with himself, a fury rose inside her like nothing she'd experienced before. She was incensed at what he'd done, with no apparent remorse whatsoever.

He grabbed her shirt and started hauling her to her feet. She tried to pull away, but his grip was too strong. Tried slapping at him, but he grabbed her wrist so tightly she screamed out.

'I don't want to hurt you, Jess.' He spoke with a forced calmness. 'Chill out, will you?'

'Chill out?' Her voice was a wild screech, unrecognisable as her own. 'Did you just tell me to chill out after everything that's happened?'

Before she knew what she was doing, she'd wrapped her hand around a fallen branch that had landed against the wall. With the full force of her rage, she swiped at him, a feral scream erupting from her throat. The effect was immediate, her blow right on target, hitting him on the side of the head. He crumpled like a puppet with its strings cut, releasing her as he disappeared from view.

She peered over the wall, saw the livid weal she'd left on his face, smeared with blood and moss and bits of rotting bark. He was out cold, his eyes closed. She thought for a moment he might be dead, but when she clambered over the wall and felt his neck, there was a strong pulse. She retrieved his phone, determined to make the call before he came round.

'There's a critically injured woman in Archallagan Plantation,' she told the operator, her voice shaking with relief as the words rushed out. 'I'm with her now. We thought she was dead, but then I saw a muscle move on her face, and she has a weak pulse. Please can you get someone here quickly. She has a knife wound to the stomach and she's lost a lot of blood.'

She paused for breath and the operator assured her she'd get someone there as soon as possible, then took the relevant details. Jess was about to ring off when she remembered Rob. 'Oh, and my ex-husband ran into a tree branch and has knocked himself out.' That was close enough to the truth for now. She didn't need to get herself into any more trouble for the time being, and hopefully Rob wouldn't remember what had happened.

There was a pause. 'Okay, can you give me his details as well, please.'

As Jess spoke, she stood looking down at this man she'd shared her life with for all those years, wondering how he had turned into a monster capable of cold-blooded murder.

Once she'd ended the call, she ran back towards the pond. She'd bring the paramedics to Rob after they'd done all they could for Carol.

Thankfully, only fifteen minutes later, a rapid-response paramedic appeared through the trees. He dropped down beside Carol, immediately starting his assessment as Jess explained again what had happened.

'Thank you for being so quick,' she said, tears of relief pricking at her eyes. 'I didn't know how long she was going to last.'

He looked up, gave her a quick smile. 'Don't worry, love. We'll get some fluids into her. Give her pain relief and get this blood loss stemmed. We've got the coastguards coming to give us some help getting her out of here. They've got the four-wheel drive, you see, so they can get pretty much to the edge of the picnic area.'

She watched as he went about his work. Quiet and efficient. There was nothing she could do but wait and hope.

Half an hour later, Carol was loaded onto a stretcher and taken to the waiting ambulance. Her pulse had improved, so that was a good sign apparently.

'Right, love. You said your husband had knocked himself out.'

'Yes, he's just a bit further into the forest, not so easy to get to.'

'Lead the way.'

She retraced her steps, confident that she knew where she was going, but when she reached the wall she thought she'd climbed over, there was no sign of Rob. She looked around, confused. 'I'm pretty sure he was here.'

The paramedic frowned, crouching down and touching something on the ground. He held up his hand, a smear of blood on his finger. 'Looks like he came round.'

So where was he?

CHAPTER FORTY-SEVEN

The police turned up then, and she spent a long time sitting on one of the picnic benches recounting the whole story and answering their questions. They organised a search of the forest, but by the time they got to the car park, Rob's car had gone and her phone with it. She had his phone, of course, but the police wanted that for evidence.

The officer who'd been asking the questions phoned her mum for her and gave her the opportunity to have a quick chat, before giving her a lift home. Except it didn't feel like home any more. She stood outside looking at it, thinking of the dreams she'd had before they'd moved in, her new life with Ben, a bigger family, support on the doorstep. It had all been turned on its head in the worst possible way, tainted beyond redemption by Rob's actions.

Where had he gone? Surely they'd catch him. It wasn't easy to get off the island at the best of times, with only a couple of ferries a day and a handful of flights. Hopefully the police had been quick enough getting his name out to the authorities so he'd be picked up on passenger lists.

Could he hide on the island? Not for long, she didn't think.

He'd be spotted by someone who knew him sooner or later. It was that sort of place. But the idea he was at large brought her out in a cold sweat. He'd been so insistent on them getting back together, so out of touch with how she felt about him. It seemed likely now that he was the one behind all her troubles, engineering a situation where she'd be forced back into his arms.

The front door opened and her mum rushed out to greet her, followed by Toby and Mo, who were chattering away, Mo jumping up and down in excitement as he told her how Gran had taken them for an ice cream and they'd been on the beach.

Jess gathered them to her, holding her family tight. The police had been in touch with Social Services, and it had been agreed that the exceptional circumstances warranted a change of approach. For now, she could live with her mum and the boys. The situation would be monitored closely, so it wasn't a permanent arrangement just yet. A sob filled her chest, but she fought against it, pressed her emotions down. There would be time for that when the boys were in bed. For now, she didn't want to spoil the innocence of their day.

It occurred to her then that Mo would probably have to stay with them for a while, the sight of his little face smiling up at her making her heart break for him. What if Carol died? The paramedics had told her to hope for the best but not to expect miracles. It was a fifty–fifty situation. But if the worst happened, there was no doubt she'd have Mo to live with her permanently, no doubt at all. He was the younger brother Toby had yearned for, the one she couldn't give him, and he was a sweet little soul who didn't deserve any more upset in his life.

Her mum rubbed her back, gave her a sympathetic smile over the boys' heads. 'I've got tea on. Let's have something to eat, then they can go and play and you can tell me what's happened.' Jess gave a nod, not trusting herself to speak without breaking down.

· · ·

It was almost ten o'clock that night when they got a call from the hospital to say that Carol had died. Twice. But they'd managed to resuscitate her, and she was now critical but stable in the ICU. She had a punctured lung and damage to internal organs. She'd also lost a lot of blood. They could ring for an update in the morning.

Jess ended the call relieved but appalled at the same time. It didn't sound like recovery was assured, and even if Carol did survive, she would need a considerable period of convalescence. Surely she wouldn't want to come back and live next door after what had happened there? But where else could she go? It was her home, after all, even if it was a crime scene for now, cordoned off with police tape, with all manner of people in white outfits going in and out.

She and her mum talked late into the night as they worked out what they might do. They agreed that staying where they were wasn't an option. Jess was terrified that Rob was still out there somewhere and might turn up, even though the police had stationed officers outside.

They also didn't want to live in a house that belonged to Rob. That felt wrong on so many levels. But her mum's house was too small for four of them, assuming that Mo would be living with them for a while. Still, they decided they could squeeze in for now, Jess sleeping on the sofa bed in the living room, the boys in the guest room. They could make it work while they looked for something bigger.

Before she finally went to bed, Jess found the new copy of the divorce papers her solicitor had sent her. They were already signed by Rob, and she signed her own name, put the documents in an envelope and slapped a stamp on it, ready to post in the morning. At least now she could aim to secure some future lump sum as a divorce settlement, whatever happened with Rob.

. . .

The next morning, the police arrived early with an update. They had no clue as to where Rob was, no leads at all, but the airport and ferries had been notified and were on the lookout.

Jess thanked them and closed the door, shaken to have her fears confirmed that he was still on the island somewhere. He was a clever man. Cunning. He knew what he'd done, knew he was looking at a long prison term if he was caught. There was no way he'd be giving himself up any time soon. She gave a little shudder, hoped that he wasn't so deluded that he'd get in touch thinking that they still had a future together.

After several more conversations with Social Services, it had been agreed that the boys could stay with her and her mum as a permanent arrangement. It was likely, after all, that Rob was the one who had been causing Toby's bruises and had somehow organised Mo's kidnap. Deborah Quirk would be checking in on a weekly basis, though, so Jess couldn't completely relax just yet.

Later that day, the hospital rang with another update on Carol. She was fully conscious now and the consultant was pleased with her progress, although she'd be in the ICU for a little while longer before being transferred to a ward. She was asking to see Jess and was insisting that Mo shouldn't be told the details of what had happened to her. It would scare him too much. They were just to tell him that his mum had been in an accident.

How would Jess explain the police activity next door, though? The fact that Mo couldn't go home to get the toys he wanted, or any clean clothes. The fact that Rob had disappeared. So much to think about, but for now, her priority was to go and see Carol, while her mum distracted the kids and packed up the necessities, ready for them to move over to her house that evening. She wanted to reassure Carol that she would look after Mo for as long as was necessary, but she also wanted to hear the other woman's side of the story.

. . .

The ICU was a world of machines and beeps, not the quiet space you'd expect. There were only six beds in the unit, arranged around a central monitoring station, and all of them were occupied.

She was shown to the first bed, where Carol was hooked up to a drip, an oxygen line hooked to her nose, her eyes closed.

'Carol, your visitor is here,' the nurse said as she pulled up a chair next to the bed. Carol's eyes flickered open, and she blinked a couple of times, giving Jess a hint of a smile.

'Just ten minutes,' the nurse said as she pulled the curtain round the bed to give them a modicum of privacy.

It felt awkward being alone with Carol after all the bad feeling between them.

'How are you?' Jess asked, a stupid question, but the only thing she could think of to say.

'Sore. Tired. But they've got me on pain meds. I just float above it most of the time.' Carol's voice was weak, hardly more than a whisper, and it was obviously an effort to talk.

'Well, that's good.' Jess inched her chair closer, wanting to be able to talk without the whole ward overhearing their conversation. She lowered her voice. 'I was so worried they were going to be too late to save you.'

'Thank you, Jess. Thank you for everything.' Carol closed her eyes, quiet for a moment. 'The police were here earlier and told me what happened.' A tear rolled down her cheek and Jess gently wiped it away.

'Hey, no need to go over it all now. You're safe, that's what's important. We're going to move over to Mum's for the time being, with Mo, if you're okay with that. I know you said you didn't want me parenting him, but... well I don't think there's really another option.'

Carol opened her eyes. 'I'm sorry I said that. I didn't mean it. It was Rob. That was the problem all along. Everything was great between us until we moved next door. I wasn't keen on the idea at first, wanted some distance between us, but he said it would only be for a year or so, until Toby had got used to the idea of his parents divorcing. The properties were a great investment, he said. As soon as we moved, though, he changed, and that's when I knew he'd been using me. I really had no idea of what he had planned. He made me do all sorts of stuff I didn't want to do, but... well, he was blackmailing me.'

'Blackmailing?'

'Yes. He said he'd been in touch with Mo's dad. That he'd had a very interesting conversation with him and if I didn't go along with what he wanted, he would make sure he got Mo back.' Another tear escaped down her cheek. 'I couldn't let that happen, because then Mo would be in Turkey and I'm certain the family would deny me access. Once he knew about my past, he understood my weak point, you see. He found my greatest fear and used it against me. Some of it was lies, though. He did give my ex my number, but he didn't tell him where we lived, so the threats of him coming to take Mo weren't real, although they felt like it at the time. Rob told me that after he stabbed me. When he thought I was dying.'

'Oh my God, Carol,' Jess gasped, appalled by Rob's cruelty. 'I thought I knew him, but I'm just... I'm so shocked by it all I can hardly take it in.'

'He's obsessed with you. You do know that, don't you? I realise now that our relationship was a sham. He was so charming, so loving, it's hard to believe none of it was real. But I can see now that everything was designed to make you jealous. When that didn't work, he set about isolating you, making everyone doubt you, breaking your life apart.' Another tear escaped. 'I wanted to tell you, but he had this threat hanging over me, and he was watching me so closely, I never had a chance to be alone with you.' Carol swallowed, ran her tongue round her lips. 'I got a new phone so he couldn't track who I was calling, but he found out about it. That's when he got really mad.'

Jess frowned. 'Did he hurt Toby?'

'It had to be him. Nobody else would benefit from that.' Carol winced, her face contorted in pain. 'I'm sorry, it hurts to talk.'

Jess reached for her hand, held it tight. 'I can't tell you how sorry I am that he did this to you. But just know that Mo is safe with us, and when you're ready, there will be a home for you as well.'

Carol nodded, but Jess could see she was suffering, could tell that her visit needed to be over.

'I'll come again tomorrow if you want.'

'Please,' she said, more of a breath than a word.

Jess gave her hand a last squeeze before releasing it, her mind busy processing new information. The fact that she'd read everything wrong. Nothing of the last year had been the truth, and she wondered what else she didn't know.

Rob's obsessed with me? He'd hidden it so well, the fact had never occurred to her before now. He hadn't come over like that when they'd been together, or in the year since they'd started dating other people. If anything, he'd been slightly remote once he'd started his relationship with Carol, offhand even.

She had to consider it to be the truth, though, and it did fit with his behaviour when they were walking through the forest. His insistence that they should get back together, even as Carol lay dying.

She shuddered to think she'd been living with a man capable of such cruelty, such manipulation and evil. And he was still out there. It was a fact that worried her constantly, making her see his face in crowds, across the other side of the car park. She'd put it down to her imagination, but what if it wasn't? What if he was following her around? Hiding in plain sight? That was the worry. She prayed that the authorities would track him down sooner rather than later, then she could rest easy. While there was a chance he might still turn up at her door, it was impossible to relax.

Back at home, she gathered the boys to her, told them about Carol's 'accident', that she was poorly but was being looked after at the hospital. She hadn't wanted to say anything before she'd seen her, just in case the worst had happened. Now, having spoken to the nurses, she felt sure she would pull through, could feel in her bones that there would be a better future for Carol and her son.

'Come on,' she said, getting up from the sofa, where they'd been cuddled together. 'Let's finish packing, shall we? Then we're all going on holiday to Gran's house for a while.'

'Yay!' Toby shouted, punching the air. 'It's way better than here. And we can play chess, can't we, Gran?'

Jess glanced at her mum over the boys' heads and saw her shrug, a delighted smile on her face.

Mo was looking a bit unsure. 'It's just until Mummy's better,' Jess said, stroking his hair. 'You'll be sharing a room with Toby. And you'll be able to look after Gran's teddy bear collection.' She winked at her mum, who gave her a thumbs up. Mo loved his teddies, but they were all still next door, and they weren't allowed in there yet.

His eyes lit up. 'Can I really?'

'Absolutely. Gran might even let you pick one for yourself.'

Her mum gave a look of mock horror, then started laughing. 'You can pick as many as you like, sweetheart. They're just sitting there gathering dust, poor things.'

Helen had started several different collections over the

years. It began with pigs, then moved on to ducks, but teddies had stuck as her favourite for quite a few years now. She picked them up in charity shops and knitted them scarves and little clothes. Something to keep herself occupied now she lived on her own. Jess could imagine there might be a few new teddies appearing now that Mo would be staying with them.

As the boys disappeared upstairs to gather the last of their belongings, Jess went over and gave her mum a hug. 'Thanks, Mum. You're the best. I don't know what we'd have done without you.'

Her mum hugged her back. 'You're not so bad yourself, and I'm sorry I got it so wrong with Rob. I thought you were mad taking up with Ben when you already had the perfect husband. I understand now that I was seeing what he wanted me to see.' She stroked Jess's hair, planted a kiss on her cheek. 'You experienced something different, and I should have trusted you on that, rather than trying to persuade you that you were wrong.'

'I still can't believe what he did. I never guessed he had that side to him.'

'We live and learn, don't we, love? No need to beat ourselves up about it. What's important is that we get it right going forwards. For the kids.'

Jess knew that her love for her mum had never been greater. She pulled away, caught her eye, a note of uncertainty in her voice. 'We'll make it work, won't we?'

'Well, if Carol comes to live with us, we'll have three wages coming in and only two kids to look after. Of course we'll make it work. We just need to find a house that's big enough for all of us and we'll be set.'

Jess grinned. 'We'll be the perfect blended family, won't we?'

It wasn't what she'd envisioned, but when she thought about it, the arrangement could work very well. She doubted that she and Carol would be going near men for the time being, and her mum would be the perfect babysitter when they needed time out to do their own thing. And the boys would be brought up as brothers, something both of them had wanted.

'The best,' Helen said, and Jess knew then that she was right.

CHAPTER FORTY-EIGHT

FIVE MONTHS LATER

Jess added the last full stop to her essay and sat back in her chair, looking out from her window across the beach. They'd been so lucky to find this house to rent, she thought. With Rob disappearing, the financial side of her divorce was on hold, and his two houses were sitting empty for the time being. This had seemed like the best option, the quickest way to move somewhere new that was big enough for all of them. Okay, so it could do with a bit of modernising, but it had all the space they could need.

It was an old guest house, much larger inside than it looked from the outside, set on three floors, with an extension on the back housing the kitchen. The boys had the attic rooms, sharing one room for now, with the other as a playroom. They also had their own bathroom. The middle floor had three bedrooms, all en suite. Downstairs there were two reception rooms and the large kitchen and utility room at the back. No garden as such, just a yard, but who needed a garden when the beach was just across the road?

She loved her bedroom. Big enough to fit a desk and a reading chair in the bay window at the front, it was a space where she could come when she needed time alone, or to study. She was doing an Open University degree in psychology. Not necessarily because she thought she'd follow it as a career, but more to try and understand what might have made Rob behave the way he did. It was part of her healing from the trauma. She'd only just started but was already an enthusiastic learner and enjoying being back in education, even if she was trying to fit it in with her job.

Carol popped her head round the door. 'How are you getting on? I'm just taking the boys swimming, I thought it would give you a bit longer to get finished.'

Jess smiled at her. 'Ah, thank you. I owe you one. I'm almost there, just got to read through and spell-check, then it's done. My first essay in God knows how many years.' Admittedly she'd been rusty when she started, but she'd talked it through with Carol, who'd made some excellent suggestions about how to structure her arguments.

'Attagirl. Okay, well I'll see you later.' Carol gave a little wave and disappeared.

Jess couldn't help thinking how strange life was. She was now sharing a house with the woman her husband had used as a weapon against her. They had become firm friends over the last few months, like sisters really, not surprising given everything they'd been through. And her mum was in her element, never alone, and in charge of the household, which was just how she liked it.

Her laptop pinged. Messenger. It was Ben.

Fancy walking the dog later?

She smiled. Replied with a thumbs up. There was no doubting she was still attracted to him, and the thought of his company made her heart give a little jig of joy. The dog was a new addition to her family, and a distraction for the boys. An excuse to get out in the fresh air. It was fun walking the coastal paths with Ben, maybe going up Peel Hill or along the river, but she knew that a relationship with him was completely off the agenda. She understood now that they needed different things. He wanted to travel. Live abroad, go where the fancy took him. Now that Ruby was back living with her mum, he had the freedom to do exactly as he pleased. Jess, on the other hand, needed stability, and that was what Toby needed too.

Her relationship with Ruby was still what you might call testy, although Darcey had made the girl come and apologise for her behaviour. Apparently she'd had trouble with someone on Instagram who was threatening to publicise embarrassing pictures if he wasn't paid. Fortunately Darcey had found out and gone and sorted him out. She was a ferocious woman and Jess secretly admired her no-nonsense approach. It was all sorted now, and Ruby seemed a lot calmer. Ben had spoken to her about defacing the divorce papers, but it seemed that had been Rob's doing too, Ruby adamant it had nothing to do with her. And when she thought about it, Jess remembered there was something about the writing that had bothered her, the 'e' completely different to Ruby's looping letters.

Her only worry, sitting at the back of her mind, was Rob. He still hadn't been found, and there had been reported sightings on the island. Even her mum thought she'd seen him looking through the window of the hairdresser's one day. The police said they hadn't given up hope, but she wondered whether things had been scaled back. She hadn't heard anything for a few weeks now.

Rob's disappearance had shocked Toby to the core, and she'd had a hard time explaining it. Especially with his constant questions. *Why did he leave? Where did he go? When will he come back?* Because to Toby, the idea that his father wouldn't come back was unthinkable. Jess thought it was probably unthinkable to Rob, too. He wouldn't leave his son. Not for ever. So she kept vigilant, just as the police had advised, and she had to trust that they were right when they said that at some point he'd make a mistake and they'd get him.

Another ping. A different Messenger chat. It was Wendy, a friend she'd made on one of the Facebook groups she belonged to. She was also a librarian, and they'd struck up an instant friendship and often chatted.

Have you read the new Jack Reacher book yet? I've just finished. Happy to pop it in the post if you fancy it?

She grinned and sent a reply. They often exchanged books and seemed to have the same taste. Wendy was such a careful reader, the books often looked like they hadn't been opened when Jess received them. She always wrote a little note to her in the front as well, so Jess didn't like to pass them on, keeping them to share with friends on the condition they were returned.

Her online circle of friends had been such a support over the last few months. There were three in particular that she'd opened up to about her ordeal – Wendy, Dee and Sue. All lovely women, who'd been endlessly supportive and never said a word in judgement, willing to share their own experiences with her. The kindness of strangers. It was like having her own little support group. They shared pictures of their families now, and their conversations were more about their lives than books. Even though she'd never met them, she considered them to be true friends.

She selected a picture of Toby, taken on the beach with the dog the previous evening, and sent it over. *Best friends*, she captioned it.

Wendy's response was immediate.

How lovely! What a handsome lad. Looks just like his dad, doesn't he?

Jess typed a reply, but her finger hovered over the send button. She sat back in her chair, gazing out at the sea. *How does she know he looks like his dad?* She had no pictures of Rob on any of her social media, having purged them all immediately after he disappeared. Her profile was in her maiden name as well, so Wendy couldn't have seen anything through following up her married name.

She shivered, suddenly cold, and pulled on the fleece that was draped over the back of her chair. A click led her to Wendy's profile. A grainy picture of a middle-aged woman with grey hair and big glasses wearing a pink twinset. Your stereotypical bookworm. She thought about their conversations, scrolled back to the start to remind herself how their friendship had begun. That was it, a post about libraries and whether they were obsolete in the digital age. Jess remembered she'd given an impassioned defence of their existence as social hubs as well as a means of encouraging reading amongst those who couldn't afford to buy books. Wendy had said how impressed she'd been with her arguments, agreeing with her sentiments.

Gradually their chats had become more personal, and it was Wendy who'd initiated the move, mentioning her grandchildren and asking if Jess had children. That led on to lots of questions about Toby and how he was doing at school. Wendy gave the impression she was a harmless grandmother, but Jess looked at their conversations through a different lens now. A lens that gave her mind a sudden clarity.

What if Wendy isn't real? What if Wendy is... Rob?

She went back to the list of people she chatted to on Messenger and clicked on Dee, looked at her profile picture. A young redhead. Their conversations were more about dating than family, some of the questions quite personal and probing, she realised, trying to get information about her love life and what she felt about people she'd had relationships with in the past. It struck her now as intrusive. *What if Dee isn't real either?*

With her heart rate increasing, she found Sue. Her profile was a dog. The same breed that Jess had – a Border collie. Their conversation had started off being about dogs but had gradually moved on to much more personal chats. Sue had a difficult relationship, she'd said, and shared a lot of information about her problems, drawing Jess in to empathise and share too. Then they'd talked about living arrangements, broken marriages and how they were each moving on.

She sat back, horrified. These three people, who'd she'd thought of as real friends, had all sucked information out of her. So much so that put together, anyone reading these conversations would know exactly what was going on in her life. And where she was living. Fear rooted itself in her chest, pressing down until she was gasping for breath.

It was Rob. She was sure of it now. But even if it was paranoia and these people were real, she had to have it checked out.

She picked up her phone to call the police, then remembered how Rob had put apps on their phones so he knew where they were. *What if he's put a spy app on here? What if he's listening?* It wasn't outside the realms of possibility.

She left her phone on the desk, ran downstairs, grabbed her car keys and scribbled a note to say she'd had to go out and would be back later. If she couldn't risk calling the police, she'd have to go and speak to them in person.

CHAPTER FORTY-NINE

Rob waited for a reply to his last message as his alter ego Wendy, but nothing came. No matter. Sometimes Jess got distracted in the middle of their chats. It was annoying, as he lived for the times he had her undivided attention, felt closest to her then, excited that he'd found a way to talk to her.

He would admit to being annoyed that Ben was still on the scene. Not in any big romantic way, though, thank goodness. At least he'd managed to nip that in the bud, with all that talk about Dubai. What an idiot. Imagine believing that a man he'd done the dirty on by sleeping with his girlfriend would forgive and forget and want to offer him a job.

Ben only had himself to blame. During their conversations when they'd been out and about on their bikes, he'd told Rob all about his many conquests and the trouble he'd got himself into over the years. Obviously Rob had prompted him, encouraged him, aided and abetted by many a pint of beer after their cycle rides. Rob considered himself a magpie, picking up little bits of information about people and storing them to be used at a later date. It had been easy pickings with Ben and simple enough to trace Ian. When Rob asked him a favour in return for a handsome fee, the man was more than willing to oblige. As they said, revenge was a dish best served cold. Ian certainly enjoyed it.

What had surprised him most over the months since he'd been gone was the friendship that had blossomed between Carol and Jess. He'd done his damnedest to make them hate each other. Thought he'd done a stellar job, to be honest, but now they were living together. Wasn't that weird? Still, given a bit of time, he was sure he could prise Jess away from her female coven and back to him.

One of the best things, though, was his relationship with Toby. His son knew him as Harvey, an eleven-year-old who was into chess and was in the astronomy Facebook group for kids that Toby was keen on. They'd had some great chats, and it was amazing how much information you could get out of a child. Especially one as trusting and naïve as his son. He'd have to have a word with him about that sometime, but for now it suited him.

It had been hard to hurt Toby with those bruises, but he'd been so out of it on Carol's sleeping pills that he hadn't felt a thing when it was happening. That side of things had worked a treat, and the social worker was quite brutal. She was relatively new to the job, wanting to make an impression. He hadn't imagined she'd be onto things quite so quickly, but then child protection was obviously better than it used to be when he was at school. And with all those recent cases, he supposed they were being extra cautious.

Little Mo knew nothing about his abduction either, not remembering his journey in the boot, nor being carried through the forest. More of Carol's sleeping tablets to thank for that.

It was tough being so far away. He couldn't risk staying on the island, though, not with the threat of prison. Thankfully, the ferry times had worked in his favour on the day of the stabbing, and he'd managed to hop on as a foot passenger before they'd even started looking for him, using his dad's ID, a driver's licence that he'd left behind when he'd moved to Spain. Thank goodness Rob had thought to stash it in the car. The two of them looked very similar, so it hadn't been a problem. His mum and dad had never married, and he had his mum's surname, so he was pretty sure the authorities wouldn't make the connection. Computers could be pretty stupid like that.

For the last five months, he'd lived in England, in a village called Ravenglass, right on the edge of the Lake District. He'd rented a mobile home, and from his window he could see the east coast of the Isle of Man. As a location, it was perfect, as close as he could be to the people he loved but quite a distance from any real centre of population. Folk here didn't ask questions, and he wondered how many other people came here to hide. Nobody would know who he was, he felt confident of that.

Of course he still loved Jess, even after she'd turned on him like that.

He'd loved her since he was eleven years old and first saw her on the school bus, with her bouncy ponytail and those great big eyes. A wonderful smile. It was strange how she didn't notice him at school. All the other girls did. Whatever he did to try and get her attention didn't work. It was only when he found out which university she'd applied for and got a place there himself that he managed to engineer a proper conversation with her.

They were two Manxies living away from home for the first time. A common bond. And he took it from there, lapping up every little detail of her life, what she liked and didn't like. Thankfully she responded well to his new tactics, and they became friends. So that was a start. She was no good at reading body language, though, and never understood his desire for her. He dated other people to try and make her jealous, but that didn't work. Finally he had to resort to that age-old tactic of getting her blind drunk and making his advances then. Okay, so she was a bit freaked out when she woke up next to him stark naked, but he gave her an edited version of the truth, how she'd come onto him, and she honestly couldn't remember anything about the night before.

It was touch-and-go whether she'd love him or hate him after that, but she trusted their friendship, because, let's be honest, he had been a bloody good friend to her, listening to all her woes and tales of rubbish boyfriends. What a difficult process that had been. Eventually, though, they were onto stage two. An actual romantic relationship. He was good at romance, and that worked for a while, until he could feel her slipping away from him.

He'd had no choice then but to pull the failed contraception ticket. Condoms with holes pricked in them. He knew if she was pregnant that she'd stay with him. She was that sort of girl. And he knew she wanted a family. Maybe not with him, but once it was a done deal, he was sure he could make it work.

His relationship with Jess was his life's work, his never-ending project, so when she'd become so desperately unhappy in their marriage, he knew there was trouble ahead. That was when he first put a spy app on her phone, so he could hear what she was saying about him and react accordingly. That was how he found out about Ben. How she had this yearning for another man, although she swore she wouldn't act on it.

Obviously it had been a shock. A very nasty shock. 'Keep your enemies close' was a motto he was particularly fond of, so he snooped on Ben and found out he was a keen cyclist. It was simple to reignite a previously undisclosed passion for the sport himself – or at least that was what he told Jess. He explained that he needed to get a bit fitter and had been in the cycling club at school. She wouldn't know that was a bare-faced lie.

He engineered a chance meeting and built a friendship with the man his wife was clearly in love with. What a buffoon Ben was. He couldn't really understand what Jess saw in him, apart from the fact he looked like Poldark, but then the grass was always greener, wasn't it? A phase, that was what it was; he just had to ride it out and let her get this ridiculous romantic fantasy out of her head.

He also knew he had to find a new romance of his own. Carol was an easy target. It was obvious she'd been through trauma; she was like a frightened deer, all jumpy and nervous, so he gave her the full-wattage charm and she fell for it. Once she'd opened up about her past and how she'd run away from a holiday romance that had turned into something abusive, he knew he'd hit the jackpot.

Looking back on it now, it was clear that he'd got a bit ahead of himself, made everything just a shade more complicated than he could manage. His web of lies got a little too tangled. Next time he'd be keeping it simple and a bit less gory. No knives. That gash on his arm had hurt like hell. And he'd admit he hadn't enjoyed stabbing Carol like that, even if it was her fault that it had happened.

He'd found her secret phone, found out she was planning on meeting Jess behind the castle, and he was, quite frankly, livid about it. Instead of caving in when he started shouting at her, though, she shouted back, said she'd had enough of his lies and deceit and she couldn't do it any more. Taking Mo had been a step too far. He could see now that it had probably been unnecessary, but then it had been part of his plan, because he wasn't sure if he'd get a quick reaction from Social Services. A double-pronged attack, as it were.

She'd grabbed a knife from the block and started threatening him. He'd defended himself and they'd had a bit of a tussle. She sliced him across the forearm and that was it, he saw red. He seemed to get this additional burst of strength and managed to get the knife pointing towards her, then drove it into her stomach.

Not nice, really not nice at all. It wasn't in his plan, so then he'd had to have a rethink. Looking back, that was another thing he didn't get right. He'd panicked. His first thought was to get her out of the house so nobody could lay the blame for her death at his door.

Fortunately she'd reversed her car up the drive, with the boot by the gate to the back garden, so she could unload some big planters that she'd bought. It was easy enough to bundle her out of the house and get her in there, along with his bike. It was more of a struggle to carry her through the forest to the picnic area, but it was amazing what adrenaline could do in these situations. Then he cycled back home. At the time, his plan had a pleasing symmetry to it, a poetic ending.

He was so sure she'd be dead by the time he got back to her, with Jess as a witness to bolster his version of events. She had to be dead.

Anyway... live and learn. Next time he'd make sure his plan was absolutely watertight.

Because there would be a next time, of that he was sure.

He just needed to lure Jess away. And he'd found the perfect bait. A literary festival in Harrogate. He knew she'd always wanted to go, but there'd never been a right time. He'd thought she'd jump at the chance, and he'd been right. His alter ego Sue had suggested they go together, and Jess said she'd love to. It wasn't until the summer, but it was best to book early, because the hotels filled up very quickly, so he'd reserved them two rooms. Well, he'd said it was two rooms, but really it was just the one. That was where she'd fall in love with him all over again.

The only downside to this plan was that Toby wouldn't be with her, but in the spirit of keeping things simple, that was a sacrifice he had to make. He'd secure Jess, then work out how to get his son. Harvey would be a big help with that.

. . .

The next day, he finished chatting with Toby and checked his other accounts. Still no word from Jess. She was being particularly slow, and he couldn't deny it irked him. The fact that she was more important to him than he was to her was something that ate away at him.

He really had no idea how to change that. Obviously he'd tried over the years, chipping away at her social circle until she just had him, but she'd still wanted someone else. Life could be cruel sometimes.

Making her love him was a challenge, but he did like a challenge, and it was one that he would eventually crack. It was like playing a game of chess with a grandmaster who was always three moves ahead. He struggled to predict what she would do. Now, though, through his online friendships with her, he was learning more, and armed with this knowledge, he was more confident that he could bend her to his will.

She would be his again.

In fact, she'd have no choice. He'd found a little cottage to rent in the Lake District, right up in the mountains. Nobody would hear her shouting for help up there. She was like a wild horse that needed breaking in. He thought he'd achieved it once, so he was pretty sure he could do it again, but properly this time. And he had more leverage in the form of their son.

He smiled to himself, letting his imagination conjure up the images he yearned for. Jess looking at him lovingly, kissing him passionately, making love to him willingly. He was certain he could manifest his heart's desire if he tried hard enough.

A knock at the door broke him out of his daydream.

Nobody knocked on his door.

Thinking it must be the site manager, looking for the rent he owed, he crouched down and scuttled into his bedroom, closed the door. Another knock, louder this time.

'Police! Open up.'

His heart lurched. No, no, no. It couldn't be the police; he'd been so careful. His mind seemed to speed up, working through the details of his life, the mistake he must have made for them to find him. The books, he realised. Sending Jess the books. And giving her Wendy's address so she could return the favour. Dammit! She'd worked it out.

A loud bang, heavy footsteps, making the place rock from side to side. The bedroom door opened at the same time as the door to his dreams slammed shut.

A LETTER FROM RONA

I want to say a huge thank you for choosing to read *The Wife Next Door*. If you enjoyed it and want to keep up to date with all my latest releases, just sign up at the following link. Your email address will never be shared, and you can unsubscribe at any time.

www.bookouture.com/rona-halsall

The story came about from a conversation with my editor when we were throwing ideas around for my next book. We were talking about family break-ups and discussing whether an amicable divorce really was possible. That's when we realised it was a perfect theme for a psychological thriller! The possibilities for conflict within a blended family are endless, and I'm sure we all have personal experience of these things, if not ourselves, then among friends and family.

I hope you loved *The Wife Next Door*; if you did, I would be very grateful if you could write a review. I'd love to hear what you think, and it makes such a difference helping new readers to discover one of my books for the first time.

I love hearing from my readers – you can get in touch on my Facebook page, or through Twitter, Instagram or Goodreads. I also have a website if you fancy having a look!

Many thanks,

Rona Halsall

ABOUT THE AUTHOR

https://ronahalsall.com

facebook.com/RonaHalsallAuthor

twitter.com/RonaHalsallAuth

instagram.com/ronahalsall

ACKNOWLEDGEMENTS

As always, I have to point out that the writing and publishing of this book has been a team effort, and I have a lot of people to thank for developing it from the initial idea to the finished article.

Firstly, there's my lovely agent, Hayley Steed, who helped with the initial synopsis and knocking my early ideas into shape. Then my fantastic editor, Isobel Akenhead, who has been so enthusiastic about my writing and made me see where the story needed tweaking and characters needed a personality transplant.

There are so many people at Bookouture working behind the scenes to bring the book to fruition and make it a success. I don't have space to mention everyone, but I want to thank you all for your tireless work and attention to detail.

In particular, I would like to thank Alex Holmes for organising the copy-edit, proofreading and typesetting. Also a massive thanks to Alba Proko and her team for arranging the production of the audio version.

The marketing team do an amazing job – thanks to Alex Crow. As do the publicity team, so a big shout-out to my publicist, Noelle Holten along with Kim Nash, Sarah Hardy and Jess Readett.

I would also like to thank my fantastic group of beta readers – Mark, Kerry-Ann, Gill, Sandra, Wendy, Chloe and Dee – who read an early draft where some things still didn't quite make sense. Thank you so much for all your comments and insights, which have made the book a whole lot better.

Not forgetting the wonderful reviewers and bloggers who shout about my books all over Goodreads and social media. I really appreciate everything you do, guys!

Finally, a big thank you to my husband for not minding that I ignore him for hours while I get busy with my characters, and constantly chatter on about plot twists when we're out for our walks with the dogs.

Lightning Source UK Ltd.
Milton Keynes UK
UKHW011959051022
410007UK00010B/103